A Place in the Country

Also by Elizabeth Adler

From Barcelona, with Love

It All Began in Monte Carlo

There's Something About
  St. Tropez

One of Those Malibu
  Nights

Meet Me in Venice

Sailing to Capri

The House in Amalfi

Invitation to Provence

The Hotel Riviera

Summer in Tuscany

The Last Time I Saw Paris

In a Heartbeat

Sooner or Later

All or Nothing

Now or Never

Fleeting Images

Indiscretions

The Heiresses

The Secret of the Villa
  Mimosa

Legacy of Secrets

Fortune Is a Woman

The Property of a Lady

The Rich Shall Inherit

Peach

Léonie

A Place in the Country

elizabeth adler

St. Martin's Griffin 🜨 New York

A PLACE IN THE COUNTRY. Copyright © 2012 by Elizabeth Adler. All rights reserved. Printed in the United States of America. For information, address St. Martin's Press, 175 Fifth Avenue, New York, N.Y. 10010.

www.stmartins.com

The Library of Congress has cataloged the hardcover edition as follows:

Adler, Elizabeth (Elizabeth A.)
    A place in the country / Elizabeth Adler.—1st ed.
        p. cm.
    ISBN 978-0-312-66836-5 (hardcover)
    ISBN 978-1-250-01442-9 (e-book)
    1. Single parent families—Fiction.   2. Mothers
and daughters—Fiction.   3. Murder—Investigation—
Fiction.   4. Domestic fiction.   I. Title.
    PR6051.D56P56 2012
    823'.914—dc23

                                        2012007562

ISBN 978-1-250-00563-2 (trade paperback)

St. Martin's Griffin books may be purchased for educational, business, or promotional use. For information on bulk purchases, please contact Macmillan Corporate and Premium Sales Department at 1-800-221-7945 extension 5442 or write specialmarkets@macmillan.com.

First St. Martin's Griffin Edition: July 2013

10   9   8   7   6   5   4   3   2   1

This is for my good friend Red Shively,
with love and a special hug.

acknowledgments

As always, enormous thanks to my friend Anne Sibbald, the best agent ever, and to all of her team at Janklow Nesbit & Associates. Thanks also to everyone at St. Martin's Press. I tell myself with each book how fortunate I am to have Jen Enderlin, the most creative editor any writer could want and always there when I need her. And of course Sally Richardson, not only a terrific publisher, but fun to have New York lunches with. I also thank my husband, Richard, who puts up with a grouchy writer in the mornings and brings her that essential cup of "starter" coffee, and brings to a much less grouchy writer in the evenings that glass of wine and two hungry cats waiting to be fed—the slinky and very vocal Siamese, Sweet Pea, and the soft black bundle of love, our rescue cat, Sunny. I could go on and name friends, helpers, family, but that would be so boring, and I never want to be that. Of course, above all I want to thank you, my readers. I like to think of you reading this book, perhaps curled up on the sofa in front of a winter fire or stretched out by a pool, or on a summer beach, or maybe stuck on another plane journey. Or simply sneaking some alone time . . . I'm with you in spirit. Enjoy.

Part One

chapter 1

Caroline Evans was having a day out from her rented London flat, driving through rainy Oxfordshire with her fifteen-year-old daughter slumped in a silent sulk next to her.

They had taken in Oxford, "city of dreaming spires," which seemed to have more traffic than a motorway in rush hour, plus a couple of thousand young people smoking and drinking coffee and hanging about outside pubs. Issy ignored it all but Caroline had fallen for the rain-slicked courtyards and the ancient colleges half-hidden behind tall gates that had been there long before Henry's time. That would be Henry VIII, who, Caroline now figured couldn't have been all bad, despite the six wives. After all, her own husband had had two, and that was before her.

"A serial husband," she had said doubtfully when James told her he was going to marry her, though she was longing to say yes because she was so besotted by him she couldn't see straight, even with her glasses on.

Forget charming the birds; James Evans could, and did, charm everyone. Caroline remembered thinking it was okay about the other two wives, she would be the last wife. That's what James told her. And she'd believed him. She was twenty-two.

Now she was thirty-eight and an ex-wife, with a teenage daughter whose name was Isabel, always known as Issy, who some days talked to her and some days did not; who looked mostly like her father; and who, Caroline suspected, was smoking. However she did not yet have a tattoo, or at least not one in any place visible to her mother.

"Oxford's a lot different from when I was a girl," she said, maneuvering the old Land Rover bumpily out of the city and onto the A40, toward Cheltenham, though she had no specific destination in mind.

"Of course it is. That was a long time ago." Her daughter turned to look at her. "You should wear lipstick," she said. "And mascara."

Caroline sighed, remembering not so long ago when her child had thought she was perfect. She fiddled in her handbag for the lipstick and Issy told her she shouldn't do that while driving. It seemed she could do nothing right.

"Bloody rain," Issy said, looking at the wipers sloshing water sideways across the windscreen.

Caroline glanced sharply at her, then caught the sign for Burford and swung right into one of the prettiest high streets in the Cotswolds. Picture perfect, lined with small shops selling the usual souvenirs and postcards, but also art galleries and antique stores, bakeries and tea shops, as well as trees dripping onto the umbrellas of the few hardy citizens who waded through the puddles, heading for shelter.

Caroline slammed on the brakes as a car pulled out in front of her. "Look, we've got a parking spot. We were meant to stop here. Let's have tea."

Issy's sigh matched the stoop of her shoulders as she clambered unwillingly out of the car and stood in the rain, looking, her mother thought with a twinge of pity, utterly helpless and defeated in her new Marks & Spencer parka. Rain slicked her brown hair and there was a look of sadness in her brown eyes. It had been there ever since they'd left Singapore a year and a half ago, and Caroline did not know what to do about it.

Now, though, she grabbed her hand firmly and hurried her across the road into the nearest tearoom. As they climbed the stairs and took the last available table, she wasn't thinking about the strawberry cream tea she would order for them both, she was thinking of James, wondering, as she had so often, if she had done the right thing, leaving him.

"Mom." They had just sat down and Issy got up again. "I'm going downstairs to look at the shop."

The tearoom was over a junky jewelry-souvenir shop. "Okay." Caroline watched her go.

The tea came, carried on a plastic tray decorated with birds of the region, by a young woman not much more than her daughter's age, but who at least smiled at her and said it was the Earl Grey you wanted, Madam.

Caroline said it was and the girl put the tray down, arranged the small flowery cups in front of her and indicated the two-tier china cake stand with its nicely browned scones and a choice of small cakes; éclairs, fruit tarts, and iced buns. There was a dish of strawberry jam and a deep bowl with cream so thick you could stand your spoon in it.

"Perfect, thank you." Caroline found herself smiling as she poured pale tea into the flowery little cup. She had been brought up in London, an English girl who'd married and gone to live in Singapore with a husband she loved, a daughter she adored, a beautiful penthouse home with a view of the river and the city and its twinkling nighttime lights.

"Best of both worlds," James said, when they first looked at it. They were young marrieds; he American in his early thirties, successful in hedge funds and investments, and so attractive and charming he didn't need a penthouse to feel on top of the world. And she was so hazy with love and sex she couldn't think of anything else.

That was then. *Now,* was this rainy English day, a steamy little tea shop, and an almost silent daughter who finally came back, taking the wooden stairs two at a time. She sat down, took a scone, sliced it neatly, slathered it with jam and a dollop of thick cream, took a too-large bite, then picked up her phone and began texting.

Who she was texting Caroline didn't know. Still, she took a scone, and smiled. "This is the best," she said hopefully.

"Yeah." Issy's thumbs were busy but Caroline noticed she was also watching her as she struggled to arrange cream on top of the crumbling scone without it collapsing entirely in her hand.

"You should cut it into two pieces," Issy informed her.

"You sound just like my mother," Caroline said, making Issy smile. It was the first smile Caroline had seen all day.

"Here, this is for you." Issy pushed over a small package, wrapped in pink tissue paper.

"*Really?* For me?"

"I said so, didn't I?"

She looked away and Caroline knew she was embarrassed and thought she was being loud, and that everyone was looking.

"A present," she said, unraveling the pink tissue. "Ohh, Issy, how lovely."

It was a tiny brooch, junky, cheap but somehow sweet. She ran a finger over the fake silver. Fake or not, she would always treasure it. "A little bird, on the wing," she said.

"Sort of like us. Birds on the wing, never alighting anywhere."

"You mean us not having a real home anymore?" Caroline felt that clench in her heart again. "We'll get one, soon. I promise you."

Her voice sounded more confident than she felt. Money was tight, to say the least. When she'd married James, she had been young, she hadn't known any better and had signed that prenup, which of course meant that all she'd gotten from the divorce and sixteen years of marriage was a very small lump sum, and child support until her daughter became eighteen.

She glanced round the small tearoom at the other people; ordinary people, mackintoshes and parkas steaming over the backs of their chairs in the heat wafting from a long white radiator under the already steamed-up windows. People, Caroline thought, whose lives were all set; who had a pattern, a routine, and probably not a care in the world as they ate their scones and jam and cream and talked about the rain, as the English always did because it always rained anyway.

"Come on, have that last chocolate éclair, why don't you," she said briskly, pulling herself together. "Then we'll get out into the country-side, see a bit more of the Cotswolds."

Issy gave her that world-weary fifteen-year-old shrug. "Whatever," she said, which Caroline guessed meant she agreed.

chapter 2

Back in the car, she turned on the heater and the wipers and drove down the high street, over the narrow stone bridge that crossed what she guessed was the River Windrush, smaller here and brown, though running quite fast on this stormy day.

Issy did not even look. She seemed not interested in any part of their weekend. She'd hated the small inexpensive hotel where they'd booked in because Caroline had seen their ad with a black-and-white drawing of a pretty timbered house. It turned out to be faux-Tudor with an air of gloom about it that made her want to check out before they'd even checked in. The only thing in its favor was that it was cheap.

She had been given a key by a tired-looking and completely disinterested woman. Ignoring the small gas fire sputtering fitfully in the "lounge," she had carried her bag up the spindly staircase, Issy clomping behind, lugging her own.

"It'll be lovely," Caroline had said, hopefully, unlocking the door to their room and taking a look. There were two narrow beds with green silky coverlets and thin blankets that promised no warmth. The single pillow on each bed had a washed-out green polyester case. A table with a brown plastic top and a single drawer stood between the beds, with the smallest bedside lamp Caroline had ever seen. Reading in bed would be impossible unless you held the lamp up over your head, plus the ceiling light had the kind of round shade that exposed the bulb, blinding you. The room had the damp chill of a place long unused.

"Bloody hell," Issy said, not even putting down her bag.

"Oh, it's not so bad," Caroline replied, but she knew it was terrible.

"Mom!" Issy pleaded. "Let's just go back to London."

Caroline noticed she had not said "let's go home."

They stood there for a minute while Caroline thought. She had paid in advance and couldn't really afford to go anywhere else. Besides, this was Oxford on a weekend, places were bound to be full. Last time she had stayed here, what seemed decades ago, they had been at the Randolph, comfily old-fashioned and warm, with a bar and a suitably proper air of "belonging" about it. The thought of her past life trailed through her mind, as she knew it must her daughter's. This place was the end of the line. They absolutely could not stop here.

She grabbed her bag, nodded and said, "You're right. Let's go. But we can't just turn around and go back to London. We'll take a look at the countryside. We can drive back later, after the traffic eases up."

Issy hefted her bag over her shoulder and led the way back down the stairs. There was no one at the counter in the tiny hall so Caroline simply left the key and they walked out.

And that's how later, they'd ended up having a cream tea in pretty Burford, and were now driving through wet countryside while Issy texted the friends she had left behind in Singapore when her mother had uprooted her, and made her what Issy now called "a displaced person."

Guilt wrapped Caroline with a chill deeper than that of the hotel room. It was all her fault.

She swung the car into a narrow lane, past an enormous house glimpsed behind iron gates with rampant lions on the stone gateposts; past a couple of fields where the long grass bent sideways under the buffeting wind, with the most miserable-looking wet sheep Caroline had ever seen. But then she had never really *looked* at sheep before, maybe sheep always looked miserable, wet or dry. Chestnut-colored cows turned their heads surprised when Caroline suddenly stomped on the brakes so hard they squealed, and Issy shot forward and dropped the iPhone her father had bought her when she was still considered his daughter.

"Sorry," Caroline said, getting out of the car. But she was looking at the FOR SALE sign and an old stone barn, set right next to the river.

It was not "love at first sight."

chapter 3

"Oh, Mom," Issy said, in what Caroline recognized as her "what the hell are we doing here" tone of voice. Why *were* they here? In the wind and the rain in England when they could have stayed in Singapore with James and had a nice life.

She pulled her woolly scarf tighter over her hair, took off the red pointy glasses she always wore because she couldn't see much farther than her nose, and wiped the rain off them. Truth to tell, she had no answer. A soggy English field with wet sheep and cold-looking cows was a long way from the Disney version of English country life. Hadn't the sun always shone in their past in Singapore? And when it did rain, didn't it come down with monsoonlike force for a few hours, then blue skies and warm breezes returned, transforming streets back from rivers, returning the market stalls to their usual glory of golden fruits, and the "hawker" food stands to their fragrant, tempting, mouthwatering goodness, with their handmade noodles and barbecued meats, their Chinese-style shrimp and Malaysian curries. You could eat at any hawker stall in Singapore and feel you'd had the best meal of your life. The rainy English high street cream tea suddenly seemed a bad exchange.

"Well," she said, as cheerfully as she could manage. "I think it looks charming." Was she *crazy*? It looked like a stone barn that had seen better days stuck next to a muddy-looking river, with only a single and currently brown-leafed tree to soften its rectangular, workmanlike outline. "It's for sale," she added. "Maybe we should take a look."

"Why?"

Her daughter was asking the question Caroline knew she should have been asking herself. Sometimes Issy was so like her father it took her breath away. Those deep-set eyes, the frown between her brows, the straight, almost aggressive nose. She had her mouth though. Not that that was too good a feature: a touch too wide, a touch too full, and a whole lot too vulnerable. Her daughter wasn't really "pretty," not yet anyway; she was all scowls and skinny legs and long brown hair. One day, though, she might be, when she got rid of the attitude and that haunted look in her big brown eyes. Looking at her, Caroline suddenly had a brain wave.

Brain wave? Crazy was more like it. But that's the way she had always been; acting on impulse, jumping in with both feet, and almost always in over her head. Her life was one cliché after another. That's how she'd gotten married in the first place.

She grabbed Issy's hand, and said, "Come on, let's take a look at it," and marched her daughter, feet dragging in her new green wellies, along the rutted once-graveled path that led between the fields to the gray stone house.

Caroline knew houses were not normally *gray* in Oxfordshire; they were built from the beautiful, honey-colored, Cotswold stone. She guessed this one was so wet it had simply given up and turned gray with defeat and age. It stood on a slight rise almost directly on the narrow muddy bit of river that snaked in a curve around it before doubling back again. It was rectangular with a small outbuilding, and close-up somehow looked more solid than it had from a distance.

The rain had stopped but Caroline could hear the sound of rushing water.

Leaving Issy standing in front of the barn, forlorn and wet as the sheep, she walked round the corner of the house to a terrace where a low stone wall separated land from water. To her right the river picked up speed and tumbled over a small weir. She didn't know whether it was the pretty, frothy weir, the rushing river, or the stone terrace, but suddenly she could imagine herself, on a calm summer evening sitting on that low stone wall with a glass of wine in her hand, watching the tiny tributary flowing peacefully past. Why, she wondered wistfully, when people dreamed their dreams, was the weather always blissful and there was always a glass of wine.

She told herself sternly to stop. She had a daughter she was bringing up alone; she did not have money; she did not have a job; she did not have a husband. Responsibility sagged her shoulders when she realized, as she had only too often recently, that she was no longer that fun, free girl who'd met the man of her dreams. She was no longer the wife with a lovely home in Singapore and time on her hands.

She had given up cursing in front of her daughter (though she had heard Issy use a few choice words on the phone when she thought her mother wasn't listening. Didn't she know mothers *always* listened; how else were they to know anything, since they were never told?). So she merely said, "You're right, honey. This place isn't meant for us. Maybe we'll go to France, be near Grandpa and Grandma."

Caroline's parents had recently sold up their London home, right before she could have used it. A free London base would have been perfect. Or would it? Issy running around London the way she was now? A city school? Good kids? Bad kids? Sighing, Caroline thought life was so much easier when you lived it young and alone and made decisions based only on what *you* wanted.

"Mom, look."

While Caroline was gazing dreamily at the river Issy was stand-ing in front of the barn. The tall wooden doors, gray as the wet sheep, were clasped by a rusty iron bar. It wasn't what she was pointing out though. Above the doors was affixed a painted sign. Worn and weathered though it was, Caroline could still make out the words *Bar, Grill and Dancing.*

Dancing? Here? The mind boggled.

"Who do you think came here, Mom?" Issy asked, suddenly inter-ested. "I mean, like— Well, there's no one around. *Nothing.*"

"True." Caroline ran her hand over wood she'd bet had been here for a very long time. "Bar and Grill and Dancing" were a long way from this barn's beginnings.

"Locals," she guessed. "Maybe people from Oxford, you know, students."

"*Drinking and driving?*" Issy wrinkled her nose.

Caroline congratulated herself that at least her fifteen-year-old knew right from wrong.

"I expect they drank Cokes," she reassured her. "But just look at this door. How old can it be?"

"Too old." Issy turned away.

Caroline knew she was remembering her home in Singapore, filled with sunlight and the freshness of new architecture, cool mar-ble floors and wooden doors that closed properly and never squeaked, as she knew these would.

"Dad wouldn't like this place," Issy added scornfully, sending a death knell through her mother's heart. It had been a year since the divorce, a year and a half since they had left. Occasionally, James texted his daughter. He never phoned though, never spoke to her, too afraid, Caroline guessed, of her emotions. Or maybe his own.

Like so many women before her, even when Caroline had known her marriage was falling apart, she'd made the mistake of staying for the sake of her child. She had asked herself what if James married again? What if he had other children? What if he cut Issy out of his new life? How could she do that to her daughter, simply because *she* had made a mistake and married the wrong man?

Anyhow, for Caroline, it had also meant giving up on love: on her home, her security. It meant responsibility. It meant being "alone."

She had found out about the other woman in the usual way: hotel bills from places James wasn't supposed to be; odd phone calls; a receipt for a pair of expensive earrings; too many nights away from home, and she had picked up her pride, picked up her kid and walked out. Leaving did not mean she didn't love James though. She still did. Probably always would.

The adrenaline of anger only got her through the first few days, the first few weeks. Then, when the adrenaline simmered down and life took on some semblance of normality, she finally had to acknowledge that knot of fear in the pit of her stomach. "Responsibility" was a big word, and now it was all hers. James was supposed to pay child support, school fees, dentist bills, and so on, and some months he did and some months he didn't.

First, they'd gone to live with Caroline's parents in Chelsea, just before they'd sold it in favor of a cottage in France. After that Caroline rented a tiny flat while Issy went to a local school, paid for by Caroline's father until James was finally court-ordered to actually pay for his daughter's education. And also pay the lump sum—very small for a sixteen-year marriage—settled in the prenup. Fool that Caroline had been to sign, but what did she know? Then she was a woman in love and that was all she'd cared about.

So now here the two of them were, escaping the confines of their small rented London flat with a weekend out in the country, inspecting a run-down barn on the edge of a river with a sign that said *Bar, Grill and Dancing,* and a door that had to be at least two hundred

years old, with a view of a field of cows and sheep, and a gravel driveway that was half mud. And she was suddenly actually thinking
about buying it. It must have been the wonderful idea of people
"dancing," as well as the pressure of her daughter's longing for a
home. Anyhow, she knew it had to be cheap, in this condition and
in the middle of nowhere, and they desperately needed a real roof
over their heads.

"I know I'm crazy," she said, taking Issy's cold hand in both hers.
"But I seriously like it."

"Ohh, *Mo-om*." Issy sounded so like her, Caroline laughed. And
then Issy said, "Ohh, *Mo-om*," again and pulled her hand away.

"Don't move," she said in a low voice. "Don't speak, Mom. Do not
make a sound."

Caroline's eyes, behind her pointy red glasses, swiveled to watch
Issy as she crept toward the river, as softly as anyone could creep in
green Hunter wellies that squelched loudly. She saw her kneel in the
wet grass. Saw her hand reach out, touch something dark. It did not
move.

Then, "Ohh, *Mo-om*," Issy said again in a choked voice, that sent
Caroline running to her side.

Issy picked up the dark blob of a kitten and held it toward her, so
tiny, and so wet it must have been dredged from the river.

"Oh, *Mo-om*," she said, choking on her tears, clutching it to her
chest; eyes pleading. "Can I keep it?"

What else could Caroline say but "yes." At least now she would
have something to love.

And that's how they acquired Blind Brenda, the cat whose pale
ice-blue eyes turned out to be completely sightless, though of course
Caroline only got to know later, after the enormous vet bills.

chapter 4

It was five o'clock that same evening when she pushed open the door of the Star & Plough in the village of Upper Amberley. A fire blazed in a cavernous grate and Mexican straw sombreros were hooked on the wall in some sort of weird decorative theme. An air of coziness locked out the chilly night. She and Issy stood there, dripping water all over the just-mopped stone-flagged floor. They were both so bedraggled the pleasant woman behind the bar immediately took pity on them.

"Evening, *amigas*," she called. "Come on in, there's a table near the fire, looks as though you might need it. And I have some good chicken tortilla soup, if you're interested. Warm you up a bit, right?"

Issy looked straight into the woman's compassionate dark eyes and held out the small fur bundle.

The woman looked at it and said, "Well, that's a poor, little wet kitten, isn't it? I'll bet it's even hungrier and colder than you are. Tell you what, I'll warm up a drop of milk, then I'll call my daughter to help. You two can take the kitten into the back kitchen and try and get that milk down it." She put out her hand to stroke the little creature. It did not even lift its head.

They waited while the woman took her mobile from her pocket and speed-dialed her daughter.

"Sammy," they heard her say. "I have a young friend here with a kitten in trouble. In the kitchen drawer you'll find the syringe we got from the vet when the starling fell out of the tree. I remember I washed it out well so now we can use it to try to get some milk into this little cat's belly."

She clicked off, smiled her lovely smile at the two of them, took a small wicker basket usually used for bread and folded a clean, soft tea towel into it. A last resting place for an almost dead kitten.

She said, "Why not take off your wet coats. And you, love." She was smiling at Caroline who found herself smiling back. "You look as though you could use a glass of wine. I know you're driving, but it's only the one glass and you should have some warm food with it. In a couple of hours you'll be okay. Think of it as medicinal."

Caroline was never so glad to see a glass of medicinal wine as she was right then. "Thank you," she said humbly, because she had come into a village pub expecting to be given the cool non-welcome issued to tourists and strangers, and now, here they were, being treated like family.

Sammy came hurrying in. She was short and round like her mother, but with blond hair and blue eyes. "From her Aztec ancestors," her mother explained proudly when they looked at her surprised. "Of course, we're Mexican."

The girl crouched, peering at the kitten and a second later she picked it up and the two were headed to the kitchen to heat the milk.

"Operation 'save the kitten,'" the woman said.

"If love can save her, then she'll make it."

Caroline had no idea where those words came from but knew

that in her heart she'd meant "love" can save anything. She had really believed that, once upon a time.

Quite suddenly she began to cry. Sometimes, no matter what strong capable face she put on things for Issy's sake, that soft wounded underbelly gave her away and the hurt frightened woman showed. She didn't want it to, at least only when she was alone in bed, never in front of her daughter, and *never* like this in public, for God's sake.

The woman fetched a brandy but Caroline refused it, saying she couldn't possibly and that she felt foolish for crying in front of a stranger, and for no reason at all really. Or perhaps it was simply *all* the reasons, catching up at once. Loneliness. Lack of money. Responsibility. Guilt.

The woman set the brandy on the table in front of her anyhow, and called her husband to come and take care of the bar. She poked at the fire with an enormous handcrafted iron weapon and threw on another log. Then she came and sat opposite Caroline.

"Where are you going?" she asked quietly, obviously not wanting to draw the attention of the three other customers, two of whom anyway were occupied with a game of dominoes. The third's only interest seemed to be his Border collie who lounged, tongue lolling, at his feet, most likely waiting for a handout of a bit of ham or a sausage.

"I realize it's not only about the kitten," the woman was saying. "My daughter's the same age as yours so I know what you're going through with her. I'll tell you what I discovered, *amiga,* until they start school your kids are all yours. They love only you. They want only you. *You* are their world. Then," she snapped her fingers, "they suddenly discover there are other people, other role models, other friends. Having a child is a full-time job, and one women don't apply for because we have absolutely no qualifications. Tell me, who knows exactly how to do it? It's all instinct. Hah, try putting that on your job application!"

Despite her sudden misery Caroline found herself smiling.

"It's true," she said. "When your child hits school your rule is over. And when she becomes a teenager, forget it."

The woman smiled her nice smile, patted Caroline's hand, told her to take a good sip of that brandy, and would she like some of her chicken tortilla soup?

She shook her head. "Thank you but I still have to drive."

"Where to? I mean, where are you going that's so urgent?"

Caroline thought about it and that hopeless feeling took over again. Where was she going that mattered? Certainly not back to London in this storm, or to another cheap hotel in Oxford and a twin-bedded room with TV she didn't want to watch and a daughter who seemed to wish she was anywhere else but there, with her. She touched the silvery bird-on-the-wing brooch pinned to her sweater that Issy had surprised her with. Well, maybe her daughter did care, sometimes.

"We have a couple of inexpensive rooms we rent out," the woman was saying. "Warm and comfortable, and no driving. How about it?"

Caroline felt the sag lift out of her shoulders. Relief took over. "Done," she said, and took a good swig of the brandy, choking as it hit the back of her throat. The Border collie gave a startled bark and the three other occupants of the pub glanced her way, but she had already dried her tears.

The woman held up a hand and high-fived her. "I'll get that soup," she said. "And then see what's doing with that poor little half-dead kitten."

Caroline called after her as she walked away. "I don't even know your name?"

"Maggie."

"Caroline."

They looked at each other, taking each other in.

Then, "It's not just my daughter," Caroline said. "It's my ex."

"I knew it," Maggie said.

chapter 5

Maggie Gonzalez had run the Star & Plough for sixteen years. It was an old stucco-faced, low-ceilinged, stone-flagged, black-beamed building, with yellowed walls and a fireplace large enough to roast an ox or brew a cauldron of stew. There was a brand-new bar counter with polished brass pulls for the draft beer, a main room, known as "the lounge"; a small back room called "the snug," which local retirees and single older ladies preferred when the Oxford young bunch rolled up and got the music going. Gleaming glasses reflected in the mirror in back of the bar and there was always a hint of freshly made tortillas in the air.

Maggie's real name was Mercedes, but this had caused some confusion with the locals and too many jokes about cars so she had settled for simply being "Maggie."

It was not so easy for her husband, whose name was Jesus, and who also doubled as the local handyman, and contractor, when he could get the work. The trouble had come when people received messages on their answer machines saying "Jesus called." It had given quite a few of the older ones a shock.

"He's a little too early, my dear," Veronica Partridge, who was seventy-five if she was a day, had said, huffily buttoning her cardigan.

"It's not my time for 'Jesus' to call." And Maggie was forced to explain it was the audio message that got it wrong and that her husband's name was pronounced "Heyzus."

Their daughter, Samantha, was almost the same age as Issy, and, like hers, somehow Samantha's name had also become shortened.

Maggie took Caroline into her kitchen at the rear of the pub, sat her at the table with a bowl of soup and told her the story of how she and her husband had come to be proprietors of the Star & Plough, a long and somewhat convoluted route from their home on Mexico's Baja peninsula where a poor girl, Maggie, had worked as a housekeeper at the local tourist hotel, changing beds and cleaning bathrooms.

Jesus was a fisherman, he knew about boats, he'd practically been brought up on one. Which was why one morning he'd been summoned to the marina and offered a job on a one-hundred-and-fifty-foot yacht sailing across the ocean to Monte Carlo, in the South of France.

They had married and ended up in England, in the rain. They got a job at a pub in Surrey, then were offered the stewardship of the Star & Plough in a straggling Cotswold village over the bridge from Burford, make a left a time or two, then a couple of rights—and here they were. And then, when Samantha came along, here they stayed. They served chicken tacos as well as ploughman's lunch. "We've become 'locals,'" Maggie said. "And friends."

Caroline knew envy was not a "good" emotion, it was probably even one of the seven deadly sins, but she wished her life could have been like Maggie's. Maggie had known poverty, but she'd worked hard and was still with her husband. "Can I become a friend?" Caroline asked.

"But you already are," Maggie told her.

chapter 6

Later that night, Issy lay in bed in a cozy attic room over the pub. The ceiling sloped to a gabled window set so low it was almost on the floor. The walls were plain white with black beams meeting in a point over the two beds, which had blue-and-white-flowery coverlets and blue-flowery sheets that matched the curtains and the rug. There was a little white dresser with a small pink-shaded lamp and a straight chair set at a tiny table under that low window. A door led out to the hallway while another led into a small adjacent sitting room with a blue velvet couch, and a big squishy-looking chair. Her mom was sleeping in an identical room on the other side of that little sitting room. Sam was down the hall and the kitten was in its basket next to Issy, who was thinking about her life.

She supposed today it had changed for the second time when she'd gotten out of the car and stood with her mom, looking at that falling-down wreck of an Oxfordshire barn with the *Bar, Grill and Dancing* sign. It was the *Dancing* that did it. There was no way she could even remotely imagine anyone dancing in that place. Even its ghosts would not dance. And she'd bet her new boots there'd be ghosts. Always were in places like that.

When her mom said she seriously liked it she knew Caroline had finally lost it. I mean, her behavior had been so totally off the wall, picking up and leaving Dad, just whisking her out of the place she had called "home" all her life (and let's not forget that fifteen years— well, she was just fourteen then—was a bloody long time).

That English word "bloody" was bloody useful and it got her off having to say "fuck," which made her uncomfortable, probably because, though she knew technically what it meant, she didn't know *"practically," if you know what I'm saying.* She loved that rapper phrase, that American black all-encompassing, "y'know what I'm saying." Made her feel part of a greater, bigger world when she used it, like she was one of them, up there to be counted. Instead of this abandoned, homeless person—she refused to call herself a "child." Fifteen these days was not a child. A "child" was when you were five or six and all was right with your world because nothing could ever go wrong. And it didn't. You were wrapped in that cozy glow of security; Mom, Dad, Home. And then they pulled the rug out from under you. And down you went. Or sometimes up, Issy supposed, though she didn't know enough people in her position to be able to make a judgment.

Now, *there* was a good grown-up statement. *Being able to make a judgment.* She'd heard her dad say that, on the phone probably, talking business in his study, where he usually was.

Her dad, James Evans, was really good-looking. Not like a rock star or a movie star; more just a tall, dark, lean, square-jawed man with an air of authority, who always wore really well-cut suits that he had made in Hong Kong. As he did his shirts, with their small raised monogram JE on the cuffs. His ties were silk and very pretty. When Issy was little she used to sit in his closet with a rack of them on her knees, folding them in her fingers, luxuriating in the softness, the beautiful colors. She had wished she could be a boy because then she could have borrowed his ties. She could have been like him.

And don't think she hadn't asked herself many times since, whether, if she had been a boy, her father would have let her go? Just like that. Pack a small suitcase and leave, with Mom clutching her hand tighter than a knot on an anchor line so she wouldn't escape and run back to him? No. Her mom said if she was going, then Issy was going too.

They'd left in a big, stormy huff. Her mom couldn't even slam the door because they lived in a penthouse and the elevator opened directly onto their floor. So they'd had to stand there, facing him, while Caroline pressed the button, and there was an achingly-slow few seconds before it finally pinged and those bloody doors, on their always perfectly soundless oiled wheels, or whatever elevators had, slid carefully together, shutting out her dad, who was standing there, arms folded over his chest, looking at them. Until the very last second.

Issy believed he had wanted to keep her face, *her agonized crying face,* in his memory so that he would come and get her, wherever she was. Wherever Mom took her. Which was actually to the Peninsula Hotel in Hong Kong.

Caroline had said she certainly was not going to the Raffles Hotel, right there in Singapore, because that's where she had met her dad. Issy had heard that story from *both* her parents many times, because she'd asked many times, thinking it was romantic and wonderful and when she grew up she wanted to meet a man exactly like her father. Now of course she'd given that up.

Because he'd given up. He never came after her. Never came to get her. Never reclaimed her. Even in the courtroom, he hadn't shown up. "The mother can have custody," he'd said in a message via his lawyers. "It's the correct thing to do. Children should always be with their mothers."

Bloody hell, what was he thinking? Issy had cried herself to sleep for over a year now. Well, *months*, anyway. Until she'd told herself to fuckin' stop it. Aw, bloody hell, *there*. She'd used that word again and she'd sworn she would not.

She thought of all the hours she'd spent in front of the bathroom mirror, checking out her image, trying to figure out what was wrong that her own father no longer wanted her. Left profile, right profile, three-quarters; allowing that her nose was too big, or was it too wide? That her mouth was big too but looked nothing like that famous movie star's; that her forehead had a definite bump, her hairline was lopsided, and her eyes a boring brown. How could a girl with brown eyes and brown hair have pale lashes? Ask her? She did.

Her father never called her on the phone now; just the occasional text message saying, like, hope your grades are good, I'm sending you a cashmere sweater; e-mail me a recent photo so I don't forget you. But he did forget her.

Still, the sweater was nice. She'd never worn it; it was preserved in tissue paper in the old Hello Kitty bag her father brought her from Japan years ago. That, and a photo of the two of them (without her mom—Caroline must have taken the picture) holding hands, walking down a country lane. She couldn't remember where that country lane was but she did remember the feel of her dad's strong hand clasping hers, and how carelessly happy she had been. She had thought he would never let go.

Oh, but she'd loved him so. Still did.

Actually, her father's and mother's stories of how they had met were completely different.

James told Issy he'd walked into the bar at Singapore's Raffles Hotel and immediately noticed the tall, dark-haired, long-legged woman perched on a stool, sipping a mojito through a pink straw that exactly matched her pink lipstick. Very pretty, he'd thought, catching her eye. As well as he could, since she was wearing glasses.

She was also wearing a very short skirt and showing a lot of thigh. "I wanted to kiss her knees they were so pretty," he told Issy. (Kiss her *knees*? Ugh! Issy remembered thinking.) "Instead, I said hello, asked where she was from, and her name.

"She said she was from London," and her name was Caroline Muggins, or Huggins or something odd like that. He told Issy he'd thought, huh she's had one too many mojitos, this girl, but then she smiled at him and said I'm going to marry you. He'd asked her why? Was it because she'd promised herself to marry the third man to walk into the bar that night? Or was she afraid of being left on the shelf? Or did she really fancy him?

Anyhow, he'd already been married. "Twice," he'd told her.

"Hmm." She'd sucked thoughtfully on that pink mojito straw. "A serial husband. But when you marry me I will be the *last* wife."

"You'll notice," James had reminded his daughter, who was curled up in bed, big eyes fastened on him as he told her the story one more time, "that your mother asked *me* to marry *her*. Not the other way around."

She asked if that really mattered and he'd said not then, but her mom hadn't liked signing the prenup.

Now, of course, Issy knew what a prenup was and it meant her mom didn't have much money.

Anyway, her mother's different story was that she had been alone in the bar at the Raffles Hotel. "Sipping that mojito," she said. "It was the first I'd ever tasted. We were more into gin and tonic when I was eighteen."

"But you didn't drink when you were *eighteen*!" Issy had interrupted. "You had to be twenty-one."

"Right," her mother had said, taking a deep breath. "Well, of course, I meant *after* I was twenty-one. So, anyway, I was sipping that bloody mojito—ooops, sorry, shouldn't have said that, it's just that I'll never drink a mojito again."

Issy had thought it must be because it didn't taste very good.

Her mother went on, "I was wearing a black pencil skirt, pulled demurely down . . ."

"Daddy said you were showing your thighs."

Caroline closed her eyes as though trying to remember. She smiled, just a faint upward twitch of the lips. "So maybe I was," she admitted. "And I had on this top from Zara, black silk jersey, and it kept slipping off one shoulder and showing my pink bra strap. Now, what kind of sophisticated young woman would wear a pink bra under her sexy black top?"

Issy didn't know, but still she was fascinated. Her mother was so pretty she could have worn her dressing gown and it would have looked all right; her tall, slender, bosomy mom, with her long, black hair cut in bangs that swept over her shortsighted greenish eyes and got tangled in her red cat's-eye glasses; with her slopey cheeks and lovely wide pink mouth that was great at giving kisses. And she had pretty hands that always held her tightly when she told this story. *"Clinging on for dear life,"* her mom used to say.

Anyway, her mom had gone on with her version of the story. "I was just sitting there, perched on a tall barstool. Showing too much thigh, when this guy came in. He stood a couple of seats away from me and ordered a mojito, exactly like mine.

"He gave me a look," Caroline remembered with a smile. "Our eyes met and linked and I thought oh my God he is so handsome, so . . . Anyway," she'd gone on briskly. "He asked if I minded him joining me. That is, if you are alone, he said. And oh, Issy I was so alone, all by myself in Singapore. I'd just finished two years of culinary school and was running away from a boy I thought not man-of-the-world enough for me. I was on my way to Hong Kong to do some boring cooking job, but you see, I didn't even get as far as Hong Kong because your father said—there and then—he said, *I am going to marry you. And I don't even know your name.*

"So I told him my name and he told me his, and instead of being Caroline Meriton, I became all at once, Caroline Evans."

"And was it lovely?" Issy always asked the same question, sucking on her thumb, already half asleep, knowing her mom would tuck the sheet up over her chest, turn down the lamp, kiss her, and always say, "It was so lovely, sweetheart. I will never forget it."

Of course now she knew her mother had meant her dad was sexy. Then, she had been too young to know about sexual attraction. She wasn't even sure now what it was, except that the word "fuck" had something to do with it.

She'd guessed she must be a late bloomer or something, but she just didn't want to know. She wanted men to be sweet and nice and to wear beautiful suits and ties, and loafers with tassels and smell of Vetiver cologne, like her dad. In fact she was horrified by the whole idea of men taking off their clothes and showing their dangly bits. Who on earth ever wanted to see that?

They'd given a talk in class, demonstrating with cucumbers and condoms, about how it was done and how not to get pregnant, while the girls *giggled* and said no way, and some sniggered and said, "*yeah right . . .*"

And then came the upheaval, her mom's unhappiness, her dad suddenly remote, hardly ever home; the fights, and then leaving, just like that, with never a thought of how it might affect *her.* She had not even had time to say goodbye to her friends, her school, her swim club, her Saturday sleepovers. It was all gone. Just like that. And she didn't know what to do. And worse, nor did her mother.

Now, here they were, in rented rooms over a pub in the Cotswolds.

The rain was still pelting against the window and the kitten moved restlessly in its basket.

She reached out, touched the pathetic little heap of cheap-looking gray fur. The milk was still warm and she inserted the dropper into its slack mouth and squeezed. It began to suck. It wanted to live after all.

Issy almost never did, she had trained herself not to, but now, quite suddenly, she began to cry.

chapter 7

In the room down the hall from her daughter, Caroline was not sleeping either. Her thoughts, as they always did, had returned to James, and what had happened. She remembered it all so clearly.

The day they left they'd flown to Hong Kong and checked in to the Peninsula Hotel. That was where James always stayed—nothing but the best for him, so Caroline determined it would be "nothing but the best" for his wife and daughter.

She'd taken a small suite and charged it to James's platinum card. She ordered room service, just the way James did, and overtipped the waiter, the way he always did. She drank a martini—telling herself she would only have one because she was in charge of a child. Well, a fourteen-year-old anyway, but when Issy had finally cried herself to sleep, she sent down for another, before she also cried herself to sleep on the sofa, only to be roused by the phone ringing.

It's him, she'd thought, waking up, startled and still in her crumpled white skirt and the yellow sweater that was years old and matted from too many washings but happened to be the first thing she'd grabbed when she was so mad she couldn't even see straight. Her hand reached for the phone and then stopped. Why wasn't James calling on her cell?

But the phone kept on, so she answered.

"My name is Gayle Lee," a woman's voice said. "I need to see you."

"Do I know you?" Caroline pushed back her tangled hair and stuck her glasses on her nose as if they would make her see the woman more clearly, or at least remember who she was. Could she be an emissary from James? A lawyer, asking them to return at once, all was forgiven? Everything back to normal?

"I am on my way up to your suite," the woman said, in such a crisp firm tone Caroline had no choice but to agree.

When she opened the door a couple of minutes later the woman walked right past her without so much as a glance or a hello, or a hand held out in greeting. Caroline watched astonished, as she stood, taking in the small and by now rather untidy suite. Issy had left her clothes exactly where she had stepped out of them, in the middle of the living room floor, and for once Caroline had not picked up after her. She supposed it was because it reminded her of James, who she was always picking up after. Her husband always left his stuff on the floor for someone else to take care of.

"How do you do," she said pointedly, in her best and most English disapproving voice, and when the English did "disapproval," people usually got the point immediately.

Not this woman, though. She walked silently to the window, then turned and looked at Caroline. They took each other in.

She was Asian, older, yet somehow ageless, with amazing platinum white hair, a clear tan skin and, Caroline was soon to discover, a brain like a machete, ready to strike. She was strikingly attractive, slender and straight and taut as an armed crossbow. She wore traditional Chinese dress, green brocade, buttoned at the neck, slit to the thigh.

The sudden sinking feeling in the pit of her stomach told Caroline she had finally met James's mistress. *This* was the woman he'd betrayed her for.

"I am your husband's business partner," Gayle Lee said.

Caroline sank into the cushioned sofa. *So that's what it was called these days.* She shook back her uncombed hair and straightened her glasses. In the middle of a crisis she was wishing she had at least put on lipstick before being taken by surprise.

"I have been James's partner for twenty years," Gayle Lee said.

But she and James had only been together for sixteen! This must have been going on since before they were married.

Gayle Lee was still standing by the window and Caroline noticed she was clever enough to keep her back to the light so Caroline couldn't see how old she really was. Older than her, that was for sure, but so perfect it didn't matter. Her unusual platinum hair was cut in the traditional Chinese bob with deep bangs. She had narrow dark eyes, high cheekbones, and a small mouth colored the reddest Caroline had ever seen. Her heart sank. Gayle Lee looked great. And she meant *great*.

"I didn't know James had a business partner," she said, still hoping she meant strictly "business." "Other than Mark Santos."

"Santos was not involved. We had a private 'arrangement,' James and I."

"*Arrangement*?" It was a dumb repeat of her word, but she couldn't think. How could she? She was being presented with a fait accompli she'd known nothing about, and she had been married to James for *sixteen years*.

Gayle Lee gave her a hard-eyed look and said, "I heard you had left James."

Caroline knew the only person she could have heard it from was her husband.

"I'm here to warn you," Gayle Lee said clearly and coldly.

Suddenly angry, Caroline sat up straighter. Who the hell did this Gayle Lee think she was anyway?

"You will not get a penny from James's and my business," Gayle Lee was saying. She walked closer and stood over her. "And I'm warning you, it will not be in your best interests to try."

"*Mommy?*"

Issy was standing in the doorway in her T-shirt and underpants because that's the way she had climbed, still crying, into bed, without so much as a shower or pajamas. She was staring, amazed, at the green brocade, platinum vision hovering menacingly over her mother.

"She looks like James," Gayle Lee said. Then she walked away.

Her hand on the doorknob, she turned. "I advise you to remember what I said. There are changes coming and they will not be to your advantage. I wish you goodnight."

And without a further glance she walked out.

"Mommy, who was that?"

Issy's voice brought Caroline back to reality.

"Oh, a friend of Daddy's. She came to say hello," she told her hastily.

"Well, she didn't say hello to me," Issy said. Then, "Mommy, I need you."

Caroline took her in her arms, put her back into bed and climbed in next to her. She held her through the longest night of her life.

That Gayle Lee was James's mistress and the source of her "betrayal," she had no doubt. She had come to warn her off and had also scared the life out of her. She had no idea what "business" she was talking about but knew she had to put the forest-green-*cheongsamed*-platinum vision out of her mind. Gayle Lee was in the past and now she had to concentrate on her future. She had a lot of work to do to make their lives right again.

Inevitably, the next day, they went "home," back to London and Caroline's own mom and dad. Where else could she have gone?

chapter 8

Now, over a year and a half later, divorced, and lying in bed in a small rented attic room over a pub, Caroline knew how much she missed James.

She had never known how completely silent a room could be until he wasn't in it. Only a woman who had been with a man for years could understand what she meant. There was that plaiting together of their lives; the where does he leave off and you begin, the shorthand of sentences left unfinished because the other person would know exactly what you meant; the perfume you wore only for him; the dress you bought because you knew it would please him; the heels you wore even though your feet were killing you because he loved you in heels; the waxing because he liked you naked "down there," even though you hated it and it was hell growing back.

She missed the sex; she missed the smell of him on the pillow she'd clutch to her face after he'd gotten up in the morning; she missed the way he always took her hand crossing the street because he was concerned she couldn't see properly and was afraid she would get run over. She missed his hand in the small of her back as he led her into a restaurant; his murmured sexy words when he thought no one could hear. She missed cooking for him, *"practicing your skills,"* he would say, because of course she hadn't really ever been a "chef" despite the culinary school training. She even missed the solitary silences when James was gone, as he so often was, wishing the phone would ring, filling her day with school runs and responsibilities, and never, ever, putting herself first.

Was it the chicken or the egg she wondered? Had she been "a woman" first? Or "a wife"? Which had James wanted her to be? Of course she would have been anything he wanted. That was how so many women lost themselves in marriage. But now, since she had supposedly become "her own woman" and left him, she wondered exactly *who* was she anyway?

One morning, a few days later she asked her new friends Maggie and Jesus that question. She had decided to leave London and she and Issy had already moved into the tiny flat above the pub.

Jesus was a true Mexican with a Latin temperament and family values. He was square-built, mustached, with black hair that stood straight up, and a deep voice. He was sitting at the kitchen table, sipping coffee he had made himself, dripped through cheesecloth from beans he'd ground directly into a tall metal pot on the stove. It was thick and cloudy with residue and needed about half a dozen spoons of sugar to make it palatable.

"It's natural for a woman to put a man first," he said, making his wife laugh.

"Women are not here simply to look after you," she said. "We have to use our brains to keep you men in your place."

"Didn't work for me," Caroline said gloomily, making them laugh.

She hadn't heard good hearty laughter in so long, she rather enjoyed it. She hadn't meant to be funny, though. What she said was true. Throughout her marriage her so-called brains had been kept on the back burner. She'd been too afraid to use them because then she would have had to face facts and acknowledge the truth about her false life and her cheating husband.

Maggie said, "As a friend, I'm going to give you some advice. You must make a plan."

Caroline stared at her, surprised. Her mind was a blank. Or maybe it was just a clean slate.

"You have been with us almost a week now," Maggie said. "And you may stay as long as you wish, but it's over a year since the divorce. Jesus and I believe it's important for you to have a home of your own."

An image of the forlorn barn dripping rain under an almost leafless tree sprang to Caroline's mind, though anything less "homelike" would have been hard to find.

Maggie said, "You told me you have a small settlement from your husband. You must make a budget, work out exactly how much you can afford. Remember, you'll probably need to make repairs, alterations, you know how we women are when we take over a house."

The cozier image of a thatched cottage flashed into Caroline's mind, but she didn't care for thatch.

"First, though," Maggie went on, "you must get your daughter into a decent school. Sammy needs to move on from the local, and tomorrow I'm taking her to look at a small prep school just five miles from here. Perhaps you'd like to bring Issy along, too? Take a look?"

Issy sat up from the kitten basket. "I'd like that, Mom," she said with the first touch of eagerness Caroline had heard coming from her mouth in a year. Indifference was what she usually got: the *whatever-you-say, whatever-you-want, I-don't-care* syndrome that drove her wild because she never knew what to do either.

"We'll go together," Sammy said. She was like her mother, warm and touchy-feely, and she and Issy had become instant friends.

"So let's do that," she agreed.

"It's private, you have to pay fees." Jesus brought Caroline back to reality.

"Yes, well, Issy's father is supposed to take care of all that. It's in the agreement, y'know; he pays for her education." She didn't add that James's payments were sporadic and that her own father picked up the slack.

"And the day after that we have to get you a job," Maggie said, bringing Caroline back to earth with a bump.

She reviewed her options, which were exactly nil. Fear clenched her throat. Without James's help she needed to make money to keep their lives going. She *had* to make money. She said, "All I know how to do is cook. I'm pretty good though."

Maggie briskly cleared the coffee cups. "Good, then as soon as Issy starts school, you'll start in our kitchen. From now on, you'll be in charge of pub lunches. And I've been wanting to do dinners a couple of times a week, so now we can. I'll still be doing my spicy tacos, of course."

"Then I'll do my Singapore wonton soup," Caroline said, full of sudden enthusiasm, then wondered where she would get the ingredients.

"Oxford." Maggie read her mind. "They have everything international now."

Caroline thought how life worked out when you took control back into your own hands. With the help of new friends, a couple of children, and a kitten, of course. And without James.

When, she wondered, did you ever fall *out* of love? *How* did you do it?

chapter 9

The kitchen at the Star & Plough was twenty-five feet square with uneven hard-on-the-feet flagstone floors, terrible fluorescent lighting, and a massive and quite beautiful, oil-fired bright-blue Aga range with three ovens, one of which remained permanently, and miraculously Caroline thought, at the correct temperature for roasting practically anything. There was another for slow-cooking, and the third for keeping things warm. There were two hotplates, also always on, though at different temperatures; you simply chose the appropriate one from boiling to simmering. Plus another perfect for a pot of soup, just to sit there, ticking over.

Agas were invented by the clever Swedes who, living in a cold country, knew how to use a stove to best effect. The pub Aga never went out; it heated the water and kept the kitchen at a useful glow. Why everyone in damp England did not have one amazed Caroline. In fact, she e-mailed her parents to tell them so. They were stuck out in some outlandish bit of the Dordogne countryside in the middle of forty useless acres that her father spent most of his time mowing, sitting on his John Deere, a Panama hat clamped on his head and an always-unlit cigar clamped between his teeth.

"Best day's work I've ever done," he would say, showing up at six

P.M. promptly for the glass of champagne he and Caroline's mother had the new habit of sipping in the evening.

"Idyllic," Caroline's mom told her on the phone. "I've never seen your father happier."

Since her father had spent forty or so years as an engineer working on other modern miracles like suspension bridges that spanned remote gorges, and pipelines that ran through frozen tundra, Caroline could understand that a day's gentle mowing and a glass of champagne at six of an evening was a pretty good exchange, lifestyle-wise. And if her father was happy then so was her mom.

She supposed she got her own ingrained "good wife syndrome" from watching her mother's happy marriage, where the husband was king and the wife the loving subject. Yet, somehow, her parents had always been equals. She had run her domain. He'd done the job he liked. They were happy. Then why had it not worked for her?

"Come live with us," her father had told her sternly, when he'd sold up their London home and they had departed for a quiet life in the French countryside. "There's more going on here socially than there ever was in London. There must be some unattached men around, we'll have 'em over for dinner. You know how your mother is, she'll cook up a storm and they'll never want to leave."

"Never want to leave *Mom*, you mean," she'd replied. Though in fact the one thing her mother did do for her, that now turned out to have a market value, was insist she go to cooking school. "At least you'll have a 'trade,'" she'd told her, fearing her daughter's romantic notions of real life.

So now, between Caroline's pies and Maggie's famous spicy chicken tacos plus the tamales Maggie cooked every weekend—the ones that were always served at Christmas in Mexico, made from *masa,* a kind of corn flour, with slow-cooked pork, shredded and mixed with diced onion, cilantro, and jalapeño peppers, then rolled in corn leaves and baked in the oven to a savory melting softness—they were a big success.

Meanwhile she was cooking steak and fries, but she'd also added chicken pot pie to her menu, American-style, served in big white bowls with the flaky pastry crusts fluffed to spectacular heights that brought gasps of admiration. She had also taken to making her own bread, round, dense, flattish loaves that she let rise overnight on back of the Aga, with a cloth draped over the tins, then baked just before lunchtime.

"With good bread and butter, you can keep the customers waiting for their food a bit longer," she told Maggie, "and they won't even notice, they'll order a second bottle of wine before you know it." She was learning the business on the hoof, so to speak.

And after long nights on the pub's infamous hard stone floors her feet felt like hooves. She longed for one of those whirlpool Jacuzzi baths they had in spas, where she could sit with her feet being gently hot-massaged while her hair frizzed in the steam and she could keep her eyes shut against the world. A world she was still afraid to acknowledge existed, where she took complete responsibility for her own life. And her daughter's.

Right now, they were living "on the kindness of strangers" as Tennessee Williams had so tragically phrased it in *A Streetcar Named Desire*. Not that she was a Blanche DuBois. Far from it. Blanche was a woman totally alone. And Caroline had Issy, who thank God, was loving her time at Upperthorpe school. The Headmistress had taken her under her wing and she was getting a good education, preparing for sixth form and boarding school, though James was still not paying for it.

Caroline's father paid up and never once said I told you so. He never said what were you thinking signing that prenup. What he did say though, was, "Look, James can't do this, he's legally obligated to pay for his daughter. Not only legally, but morally." Her father was a moral man.

Meanwhile, Caroline was getting on with her new life. She'd met some of the locals who seemed to know more about her than she did them, via the "pub grapevine," she supposed, and received many a cheerful good morning while shopping on the high street, or queuing at the post office where the line was so slow you could read the morning paper while you waited, because everyone had to have a chat and a laugh. And of course she became familiar with the regulars at the pub, who came for her pie and Maggie's tacos, as well as the cute young guys whose eyes fastenened onto her as she walked across the lounge to serve them, making her blush, which of course made them laugh and tease her.

"I'll have you know I'm old enough to be your mom," she would say sternly, folding her arms over her sweatered bosom. Oh, go *on*! they'd reply, or words to that effect. You're not old enough to be anyone's mom.

There was one face, though, Caroline found herself looking out for. He wasn't "a regular," he only popped in occasionally, and he was never "dressed up." Middle height, dark hair, a bit beaky-looking. Hawklike some might have said. Maybe he had a sexy mouth? What did she know? She certainly wasn't thinking about "sex." Anyway, he came in early, sixish usually for a beer, and his sweater always seemed to be dotted with bits of wood shavings. Caroline assumed he was the local carpenter, though she never asked. She wasn't *that* interested. Or was she simply being cautious?

Every morning, Caroline got up early, gave the girls breakfast and drove them to school. Maggie picked them up in the afternoon. They were inseparable. They did their homework together; ate breakfast, lunch, and supper together. They gossiped and flirted with boys online. They went to the movies and shopping in Oxford, hung out with boys in cafés, and had a good time. Then, back home at the Star & Plough, watching TV they cuddled Blind Brenda on the sofa between them.

Two months passed and Caroline knew the time had come to take life into her own hands. She took a leap of faith and bought the broken-down barn grill & bar that cost every cent of her settlement from James (at least she'd gotten that up front.) She bought it because it was quite simply the cheapest place for sale around, and she had exactly enough for a low bid. The owner was desperate and accepted; he'd been trying to sell it for years. Looking at the place, in the clear light of day, Caroline understood why. The whole place needed restoration.

Still, there was something about it; its solitude, its age, its history she felt comfortable with. She loved the sound of the slow-flowing river; loved the stone that turned out to be honey-colored after all; loved the way it sat at the end of the rutted once-graveled drive (don't even ask what gravel cost and how much to deliver and spread it around!). Somehow, there was a connection. Possibly it was the sign, *Bar, Grill and Dancing,* that did it. She had always been a dreamer.

They were still living at the pub, wondering how to put their new "home" in order, when a few weeks later, James's business partner, Mark Santos, came to see her.

chapter 10

It was seven o'clock on a Friday night and the pub was packed with mostly young people, ten deep at the bar, with the old-fashioned juke box Jesus had rescued from somewhere, blasting the dated seventies pop he loved, and people shouting over everyone else to make themselves heard.

Every table was taken in both the lounge and the snug, and orders were coming in thick and fast, especially for the chicken pot pie with its billowing crust. The smell of beer, of bread, baking and *pico de gallo,* hot sauce and tacos leaked out into the street, where cars were crammed into tiny parking spots and smokers leaned up against the walls, lingering over cigarettes. Friday nights were always like that.

Caroline was in the kitchen, hovering over the Aga, pink-cheeked from the heat, helped by her Friday assistant, a young single mom called Sarah, who lived on her own with her baby, Little Billy, in a cottage nearby. She brought him to work and mostly he slept through all the noise, in his carrier. Teenager Lily who also babysat for Sarah, from time to time, helped with the dishes, mostly by dropping them.

Issy and Sam were too young to work in the pub but usually helped out in the kitchen on Fridays. Tonight, though they had been given a reprieve and were in the upstairs sitting room, homework done for the weekend. Blind Brenda was slotted between them on the sofa, and they had their bare feet on the green velvet ottoman, watching TV, and texting friends.

Caroline was wearing jeans, her old yellow sweater, and scuffed white clogs that made her feet look enormous. Her hair was stuffed under a denim Club 55 baseball cap and her red cat's-eye glasses were sliding down her nose from the heat. Sweaty, was how she would have described herself, when Maggie came in carrying a load of empty dishes and told her there was a man at the bar who wished to see her.

Caroline froze. Her eyes met Maggie's in a question.

"It's not him," Maggie said quietly. "This one's tall, with a beard, glasses too. In a nice jacket. Cashmere, you can always tell. Better go wash your face. He'll wait. I'll take over in here."

Still, Caroline was nervous seeing Mark, it would bring back her past. He was James's longtime friend as well as his business partner, a solid, quiet, bearded man you just knew you could trust. In fact, he was the first person she had called, from the Peninsula Hotel in Hong Kong, to say she had left James.

He had kept in touch, checking on her via e-mail or phone, always asking if she needed help. Was James doing his duty? Did Issy need anything? Of course Caroline always said she was fine and refused any help. She had made her choice and must live with it.

Now she looked unhappily at herself in the mirror. Her sweater was too snug; she'd bet she'd gained five pounds since she'd become a cook. She rinsed her face, dabbed in some perfume—Cartier's So Pretty, a gift from the ex that she had not used in years—and put on a clean white shirt, and a pair of gold sandals (it was cold but she was still hot from cooking), ran a brush through her hair, fluffed up her bangs, cleaned her red glasses and put them back on. Oh, she'd forgotten lipstick. She smoothed on Revlon's Just Enough Buff, then took a deep breath and went downstairs.

"You haven't changed," were Mark's first words, when he saw her.

chapter 11

Still sitting on the couch upstairs, Issy lifted her eyes from the tweet she'd just gotten from Lysander, an older boy (seventeen for God's sakes, and *cute* with it—and with whom she hoped to get a date) just in time to see her mom hurrying past the open door in a clean white shirt, hair combed and, Issy could *swear,* wearing lipstick.

"Sam?" Issy turned to look at her friend, thinking Sam had a perfect nose, small and straight with a short upper lip that made her mouth appear to smile all the time, and blue eyes with long dark lashes. How a blonde like Sam got dark lashes while she, the dark one, got pale, was something that bewildered Issy. Life, she had decided, long ago, simply was not fair.

"What?" Sam's gaze hovered between a dance program on the telly where a skimpily-dressed young woman was being twirled around by a man in tight black pants while the audience applauded and scores were tallied, and a text message from a boy who Sammy knew fancied her, though she did not fancy him. "Do you think she's wearing Spanx under that dress?" she asked.

Issy studied the woman. "I don't see how she can. I mean she's almost not wearing anything."

Sam twisted her blond pigtail, thoughtfully. "I wish I was her," she said. "I'd like to be a dancer."

"You're too short," Issy said, though of course she would never have hurt Sam's feelings by telling her she was also too plump. Which was the truth. Sam was. A bit.

"And you're too tall," Sam said. "Do you think Rob Maclean fancies me?"

"No."

"Oh."

Issy frowned. "Sam? Something's going on with my mom. She just dashed up here, then dashed back down again, all done up."

This time Sam turned to look at her. "You mean, like, in a dress and heels?"

Issy hadn't seen her mother in a dress and heels since Singapore. "No. But she'd changed her sweater and combed her hair, and put lipstick on."

Sammy laughed.

"You don't get it!" Sam had not seen her point. "Mom was going downstairs to the pub with lipstick on and her hair combed. That means she was going to see *a man*."

"What *man*?" Sam had never seen Caroline with any man.

"I think it might be my dad."

Shocked, Sam sat up. "Are you sure?"

"Who else would she dash downstairs to see without even stopping to tell me?"

She picked up Blind Brenda and buried her face in the cat's scrappy fur. "I'm scared to go and look," she mumbled. "Imagine, Sam, I'm scared in case it's my own dad."

"I'll go." Sam got up, turned the TV volume down and tripped over the pizza box. "I remember what he looks like," she added, because of course Issy had shown her photos of her good-looking

father who Jesus called, when Sam wasn't meant to hear, "a dead-
beat dad."

Alone, Issy waited, anxiously stroking the cat for comfort. It
seemed ages before Sam got back, but it was really only a few minutes.
"Well?" she asked.

"It's not him. It's a big man with a beard."

"That's Mark Santos. Dad's partner. I wonder why he's here."

She hoped he'd come to tell them her father wanted her back,
that he would also tell her mom to get rid of that filthy old barn. She
so wanted her old life back, a girl with a proper home and a normal
mother and father. She just wanted everything to be all right again,
and maybe Mark Santos could make that happen.

chapter 12

"*Liar,*" Caroline said, when Mark told her she looked exactly the same. She threw her arms round him in a hug, then they stood back and smiled at each other.

"At least *you* haven't changed," she said, meaning it.

He looked the same as he always had. His skin was slightly tanned from sailing the boat she knew he kept out at Lantau, the once-quiet island off Hong Kong that had suddenly developed from an isolated fisherman's paradise and blossomed with big new resorts. His eyes were gray, or were they brownish? She could never quite tell, hidden as they were behind his square, horn-rimmed glasses. But then, he probably couldn't tell her eye color either. Glasses were an impermeable barrier between friends and lovers. She knew that for sure; she had taken them off often enough in the cause of love, God knows. She thought Mark seemed taller, broader, *bigger,* than any other man in the room. And that included the carpenter, whose eyes had connected with hers as she'd pushed through the bar crowd. He'd given her a smile.

Jesus was tending bar alone since Maggie had taken Caroline's place in the kitchen. Now he placed a glass of red wine in front of her and she introduced him to Mark, who leaned across to shake his hand.

"I heard all about you," Mark said to Jesus. "The lifesaver."

"To old friends and new," Caroline said softly, as they touched glasses.

"You've come to tell me about James." She was suddenly afraid of what he was going to say.

He shrugged and took a sip of his beer. "Actually, I'm here because I wanted to see *you*."

Caroline leaned affectionately in to him, resting her head on his shoulder, remembering his scent, Chanel's Égoïste, from long ago. She had always thought Mark was a little in love with her; she'd felt his eyes follow her across a room; and the way he held her, too carefully whenever they'd danced. But Mark had never made a wrong move. Now, though, he had come all the way from Singapore specially to see her, and somehow she knew it couldn't be good news.

He said, "I came because I was worried. James told me he'd heard from his lawyer that you'd blown your divorce settlement, such as it was, on a bad piece of property out in the boondocks." He shook his head. "Not a good idea, Caroline."

She got that sinking feeling again. Mark was a good businessman, but good deal or bad, she'd fallen for that barn and she intended to keep it.

"I'll see if I can get you out of it," Mark was saying, taking over. "Then we'll look for a better place. Issy needs a proper home and it's your responsibility to give that to her."

Caroline was suddenly rattled. Here she was doing her best, cooking in a pub to make a living, buying a house, trying to figure out the next move toward a more secure life for them, and all she was getting was criticism.

"I'll help you," Mark added.

She knew he meant it. All she had to do was say the word and he'd have had her out of the deal and into something better, with his financial help of course. She thought maybe he was still in love with her. That "maybe" was the reason she knew she could not accept. She needed to keep her independence; she'd managed so far and she wasn't about to succumb now.

"You know how much I care about you, Caroline," he was saying. "I always have. I could take care of you, you know. Life could be good again, you and me, together."

Was he asking her to *marry* him? *Well, why don't you?* a weak treacherous little voice inside her asked. *He cares about you. You could have security. A good home. Your daughter would have a better life than living over a pub with a tired financially-stressed-out mom. What woman would not think about that? What woman wouldn't say "grab him with both hands"?*

But she was not in love with Mark, she simply did not have that special feeling for him. That spark—that *sparkle* that happens between a man and a woman. She did not want Mark as her "lover," or her husband.

She said quickly, "Thank you, Mark, it's better if I'm on my own right now." Then, "Tell me about James."

He shrugged. "We don't communicate much, except for business."

She looked at him, astonished.

"He's away most of the time, Hong Kong or Macao, or . . . who knows where."

"I'll bet he's with Gayle Lee Chen."

"You know about her?" He sounded surprised.

"I never told you, but she came to see me, right after I left James. She came to warn me off. You know she was James's mistress, for *twenty years,* and I knew nothing about her?"

"It's easy to dupe the innocent."

"But, in my heart I *knew* there was someone else, I just refused to acknowledge it." Caroline sniffed back tears of humiliation. "It's very easy to fool someone who's in denial."

"There are women in this world," Mark said quietly, so only she could hear, though the pub din was loud enough to drown out almost anything. "Women who can take over a man's mind with flattery, with sexual favors offered. They can take over so completely a man can be totally controlled. He does as she says, he even uses her words; smiles exactly the way she does; uses her thinking in business, her logic. He gives himself over to her. His entire life is thrown away. And she gives up nothing, not one scrap of her own life. For her, every-thing remains the same. It's the man who ends up the loser. James lost you, and he lost his daughter."

Caroline thought sadly about the James she had first known, the astute businessman, the man about town, the charmer, the caring lover, the good father.

"James is in trouble," Mark said. "I don't know yet exactly what *kind* of trouble, but something's wrong. Money went missing then was replaced. He's not always where he says he is going to be." A frown creased Mark's forehead. "He's not always doing what we had planned on doing. He's lost me clients because of it."

Caroline stared at him, stunned. James had always been the per-fect executive; showing up for meetings anywhere in the world, al-ways correct, always on time, always there for his clients. And his partner.

"That's why I asked about your payments," he said. "I wanted to know he was being straight with you."

"He isn't," she admitted. "Well, sometimes. I mean I get some money and then I don't, but I thought that was just James being mean. If he were a woman I'd say he was being bitchy."

Mark laughed. He said, "Now, tell me about Issy. She'll be growing up so fast I'll hardly know her."

"Of course you will," she said. "Issy will never change."

"We'll take her out to lunch, tomorrow, if that's okay?"

"More than just 'okay.'"

It was time for him to leave. A black Mercedes with a driver waited for him, parked illegally across the street. Men like Mark always parked wherever they wanted, Caroline thought.

"I'm at the Randolph, in Oxford," he said. "I'll call you first thing, make arrangements to pick you up."

She waved him goodbye then stood for a minute, staring at the empty spot where his car had been. Had it been a mirage? Had James's old friend come to find her and offered to take care of her? Had he *almost* asked her to marry him? She looked across the road at the reality of the Star & Plough, at the young people leaning up against the wall, smoking, chatting, laughing. Flirting.

The door opened and another crowd spilled out. Among them was the carpenter. He spotted Caroline and lifted a hand in a good-night salute. She waved back.

Of course she wasn't flirting. She didn't even know how, anymore. Still she felt better.

chapter 13

Mark returned the next morning and picked them up in the chauffeured black Mercedes.

"Look at you," he said to Issy, teasing. "I'd swear you were twenty-three."

Caroline saw the blush rise all the way up her daughter's neck. She also noticed she was wearing the precious cashmere sweater her father had sent from Hong Kong months ago, and that she knew Issy kept hidden in the old Hello Kitty bag under her bed.

She also knew how much that sweater meant to her; it meant her father had thought about her long enough to go to the store and pick it out for her and have them send it, with a little card that said *With love from Daddy*. Despite his neglect, James must still love his daughter, he was just too ashamed and guilt-ridden to come to see her. James's mind was elsewhere these days.

The sweater was a pale blue crewneck. Over it Issy wore her parka and her red school scarf. She'd pulled her hair into a ponytail and wore pink lip gloss.

Caroline was in a brown wool dress. She wondered when she ever thought *brown* was a good color for her? She'd bought it five years ago on a trip to Hong Kong, in their famous department store Lane

Crawford. It wasn't the most attractive dress there, but it had fit perfectly and required no alterations and, since she'd needed it for a dinner that evening, that was what she got. And the fact was now it was the only one of her old dresses that actually did fit, thanks to those extra pub pounds. She'd vowed late last night a diet was absolutely necessary. Did she remember that though when they ended up for lunch at the famous Manoir aux Quat' Saisons? Of course not.

Sitting opposite Issy, with Mark between them, at a window table with a view of the rolling lawns dotted with shade trees, Caroline thought that to the other diners, they must look like the perfect family, a daughter having lunch with her parents.

To Caroline's surprise, Issy decided to have oysters. She sipped champagne, feeling good. Her brown dress looked nice, thank-the-Lord not too tight, and she'd filled the deep V-neck with a faux-gold tangle of necklaces. The narrow skirt stopped just above the knee and she'd added a gold mesh bracelet, bought at Agatha in Paris a decade ago, and gold stud earrings. She'd also slung a pashmina round her shoulders, a little dated perhaps but those shawls served a multitude of purposes; they kept you warm and added a spot of color where needed—bright turquoise in this case—and also hid a multitude of sins, like an added pound or so. Her shoulder-length black hair was brushed smooth, the fringes carefully swept to one side so as not to tangle with her glasses, horn-rims today, sort of like Mark's actually. They went better with the brown dress, even though Issy had said they made her look like a schoolteacher.

"It's better than looking like a pub cook," Caroline had said.

"You know, Issy," Mark was saying, "I wish your father could be here. He's just so busy these days, but I know he thinks about you."

"He was *always* too busy for us," Issy replied, unwilling to be fobbed off with platitudes about her dad loving her. "At least he could find the time to call me, or write."

Mark sighed. "There's nothing I can do about that."

"Never mind." She sounded so grown up and composed, Caroline wanted to cry for her. Then the oysters came and Issy even decided she liked them.

They drank a bottle of excellent Puligny-Montrachet and a lot of laughter and good food later, Caroline decided it was time to take Mark to look at their barn.

First though, she and Issy went to the ladies' room. It was beautifully done up, with pretty wallpaper, linen hand towels, and mirrors that allowed you to believe you didn't look half-bad, especially after a bottle of wine.

"Mom?" Issy called from the stall.

Caroline was combing her hair, adding some lipstick. "Yes?"

"I really, *really* like Mark."

"Good," she replied cautiously. "I like him too."

Issy emerged, standing next to her, washing her hands. "Mom?"

"What now?"

"He'd make a very good substitute father. And besides I know he likes you. I saw the way he looked at you."

"Mark is a very good friend," she said, noncommittally, waiting for Issy to dry her hands.

"Yeah, that's good too. But with Mark we could go back and live in Singapore."

"Isabel Evans you are getting way above yourself," Caroline said, shocked. "Enough. Right now, we're going to show Mark our new home."

Standing at the bottom of the rutted driveway, Caroline thought her future home looked a lot better under the spring sunshine. The little tree had sprouted a few green leaves and the river slid gently past, throwing off sparkles here and there. She had been to look at her barn so many times by now she knew its layout and its history by heart.

"It dates from the early seventeenth century," she told them and saw Issy turn away, deliberately not listening. "The stone was hewn by local men thought to be monks running from religious persecution under Cromwell, hiding out in the deep countryside, building their little house and the tiny secret chapel. Of course the chapel has long since disappeared but some of its stones can still be found under the grass."

She pushed open the squeaking barn doors and stepped into the flagged hall, which led into another enormous room. The floor was covered in worn linoleum, and there was a raised platform at one end, for the band and the dancing, Caroline supposed. A passage off the hall led to a squalid kitchen with an ancient cooker and a worn stone sink. Double French doors opened from that onto a small walled courtyard. A spiral stone staircase led up to a beamed room filled with a watery-river light. Another short turn in the stairs led to three more rooms and a fifties-style pink-tiled bathroom that matched the kitchen in its squalor.

Outside, across the little courtyard and through a gate, was a tiny cottage. One corner had been made over into a kitchen and upstairs was a bedroom and small bathroom.

Best of all, though, Caroline thought proudly, was the terrace: the lovely curve of the river, and she imagined herself sitting on that low stone wall on a lovely summer morning, with a cup of coffee, and her dreams.

Looking at the two of them, though, she realized they didn't understand. Only *she* saw the barn this way. Only *she* saw the bones of the place, stripped of its ugly linoleum and Formica, its sordid kitchen and bathroom. Only *she* could imagine it, warm and cozy with an

Aga in winter, cool and sunny and filled with light in summer, alive with Issy's young friends while she barbecued burgers on the terrace for them and eavesdropped on their conversations.

Mark was looking at the faded sign, *Bar, Grill, and Dancing.* He said, "They must have had a license for this place. I'll bet you could reapply for one."

She stared at him, astonished. "Run it as a bar, you mean?"

He shrugged. "You're a cook, aren't you? Why not open it as a restaurant?"

It certainly gave her something to think about.

chapter 14

A few weeks later, on a bright, sunny morning Caroline went with Maggie and Jesus to clean up the barn.

"Daunting" was the first word that came to her mind when she looked at it. "Impossible" was the second, after Jesus had jimmied open the front door which had swollen in the recent rains. "*God!*" was the third when she stepped over the threshold into the black hole that was supposed to be her new home. And also her restaurant, if the council ever came through with that license, a new battle in which the words "inspection" and "original footprint" featured frequently.

"Well, then," Maggie said, sounding deliberately cheerful, pushing past in the dark and heading as though she had built-in radar, toward the row of French doors, throwing them creakily open onto the terrace. A couple of ducks glanced lazily over their shoulders, then continued cleaning their feathers, enjoying the sun.

A battered skip stood outside the door, ready for whatever they chucked out, which promised to be a lot, and then some. Knowing it was going to be dirty work, Caroline had worn old sweatpants with SINGAPORE FLING GYM on the backside, and the old yellow "running-away-from-home" sweater.

Maggie went to the truck and came back with hard hats and

thick gardening gloves. "You never know what's in there," she said, handing them out. Jesus was on his knees levering up dead linoleum. It cracked like pistol shots. He said that was a good thing, it meant the floor itself must be dry.

"One bit of good news today, then," Caroline said pulling on a pair of the thick gardening gloves. She saw Maggie already cleaning off shelves, running her arm along them and letting everything drop into her trolley with a satisfying crash.

Caroline decided to start on the kitchen, but first she took a look at the courtyard. In the center was an overgrown flower bed, divided into four squares by low, box hedges. She leaned over and picked a sprig of lavender. *Real lavender.* And next to it was . . . could that be *true? Basil. And parsley, and lemon-thyme?*

"Mags, Mags, we have our own herb garden," she yelled, thrilled.

Maggie came and stood in the doorway, hands on her hips, but she was staring horrified at the kitchen, and the cooker that was encrusted with enough grunge to earn a fail rating from any inspector.

She said, "This is about the worst I've ever seen. And don't forget, I know what I'm talking about. I was a poor girl in Mexico."

Caroline's heart sank as reality finally set in. What had she done? Her daughter was right and no amount of work or money would ever put this place into habitable condition, let alone turn it into a restaurant, even if she was an experienced cook, and even if Issy would come and live there, which she said she definitely would not. And even if James came and rescued her and said he would take care of it all for her, which he most definitely would not . . .

Jesus came to take a look at the cooker, and immediately got on his mobile.

An hour later a large pickup trundled up the drive, listing from side to side in the deep ruts carved by the mud. To Caroline's surprise the driver was the dusty dark-haired carpenter from Friday nights at the pub. So this is what he did? Shift people's junk for them.

"Hey," he said, strolling over, thumbs stuck in the pockets of his jeans.

She noticed they fit him very well; in fact they fit exactly the way jeans should.

"Hey, yourself," she replied, still caught up in admiring his butt.

"It's about a cooker?" he reminded her.

"We know each other." Caroline got herself together and smiled at him. "I've seen you in the pub."

"Right." He waved his mate over, the huge giant of a man who looked capable of shifting the old stove all by himself. "This is Georgki, he's a stonemason. Heard you might be needing a bit of help." He glanced at the barn. "Certainly looks as though they were right."

Caroline led him quickly through the little courtyard-garden into the old kitchen. Thumbs still in his jeans pockets, he studied the situation.

"Lord save us," the giant named Georgki exclaimed, looking at the stove.

The carpenter said, "If anyone ever ate anything cooked on that bastard, he would have ended up at the Radcliffe Infirmary."

"More like in coffin," Georgki added, in what to Caroline sounded like a Russian accent.

The carpenter turned to smile at her. "Not to worry, we'll have this out in a flash. By the way, my name's James."

"Oh, no!" Caroline stared blankly at the hand he held out for her to shake. A nice, square, long-fingered hand, nails clean and everything, even though he was a manual laborer.

"I don't usually get that kind of reaction," he said mildly.

"Oh," she said. "It's just that my ex's name is, *was*, James."

"Is? Or was?" He was laughing at her.

"Hmm, what I meant is that he *was* my husband. *Now,* he is my ex."

"If it makes it any better I'm usually known as Jim. Jim Thompson."

It did make it better; easier anyhow. "Okay, Jim," she said. He was definitely easy on the eye, as she had noticed in the pub. Medium height with a compact body that looked muscled from hard work and not merely from a workout at the gym; dark hair short-cropped; lightish-brown eyes that seemed to see everything, notice every-thing anyhow, because the next thing he said to her was that she was wearing that same yellow sweater the night he'd first seen her in the Star & Plough.

"Never forgotten it," he added, with an admiring grin.

Caroline wavered for a second or two, trying to decide whether to be insulted or grateful that she had been appreciated. Smiling, she decided to allow herself to be appreciated.

"It's long past its sell-by," she said, folding her arms over her breasts where the sweater definitely stretched too tightly. She told herself she had to stop eating Maggie's leftover tacos, sneaking downstairs late at night, followed by that little wraith of a blind cat, who she'd found also appreciated a cold taco.

Then, with a smile that included Georgki, who had not uttered a word since the first shocked, "Lord save us," she asked what they thought of her barn.

"Lotta work," Georgki said, heaving his bulk over to the wall and running a hand over the stone, which crumbled under his touch. "Beautiful, though," he added, making Caroline's heart sing. At last, here was someone who saw the beauty she saw.

"Can be done, though. Maybe." Georgki took in the sagging plas-ter ceiling held together by a crisscross of scabby black beams. "The bones is good."

She said, "Yes, I think the bones is good too."

"Georgki is a stonemason. He's the best." Jim went and looked at the stove. "Okay, so we'll get the equipment and lift her out of here. Send the poor old thing back to her maker."

Jesus came in to see what was going on. He was acting as Caroline's contractor, he knew what he was talking about and exactly what was needed to put this wreck back into shape. He also knew what workers he needed and how to lay his hands on them. Certainly one way was via Jim Thompson, who knew everyone, from electricians to plumbers, to backhoe drivers, floorers, and roofers. And of course, Georgki, the best stonemason in all of Oxfordshire, who, while Jim was conferring with Jesus, said to Caroline, "I like this place. It speaks to me."

Caroline was thrilled. She asked him what it said.

"It says thanks Lord, I have good heart." He thumped his chest with a hand big as a soup plate. Georgki must have weighed all of two hundred and fifty pounds and when he struck himself on the chest, it rattled. For a second, Caroline thought he was going to fall over in a heart attack, but he grinned and said, "Just some bits of stuff where they fixed my bones after the war."

"What war?"

"Oh, long ago now. In Serbia, when there was wars there. I am Russian, from Ukraine, but that's where I ended up, in Serbian hospital. They very good to me. I like."

Serbia? A hospital? Metal bits rattling? A Russian stonemason, who was only the best in the area and who, it turned out, was booked into all eternity by those super-rich, newly-moved-to-the-Cotswolds international wives, who needed him to restore their enormous old country houses that made Caroline's little barn look as though it belonged in a toy shop.

"I come to you for good price," he said, without even asking *if* she wanted him, or, as importantly, *telling* her what that price might be.

Caroline was beyond caring. He was the best. He would create her new home. It was a done deal. She put her trust in him.

Besides, she thought as they shook hands, or rather when Georgki covered her hand with his and squeezed so tightly she had to stop herself from gasping with pain; besides, it just might change her daughter's mind when she told her it was all arranged and their barn would, before too long, become a proper home.

chapter 15

Issy decided not to go down for dinner. Caroline found her in her room, still in jeans and boots, and with Blind Brenda, her new love object, clutched to her chest.

"What's up, sweetheart?" she asked, knowing there was trouble.

"I hate it." Issy turned her face away.

"You hate our barn?"

"It's not *our* barn. It's *yours*, Mom. All *yours*. I'm never going to live there."

"Oh?" Caroline kept her voice neutral. What was wrong with Issy? She'd just found a way to get them a home and now she was acting like she was being tortured.

"And so where will you live then, Issy?"

"As soon as I'm sixteen, I'm off to boarding school."

Issy hugged the cat tighter, practically flattening it against her chest, trying to keep back the tears of anger, of frustration, of help-lessness at not being old enough to run her own life, the way she wanted it. "In the breaks," she said, "I'll just get on a plane and go back to Singapore. You can bet when I show up my father will be so pleased to see me, we'll be happy together. Without you."

"And if he isn't?" Caroline felt her own anger rising.

"Then I'll just stay where I am. At my home. The Star & Plough in Upper Amberley."

Eyes locked, they stared silently at each other for a long moment, Issy seething with despair and anger and a loneliness she knew her mother could never understand. Only Sam *really* knew her, and maybe Lysander, the student she'd met in Oxford, and who lived in London and whose own parents had gone through a divorce when he was ten years old.

"The trouble with you," she yelled, "is you still think I'm a little kid you can boss around, tell me what to do."

"I never 'bossed' you." Caroline stopped herself just in time from yelling too. "I was a good mother," she added quietly, wondering where she had gone wrong and become the "bad mother."

"Yeah. Right. You always knew best. Mothers—as a breed—just don't get it."

Issy was lying on her back with Blind Brenda still clutched to her chest.

Caroline leaned over and shoved Issy's booted feet off the bed-covers. "Well, I *am* your mother, and like it or not, I'm all you've got. And I've gotten you this far in life without deserting you."

"Like my father, you mean?" Issy glared at her, her face red, her eyes angry. "May I remind *you,* Mother, you left *him. I,* did not. You took me with you because you didn't want him to have me. You wanted to *hurt* him. You wanted out and you *used* me. So now I'm stuck."

She clutched the cat even tighter, but it sensed conflict and strug-gled free. "See, even the fuckin' cat can't stand me," Issy yelled.

Caroline sank onto the bed next to her, but Issy pulled away and turned her back.

Caroline got up and went and sat on the chair. She put her hands to her face. She could *not* cry. She *must not* cry. She was the strong one, the responsible one, the mother.

Blind Brenda went and sat at Caroline's feet. She picked her up then went to lie down next to Issy. She pushed the little cat over the bump of Issy's back, saw her arm reach out to hold it.

"I'm so sorry," Caroline said softly. "Trust me, baby, I love you. I know you're almost grown up but you're still my girl. I don't mean to treat you like that, it's just that . . ." She sighed, thinking of what to say, how to say it . . . "It's just that I'm a mom. I'm learning on the job. It's the only way moms know. I can only hope I'm doing the right thing. I *believe* I'm doing the right thing, but you must understand, I have to at least *try*. I can't depend on your father, I have to look after you. Won't you at least give me a chance?"

A tiny meow broke the silence. Issy's back unstiffened and she sat up. She said, "Oh my God, Mom! Blind Brenda *spoke*! Her first *meow*!"

And then she turned over and hid her face in her mother's shoulder and cried.

chapter 16

The barn was finally cleared out; the black-varnished beams were stripped. They smelled of whatever was used to remove the paint before they were sandblasted, which would cause another mountain of dust, similar to, though possibly not as large, as the one Georgki was creating every evening when he blasted the stone walls clean of ancient grout and filth and a great many spiders, for which Caroline was deeply thankful. She would rather face a dragon than a spider, especially in bed at night with bare feet.

He was enveloped in a sort of canvas shroud with a visor covering his head and shoulders. He looked like a moving tent, blaster held out in front, a fine spray of dirt and old stone drifting round him like a cloud.

Caroline stood, arms folded, in the open doorway. The doors themselves had been removed and were propped against the out-building, currently known as "the cottage." She had to get back to the pub where she was expected to cook steak pies.

Georgki pushed up his plastic visor and said to her, "We go out tonight. There is pub in Pangbourne. On river. Swans. You'll like. And they do good food, in a basket. I buy wine."

From under the up-tilted visor, he gave her a smile of beaming sweetness and she realized he was asking her out on a date. "Pangbourne is a long way, the other side of Oxford," she said quickly. "In Buckinghamshire."

"Oxfordshire. I know for certain."

"Hmmm, right, well . . . actually, Georgki, I'm supposed to work tonight. Remember? I have a job? Tell you what though, why don't you come to the pub later and I'll fix you one of my chicken pot pies. My treat."

She saw his big shoulders droop under his tent and hated herself for doing it. "Tell you what," she said, "tomorrow, I'll bring a picnic. We can eat it here, just you and me. I'll bring the wine you like . . ."

"Beer," Georgki said quietly. "Remember I like beer."

Of course she knew that, how could she have forgotten! "So, let's settle for the pub tonight then. I'll buy you a Sam Adams," she added, with a warm smile that she really meant, she was so grateful he'd cared enough to ask her out.

"Watneys," Georgki replied, and slammed back his visor, switched on his blaster and got back to work.

He did not show up at the pub that night, though, and Caroline worried she had hurt his feelings. But he was back at work the next afternoon, and nothing more was said.

The following day, Caroline drove into Oxford to get her hair cut. When she got back Maggie sat her down at the table, gave her a cup of coffee and said she had three things to tell her.

"Three? I've only been gone a few hours." Caroline fluffed out her hair. "What do y'think?"

"Expensive," Maggie said. "But worth it."

"Thank God." Caroline slumped into the chair nearest the fireplace and swung her jeaned legs over the arm. "What do you mean, *three* things? What's happened?"

"Nothing bad. First, Issy's been invited to a party Saturday night. By a boy. A seventeen-year-old. Name of Lysander Tsornin."

"Seventeen! That's too old! And anyway, how can anybody be called *Lysander Tsornin*? Who is he? And how does she know him?"

"School, parties, other girls, they all know each other, you know how it is."

Caroline thought how much she apparently did not know. Of course she drove Issy and Sam to the movies in Oxford, and she knew after they went to a café for spaghetti or whatever was cheapest, but they were still too young to go clubbing. They hung out at their friends' houses, but she always knew exactly where they were.

Maggie said, "Issy was afraid to ask you, so she asked me to. It's an overnight party, she's been invited to stay at the house."

"*Lysander asked* her to stay at his house!"

"It was the mother who called, not the boyfriend. Mrs. Tsornin. Arabella Tsornin to be correct. She left her number if you want to call."

"Mom?" Issy was standing in the doorway, radiating anxiety. "You won't mess it up, will you? I can go, can't I?"

"You can go if Sam goes too." Caroline quickly decided two was definitely better than one.

"But Sam's not invited."

"Oh? And why not?"

"Well, Lysander is kind of *my* date."

She twisted her hands together, her face scrunched. "Mom, I've got to do some things on my own. I'm going to be sixteen in a couple of weeks."

So she was, Caroline had almost forgotten. Or at least she had put it out of her mind. This would be her second birthday without James being there to celebrate.

"You're asking to go to a party with a seventeen-year-old boy I don't even know, and stay overnight at the house of people I don't even know?"

"But you *can* know them, Mom. Just call them."

Maggie handed her the piece of paper with the Tsornin number. Caroline saw the area code. "London? You mean the party's in *London*?"

"I can get the train to Paddington," Issy said quickly. "All you have to do is drive me to Oxford station."

Caroline suddenly gave in. This was Issy's world and she had a right to it. She would call the mother, it would be okay. "So, what are you going to wear?" she asked, smiling.

She called Arabella Tsornin, who was cool and polite and said she was glad she had called and please not to worry, she would take good care of her daughter. "There'll be fifty of them," she explained. "Lysander said he needed a celebration, he's at a tutorial in Oxford and it's hard work. Anyhow, tell Isabel to arrive at teatime. We'll be expecting her."

Caroline sat back in the chair and looked at her daughter, wide-eyed and expectant. "They'll expect *Isabel* at teatime Saturday," she said.

"Ohh, Mom, *thank you, thank you* . . ." Issy was in her lap, her arms around her neck.

Caroline looked at Maggie. "You said *three* things. I hope the other two are better than this."

"Georgki called to say that the stonework is completed. He's got a blower and is cleaning up the mess."

"More like shifting the dust from one place to another."

"And he wants to celebrate. With you. At The Swan in Pangbourne."

"Uh-uh!"

"I told him you were working but I'd give you the message. And he said to come over and take a look because you're not going to believe it. At least that's what I think he said with his accent. I can never quite tell."

"Me either. Oh, Mags, what shall I do?"

"I think you should go," Issy spoke up. "You owe him, Mom."

She was right. "Okay. But *I* will take *Georgki* out for dinner."

"And three," Maggie said, ticking the numbers off on her fingers, "Jim Thompson called."

Caroline's ears seemed to stretch forward, waiting for her next words.

"I said you'd call him back." Maggie leaned smugly back against the sofa cushions.

"Hah!" Caroline didn't want to say too much in front of Issy, but she couldn't help a pleased smile.

"So call him, too, Mom," Issy said, adding generously, "It's time you got out a bit more."

It was the first time her daughter had even acknowledged the fact that her mother and her father were no longer a pair.

chapter 17

"I won't call him back right away," Caroline told Maggie later. "That would look pushy."

"Trust me, *amiga,* push." Maggie gave her a long look that meant just get on with it.

She went outside to make the call, tapping her black-booted foot nervously while it rang. And rang, and rang. Didn't the man have an answering machine?

"Jim Thompson."

She was taken aback when he finally did answer. Suddenly nervous, she ran a hand through her newly-cut hair, and said, "How very formal. I only ever answer 'yes.'"

"Then how does anyone know who you are?"

"I expect they know because they called me."

He laughed. A nice round sound. Warm, she thought.

"You're right, Caroline Evans, and I did call you. Look, I'm sorry I haven't been around lately, but I was away, on business. I did my best for you though, got you all the good workers. And Georgki."

Oh my God... She remembered the dinner with Georgki... She said, "Yes, thank you. The barn's just about finished. I can move in soon, maybe next week."

"I know a guy who can help you."

"I might need two guys."

"One like me, young and strong, does the work of two."

Caroline laughed. "How old are you anyway?"

"Twenty-seven."

Jesus! *Twenty-seven.* She wished she'd never asked.

He said, "So how old are *you*, then?"

"Let me tell you I have a daughter almost your age."

"No you do not. Issy is fifteen."

"How do you know about her?"

"I made it my business. That's how I know about you too. Live in a village, hang out at a pub, and everybody knows everything about everybody else. No secrets in Upper Amberley. Veronica Partridge is the worst. Gets all her info from church, she tells me. And the post office."

"I'll never go there again," Caroline said, thinking now he knew all about her anyway, she might as well relax into it. "So, I'm thirty-eight. And divorced," she added.

"And still not over it," he said.

Caroline felt herself freeze, this was becoming way too personal. "So, why did you call, anyway?" she asked sharply.

"I wanted to invite you to dinner, Saturday night. I was hoping you might be interested?"

"Ohhh," she said, thinking about it. *She hadn't been out with a man other than James in seventeen years. She wasn't sure she still knew how to be a simple woman on a date.* "Dinner," she said. "How lovely. Thank you." *She was accepting, not even hesitating. God, she hadn't changed; she still jumped in with both feet.*

"Wait a minute," she added. "I work Saturdays. I can't do it."

"Don't worry, I'll bribe Maggie. Look, it's actually a dinner party, sixteen people. I think you'd like them, well, some of them at least. Maybe you even like me enough to say yes?"

"Okay," she said, laughing now.

"I'll pick you up at seven thirty," he said. "Oh, and by the way, don't wear the yellow sweater." He was laughing too when he rang off.

Caroline ran back into the pub, slamming the kitchen door behind her.

"I have a date," she said, with a note of wonder in her voice.

"Then you'll need a new dress too, Mom," Issy said.

chapter 18

Ever since she'd seen Mark, Caroline had been mulling over his offer of financial help. She desperately needed it but was reluctant to give up her new independence, and besides, she didn't want him to think she was interested in a closer relationship. Finally though, he called and said, "Listen, it's not just restoring the old barn, you'll need a proper restaurant kitchen and that costs. Plus you'll need to get it into shape, furnished, y'know chintz sofas, nice comfy chairs, silver cutlery and candelabra. Face it, you'll need financing, Caroline."

"Everybody with a country restaurant has flowery sofas and silver candelabra," she protested. "My place in the country is going to be different."

"Different still costs. Face it, I'm your only option. You'd better take me in as a silent partner. I promise I won't interfere, you can do whatever you like. I'm faxing an agreement and I'll open a business account for A Place in the Country."

She didn't know whether it would be her salvation, or her undoing, but money certainly wasn't growing on any trees near her and she had no choice but to agree.

Finally the restoration was complete and she took Maggie and

Jesus to inspect the result. They stopped at the end of the driveway so they could look at it. The only sounds were of the cows slurping up the long grass in the nearby field and the river slithering silkily by. No ducks racketed around today, there was no noise of drills, no workmen. It was quiet and beautiful.

Why then, did Caroline feel a sudden sinking of the heart? A clench of fear as she thought of what she had taken on, the debt, the responsibility? How could she ever have thought that she, inexperienced and unprofessional, could ever open a restaurant never mind make it a success?

Georgki was waiting to show them round. Her future restaurant was just a big bare room with a white plaster ceiling and four sets of French doors leading onto the terrace.

"It looks very *empty*," Maggie said doubtfully.

"It's that ceiling. Barns usually have enormous beams but whoever converted this made it into two stories." Looking at the blank ceiling, she suddenly had another of her brain waves.

"We'll hang a sail over it," she said. "Billowing cream canvas, pegged wall to wall, like it's blowing in the wind. Romantic, you know," she added, beaming with pleasure at her own brilliance.

"Hmm," Maggie said doubtfully, while Jesus just looked bewildered.

"And I'm not having any flowery chairs either. I'm having Philippe Starck Ghost armchairs, padded in deep bronze canvas. And I'll have taupe-colored tablecloths. I hate placemats," she added. "So cheap looking, as if they can't afford the laundry for the cloths and napkins."

"You can't," Maggie reminded her.

"Oh. Well, yes." Caroline wasn't about to be brought down by mundane thoughts of laundry.

"A single flower floating in a glass bowl," she went on. "A dahlia, or Gerbera daisy, or perhaps a rose from the garden."

"You do not have a rose garden," Jesus reminded her.

She lifted her shoulder in a little shrug. "You know what I mean. A cowslip would do, or Queen Anne's lace picked from the hedge-row . . ."

"You'd put *cow-parsley* on your table?" Maggie was shocked.

Deflated, Caroline said, "Well, anyway, I'll also need to find a couple of old wooden sideboards to go along the two walls, and lamps and things." She knew she sounded like a housewife with delusions of restaurant grandeur.

They walked upstairs to view her new "home" quarters.

"Is good, yes?" Georgki said.

The chestnut floors were smooth, the limestone fireplace all clean and swept, and the windows sparkled. Up another little flight of steps, in the mezzanine, was a small private kitchen, and up yet another twist in the stairs were now two bedrooms and two bathrooms. Caroline had gone for broke and installed an expensive Jacuzzi tub that would rescue her feet from their nightly stint on the flagstone floors.

Looking at it all, A Place in the Country suddenly became a reality. She was scared. She was in debt up to her ears; she had committed to bank loans and a loan from her father, as well as Mark, her silent partner. And the restaurant did not even have a kitchen yet.

Jesus went and got the bottle of champagne he'd brought to celebrate, and they sat on the terrace toasting Caroline's future, while the river unfurled slowly to the weir, the way it had done since the beginning of time. And would, Caroline knew, for ever more.

She felt the weight suddenly lift. The responsibility would become a pleasure, the work a necessary part of her life. She would enjoy this place, this home. She would be her own woman, at last.

chapter 19

Caroline called the kitchen people as soon as she got back to the pub to confirm Monday's installation, then she called the cheap moving company, run by Oxford students, and confirmed Monday's move.

This weekend was Issy's London party, and Caroline was still worried that it was in London, and that he was seventeen. Too late to change her mind now. Anyhow, she'd better take her to Oxford to buy a new party outfit. She would need one too for the dinner party. An *English* dinner party, all pearls and small talk, she'd bet. Still, she was looking forward to seeing Jim. *Cute Jim. Too young Jim,* she thought. Then told herself what the hell, enjoy it while you can.

Issy and Sam looked through the racks at Miss Selfridge and Zara like professionals. Issy held up a black dress for Caroline's approval.

"No black," she said firmly.

"Red, then?" She held up a scrap of a skirt that would fit a six-year-old, and an even smaller strapless top.

"No red," Caroline said, even more firmly. "Besides, your boobs will fall out of that."

The girls giggled, and Caroline sighed. She'd thought she'd never get them out of there. Finally though they found something Issy liked and that Caroline approved of. It was a simple blue dress, shorter than she thought appropriate but Sam told her everybody wore them like that nowadays. It had skinny straps so she insisted on a little mesh shrug to go over it. Since the shrug was black, Issy agreed, but despite Caroline's protests that they were too grown-up and too high, she also talked her into a pair of black peep-toe, sling-back, platform wedges. "I *am* almost sixteen, Mom!" she argued. Her legs were winter-white and she refused to even think of tights. "Nobody ever wears those, Mom," she said. "Especially not with sling-backs." So they went to Boots and bought a tube of instant golden tan. They found her a black skirt and a white cardigan, for daytime, and Caroline had a nice trench coat she could wear. After that they went to M & S and got underwear and Caroline couldn't believe it when they bought thongs. After that, she dropped them at a café, while she went on the hunt for something for herself.

Of course she was really too old to shop at Zara, but she'd spotted a dress there. She hadn't had the nerve to try with the girls looking on. Now, she grabbed the size ten and went to the changing room. It was a bias-cut pale green silk jersey with a sweetheart neck, cap sleeves, and a narrow skirt. Every line of her underwear showed. And more.

She took another shocked look at herself in the mirror. No way could she wear this.

The salesgirl popped her head in. "Try the twelve," she advised. "It's cut real small."

The twelve hit all the right places nicely but she still wouldn't be able to wear panties. Well, maybe a thong. She bought the dress, and a pair of nude suede shoes with four-inch heels. She also picked up a thong en route to pick up the girls, then drove them home. She hoped her credit card would stand up to the onslaught.

Of course she had second thoughts about the dress later, when she modeled it for Maggie, who assured her it looked terrific.

. That Saturday night they arranged for Sam to stay with a friend and Sarah agreed to take over in the kitchen. Lily was to act as assistant, while her sister would mind Little Billy in the living room upstairs.

It was all set. Issy's party. And Caroline's date.

Alone though, later that night, she admitted the truth. She wished her date was with James, and not Jim.

chapter 20

On the day of the party Issy stood in front of the long mirror in Sam's room, in her new black skirt. It wasn't exactly pencil but it was short, and, though she did say it herself, she had nice legs.

"What d'you think?" She frowned, inspecting the snug little white cardigan she had gotten past her mother's eagle eyes, purely on the basis that it was only a cardi so how could it be wrong. "Do my boobs look too big in this?"

"Not exactly *big*," loyal friend Sam said. "But it is a bit tight."

"That's the way everybody wears them." Issy took another anxious look. "I can always unbutton it and put a T-shirt under," she added, still doubtful she had enough nerve to show off her body to Lysander, not to mention the other partygoers, who she knew for sure would be older than her, because Lysander was older and they were his friends.

"When are you going to tell Lysander how old you *really* are?" Sam leaned back on the pillows, arms folded. Blind Brenda squeaked and emerged from under the pillow. "Oops, sorry, kitten." She picked her up and cuddled her.

"He thinks I'm sixteen. Anyhow, I will be in a couple of weeks, so what's the difference?"

Still, Issy sat down next to her friend, suddenly nervous. "Should I really go to this party? I mean, I don't know anybody except Lysander, and truthfully, I hardly know him, except for seeing him a few times in Oxford."

"And then only in public places, like the café, or hanging in the street, smoking."

"You know I don't smoke."

"You might, by tomorrow." Sam had seen it happen before, peer pressure was a bitch. "I'm worried about you going alone," she added, sitting up and pulling her blond hair into a ponytail. "Lysander's different from us, he's always going to parties. He makes me feel like a kid when I'm with him."

"Well, we are *not* kids. And time I learned how the real world lives instead of just school and Oxford and that bloody barn my mother thinks is going to be our home and make her her fortune. She's nuts." She sounded sure of herself, but the truth was she was nervous about going alone.

"It's not too late to cancel," Sam prompted.

Issy turned back to the mirror. Maybe the sweater looked okay? She undid the top three buttons and added her mom's gold chain necklaces. Her small duffel bag was packed. She was ready. Caroline was to drive her to the station then drop Sam off at her friend's house in Oxford.

"I'll call and tell you everything," she said, putting on Caroline's good cream trench coat that fit her perfectly and looked terrific with her black ankle boots, especially with the golden-tan stuff on her legs.

"Pretty good, though I say it myself," she said to Sam with a big, nervous, grin.

"Terrific," Sam agreed loyally.

chapter 21

The London train was one of those rattling old ones that stopped at every small station. Her mother had bought her a magazine but Issy was so worried she would be late she couldn't even read it.

What if tea was already over and everybody had gone on somewhere else, and there was nobody at the house to meet her? What if Lysander had forgotten all about her? He couldn't have; he'd called her that morning and said see you later, girl.

Lysander always called her "girl," and Issy didn't like it. She would have preferred him to use her name, but he'd laughed when they'd first met, three weeks ago, in the café where everybody hung, and she had told him it was Issy.

"Kind of a 'Bambi' name," he'd said, mockingly, making her blush and she'd told him quickly she was really Isabel but that her father had always called her Issy.

"So where is your dad, anyway?" Lysander was sharp enough to catch her hesitation when she'd mentioned him, and she told him quickly he worked in Singapore and came here whenever he could.

"Yeah right," Lysander said, seeing the truth, that her parents had split up. He'd told her about his mother and father divorcing, and that he'd gotten over it. He gave a devil-may-care shrug and a cocky grin and told her just to get on with it.

He was at a tutorial in Oxford, and Issy had met him in a café and been instantly smitten.

She had seen him a couple of times since. They'd gone to the movies, with Sam too, of course, and Lysander had held her hand. Actually what he'd done was take her hand and put it on his lap, which had startled her. Still, it was friendly and sexy and she hadn't actually *touched* him. And he hadn't kissed her then, because Sam was there. She had been kissed before and not thought much of it, but later when he kissed her goodnight and put his tongue in her mouth, it had given her a terrific thrill. He'd run his hand quickly over her breasts and kissed her again, no tongue this time, and told her she was cute and very pretty and sexy with it. He'd mentioned his party and said he would invite her, and now she was so nervous she was almost wishing he had not.

Thank God, the train was finally crawling into Paddington. She grabbed her duffel and was off before anyone else had even moved. Then there was a queue for taxis that took another agonizing ten minutes before she was on her way.

Lysander's house was on a smart block in fashionable Bayswater, near Hyde Park. It was white with black shutters, gleaming windows, and a shiny black front door with a pair of twirly topiaries at the top of the steps.

Issy had to press the brass doorbell twice before it was answered by a tall model-type girl with enviable straight blond hair and wide, shadow-smudged blue eyes. She had long legs in narrow jeans and wore flip-flops. Her toes were painted a perfect turquoise. Issy had never seen turquoise toenails before.

The girl checked her over. "I guess you're expected."

She stood back to let Issy in then closed the door and walked away, leaving her just standing there.

"Who is it?" A thin woman clutching a sheaf of papers came down the stairs. She looked at Issy as though she had no clue who she was, or even that she was expected.

"I'm Lysander's friend, Isabel?"

"Ah! *Isabel.* Of course." Mrs. Tsornin gave her a smile. "Just drop your bag and coat there, my dear, on that bench, and go along into the drawing room. They're all in there. Lysander will show you your room later, I'm afraid I'm busy right now, all the organization you know . . ."

Issy took off her coat and left it, as instructed, on the hall bench. She wished she had worn jeans and a T-shirt like the model-girl, and thought her legs looked too-fake-tan in this light. She might have stood there forever, alone, if she hadn't finally gathered her courage and her nerves and walked as inconspicuously as she could, into the room where all the noise was coming from.

She spotted Lysander chatting to a group of people and by some miracle he spotted her too. He came over and kissed her on the cheek.

"Glad you made it," he said. Then took her hand and led her over to the group of young guys who were smoking like chimneys and looking at her.

"This is Issy," he said, throwing a casual arm over her shoulders. "She's come all the way from Oxford," he added, which for some reason made them all laugh, probably because they were all at the university there.

"Come on," he added. "Let's get some tea. Then Miranda will show you your room."

"Who's Miranda?" They were the first words she had spoken, except for the quick hellos.

"You'll soon find out," one of his friends said with a mocking grin, but Lysander took her arm and got her a cup of tea and a piece of cake she didn't want. He was really cute, tall, wide shoulders, skinny hips, blue eyes and blue jeans, dark hair all rumpled, and a wicked mouth.

"You're gonna have a good time," he assured her, smiling.

Then he showed Issy her room on the second floor, and it was time to get dressed for her first big party.

chapter 22

Back at the Star & Plough, Maggie was in the kitchen, supervising Sarah, known to all now because of her year-round indoor pallor, as "Winter-White Sarah." Promoted for the night to chief cook, she was coping with the Aga and the steak pies and fries, while Lily, appointed chief helper, dashed in and out carrying three plates on one arm and two in her other hand, shoving through the kitchen door with her shoulder while dying to get back into the bar and chat up the guys. It was, Lily said, beaming and tossing back her long red hair, a lot more fun than babysitting a usually-squalling kid and watching TV, alone.

"She's gonna drop those plates," Sarah said, in a resigned tone. "She drops everything, including my son."

"She *dropped* Little Billy?" Maggie asked, shocked.

"Only onto the sofa. She says she does it to keep him amused, and he does giggle. She sort of holds him up a couple of inches then lets him go, onto the cushions."

Maggie shook her head. "Better stop her right now, that girl doesn't know what she's doing."

"Oh yes I do," Lily said. "I have three younger brothers and I've dropped all of them on their heads. Brains are still ticking over all right." She gave them a jaunty grin, grabbed a couple of salads and said, "Better hurry up, Sarah, or Maggie'll be on your tail instead of mine."

"Fuck off," Sarah said smoothly, while turning yet another flatiron steak.

"Sarah!" Maggie exclaimed, shocked. "You must not talk like that. Remember your child."

"Oh, I never curse in front of Little Billy." Sarah filled a couple of warm tacos with the pork mixture then set them on a plate with a dab of sour cream and a spoonful of the chopped tomato, cilantro, and onion mix with a hit of Tabasco, called *pico de gallo* that, depending on how fast Sarah was moving, might be mild or, in moments of pressure, so spicy hot it could take the roof off your mouth. Either way, the customers liked it. Or at least there were no complaints.

Maggie sighed. She did not understand young people these days, having babies and no husbands, struggling with a life alone, trying to make ends meet. Though when she thought about it, Caroline's situation wasn't much different from Sarah's; just that she was older, and Issy wasn't a baby anymore.

It was seven twenty-five and Maggie was waiting for Caroline to make her appearance. She thought Caroline was in for a surprise with Jim Thompson. Maggie didn't know Jim personally, only from his visits to the pub, but she knew all about him. She guessed everyone did, except Caroline, and she'd decided not to fill her in because it was better if she made her own judgment. Woman-to-man judgment. The way it should be.

"So, here I am." Caroline walked into the kitchen looking about a foot taller than she usually did in the four-inch heels and the short skirt. The pale green silk jersey dress narrowed her thighs and exposed the pretty upper curve of her breasts that, Maggie noticed, she had attempted to cover up with a rope or two of crystal beads, and the little fake silver bird-in-flight pinned in her cleavage. Issy's present. "For luck," Caroline told her now. She wore the plain diamond stud earrings Maggie knew the ex-husband had given her years ago, and the narrow diamond wedding band on her right hand instead of on the left. Her black hair hung smooth to her shoulders and she'd clipped back her shaggy bangs with a small diamanté arrow. Maggie thought it made her look younger.

Caroline did a nervous pirouette. "You think I'm overdressed for an English country dinner party?"

Sarah turned from the stove to take a look. "Who cares? You look fantastic," she said, smiling for once, which Maggie thought made Sarah look all of seventeen, though she was still only nineteen anyway.

Sarah gave Caroline a hug. It was the first time she had seen her looking like a real woman, and not the usual harried-mom-in-jeans-and-boots-and-sweater. She took another critical look. "Did you ever think of wearing contacts?"

"I've tried, they kill me. It's contacts and watery eyes or old-lady glasses, and since I can't see a thing without them, I'll go with the glasses. He can take it or leave it."

"Trust me," Sarah said, looking Caroline up and down, "he'll take it. He'd be crazy not to."

The three of them giggled just as Lily waltzed back through the kitchen door, dropped two plates, said, "Oh shit," then looked up and saw Caroline.

"Jesus," she said, awed. "I didn't know you existed under that mom outfit you always wear."

"Well, she does, and don't you be so rude, and anyway, get those plates swept up before somebody breaks their neck on them," Maggie said sharply, but she was smiling.

Caroline wrapped the turquoise pashmina around her shoulders, carefully covering all feminine body parts.

"Just in case he should notice you are a woman!" Maggie adjusted the shawl so that it flowed around her and not over her. "Remember who you are, Caroline Evans," she added, handing her the little black evening purse and walking her to the door, where she knew Jim was waiting, because Jesus had told her the moment he'd arrived.

"Have a good time," she said, as Caroline gave a nervous smile over her shoulder and went out to meet her first date in seventeen years.

chapter 23

He had on a jacket and tie and was standing in front of a long, lean silver sports car, waiting for her.

"Wow," Caroline said. "I miss the sawdust."

"I cleaned up for you."

"Me too."

They laughed, and his eyes admired her. "You look wonderful."

"Sure I'm not too fancy for a country dinner party?"

"You're perfect for any dinner party." He helped her into the car.

"I thought it would be the truck," she said, looking at the expensive leather upholstery. "What is this anyway?"

"A Maserati. Just a small one."

"Hah! Then I must be paying you too much. Or else you've borrowed it to impress me." She nudged him jokingly with her elbow as they drove, smooth as silk, across the bridge and into the black country night.

"The car's all mine." He turned down the lane that led in the direction of her barn. "And paid for by my own hard work."

"All those rich wives with their enormous country piles paying you and Georgki a fortune to redo them." She sighed, suddenly remembering. "I have a date with Georgki. He's taking me to The Swan in Pangbourne."

"You'll like it. The swans are beautiful, if a little aggressive, the river is wide there, and there are proper falls."

"Not like my tiny little river and baby little weir and my humble mallards, you mean," she said, trying to sound affronted and succeeding in making him laugh.

Looking at him, quite suddenly, she really wanted to kiss him. Could she possibly ask him to stop right there and then and just do that? God, of course not! He'd probably think she was some frustrated divorcée who couldn't wait to get her hands on him. In fact that was the truth.

"Caroline, you are a flirt," he was saying.

"Was that flirting?" She smiled. She knew how to do this, after all.

He turned into the side lane that led to her barn and she said, surprised, "You're not taking me for dinner at my place, are you?"

"I am not."

He turned again, this time between the stone gateposts with the rampant lions. At the end of the driveway Caroline saw the lights of a Jacobean manor. "I'm taking you to mine," he said. "My family's, anyway."

She fell back against the soft smooth expensive leather. What was he doing, taking her to meet his family? What was he *thinking*? She was a married woman, divorced anyway, and with a fifteen-year-old daughter. *And* she was eleven years older than him. She worked in a pub for God's sakes, and he lived in a manor house dating back centuries. All her insecurities flooded her. She should leave immediately, get back to the safety of her anonymous role as the pub cook; hide from people like his family, who would probably patronize her thinking she was Jim's little-bit-of-older-sex-on-the-side. Until he married some girl exactly like them that is.

"You're not happy," he said.

"What makes you think that." Her tone was arctic.

"This is not what you think."

"And what *do* I think?" She shoved her red glasses further up her nose and turned to look at him. The diamanté arrow slid off and her hair tumbled down.

He said, "You think I've one-upped you. You thought I was just the local carpenter, which, in a way I am."

"In what way are you?"

"I *am* a carpenter, only I don't just fix things, I make them too. I make furniture, and I wanted to bring you here tonight because I've made something for you."

Softening, she turned her gaze full on him. She said, "I kind of miss the sawdust."

"I told you I cleaned up for you."

There was a small silence. "And just look at us now," he said softly. Then he leaned over and planted a kiss on her mouth which fell half-open with shock, so he kissed her all over again.

"I've wanted to do that ever since I first saw you in that yellow sweater that's fabulously too tight," he whispered.

"Oh my God, oh my God," Caroline whispered back, but she didn't tell him it was because this was the first time she had kissed any man since James, and she didn't, right now, want to remember how long ago that was. And this man's lips were really quite—*lovely*—was the only word she could think of. It made her knees go weak. Tremble.

She moved away, nervously fishing a lipstick from the little black evening purse, skimming it over her just-kissed lips.

He got out, came round her side, took her hand and unfolded her from the Maserati's innards.

"Wait a minute," she said, remembering. "I have to call my daughter, see how she's getting on at her party in London."

There was no answer. Slightly worried, she left a message saying, *"Call your mom immediately Issy Evans, and tell me where you are and that you are okay."* Then she walked up the wide, shallow front steps into a Jacobean mansion with her date, the really quite good-looking and really, *really* too *young,* Jim Thompson.

chapter 24

The doors of Thompson Manor opened onto a large hall whose dark wood floors were polished to a labor-intensive gleam, and whose fourteen-foot ceilings were embellished with plaster cornices of cherubs and flowery wreaths and heraldic shields that, Caroline had no doubt, told the family's history. And that "family" was standing about in the hall, drinking what looked to be Pimm's from silver cups with little sprigs of mint sticking out the top, wearing long evening gowns and looking like a picture straight out of *Town & Country* magazine.

She gave Jim a quizzical look out of the corner of her eye. "Thanks for warning me not to wear the yellow sweater."

"You look wonderful," he said, taking her hand and leading her in toward a woman with piled-up auburn hair, and a long, red dress.

"Caroline, I'd like you to meet my sister-in-law, Jenny."

"How lovely to meet you." Jenny gave her a welcoming smile. "Though when I heard what a wonderful cook you are I was afraid my little dinner wouldn't live up to your expectations."

A man who looked a lot like Jim, though a bit older and maybe a bit better looking, with sandy hair and a trim mustache, and who was obviously Jim's brother, hurried over. He gave Jim a hearty slap on the shoulder and said to Caroline, "Better watch out for him. He's only the local carpenter, y'know."

She laughed and said, "So I discovered."

"It's so nice to welcome you to our small community," Jim's sister said. "Now, tell me all about your daughter. I hear she's at Upperthorpe. Where is she planning next?"

Before she knew it Caroline was absorbed into the small crowd. They all seemed to have heard about her restaurant and wanted to know all about it.

The dinner table was beautiful, all white roses and polished silver and candlelight. "Of course we'll all come to your opening," an American sitting on her left, whose name was Bradley, told her. "I've already sampled your pies at the Star and Plough."

"And how about those tacos," said the man on her right, who turned out to be a TV producer and who was way too handsome, Caroline told him, in a definite flirt, saying he should be *on* screen and not off.

"We need a good restaurant round here," Bradley added, spooning up his dessert which was called Eton mess, a "mess" of crushed meringue and strawberries mashed with enough cream to add five pounds onto any girl's hips practically overnight.

"You should ask Jim to show you his studio." Bradley poured a chilled Sauternes into her glass to go with the dessert. "He's an artist you know. In wood."

She glanced at Jim, sitting opposite. Their eyes met and he smiled.

"I need to see your studio," she said.

"Then you shall." He saluted her with his glass.

Soon after, Jenny rose to her feet, summoning the women with a glance and they left the men with a decanter of port making the rounds and went to Jenny's bedroom to freshen up. It was enormous and slightly chilly though very pretty, with two sofas and a huge four-poster, covered in what Caroline thought must be the original blue-silk-damask because she could see it was worn through in parts. The women powdered and lipsticked and gossiped about children and help and gardens, then they went down to the drawing room, where they joined the men, and soon it was time to leave.

It was freezing cold out and Caroline wrapped her shawl closer as they drove round the corner of the house and to what used to be the stables and was now Jim's studio.

His walls were covered with pegboards on which were pinned hundreds of drawings, some technical, complete with measurements and notations, others just beautiful sketches of entire sets for stage, or TV.

At the far end of the workspace was a half-built spiral staircase. The steps were already in place and Jim was obviously working on the banisters that curved sinuously in what seemed to Caroline to be a miracle of craftsmanship. She had no idea how you got a solid piece of wood to actually curve. "It's beautiful," she said.

"I was the best kid at woodwork in my class," he said, making her laugh. "Not that I'm too grand to make a door or fix a broken cabinet." He lifted a shoulder in a shrug. "I have to work for a living. A job is a job and I rarely turn one down."

"But you have all *this*. Your wonderful house that's been in your family for generations, and . . . oh, I don't know, I suppose the history."

"Don't believe everything you see." He loosened his tie, took off his jacket and undid the top button of his shirt. "God, that's better," he said. "My brother inherited it, and let me tell you, this house eats our family up, what with a new roof and plumbing and heating and general upkeep. Believe it or not, in my grandfather's day we had fourteen indoor servants and ten gardeners. Now we have two gardeners. Jenny is a miracle worker. Two women come in from the village every morning to clean and vacuum and keep the dust at bay. When she gives a little dinner, like this, they come in to help. That's the way it is with families like ours these days." He came over and stood beside her. "I'm not moaning," he said, "I'm a very lucky man. I live in a beautiful place. I love what I do."

"Then you'd never think about selling?" Caroline knew the estate must be worth a small fortune, especially with all the new money around. "The Russian oligarchs and their spectacular wives would really go for this."

"We're not at that place, yet," Jim said. "And I hope we never will be. There's a couple more paintings we can sell, and my brother's doing well in hedge funds."

Hedge funds! That brought her quickly back to reality. "My husband's in hedge funds," she said. Then, "I mean my *ex-husband*."

"Glad you remembered." He took her hand and led her to the living area where a fire flickered in the grate. The scent of wood smoke mingled with the fainter stable smells of horse and of hay and wood shavings. Aromatic. Masculine.

She sat on a sofa and he put a parcel, clumsily wrapped in brown paper, on the low table in front of her. "A small thing, but mine own," he misquoted from somewhere.

She clutched a hand to her breast and gazed up at him over the tops of her red glasses. "*Really*? For *me*?"

Jim rolled his eyes. "For heaven's sake, open it. Tell me you hate it if you must, but at least get on with it."

Laughing she untied the string. It was a small wooden box, perhaps nine inches long and less than an inch thick, curved into the shape of a leaf. She turned it over gently, marveling at the intricacy of the woodwork, at the thin layers of different colored woods.

The top had an inlaid marquetry design, very simple, and the narrow sides showed the three layers of different woods. When she opened the box, the inside was as beautifully fashioned. It smelled of new woods, and faintly of wax polish.

"It's lovely. A treasure. A true work of art." Her eyes linked with Jim's. "And you made it for *me*? But you hardly know me."

"I didn't have to know you. I know who you are."

He went and stood in front of the fire, kicked the log into action, then leaned an elbow on the pine mantel, looking at her. "Sometimes it happens like that," he said simply.

"It must have been the yellow sweater," she said after a moment, and then they both laughed nervously, and he came and sat next to her and began kissing her.

Time passed. It was wonderful, exciting, and sexy. Caroline knew she had to leave. This was a first date and the romantic gift and kisses aside, she had to get herself together before it was too late.

She put her glasses back on so he would know she meant business, but Jim merely laughed. "I guess I've got to take you home now," he said.

"Next week, we'll be neighbors," she said. "I could almost walk home then."

"I'll walk you. *Then.*"

He helped her with her shawl and put a hand on her waist as he walked her out. She was super-aware of him, sitting next to her as they drove. He parked outside the pub this time, because it was late and there were no other cars. She had forgotten about the time; and also had forgotten about Issy and her London party.

"It's after one o'clock," she said, leaning over to give him a good-night kiss, on the cheek this time. "They'll be wondering where I got to."

He took her chin in his hand, held her for a second in a deep intense look. Then he let her go, got out of the car and came and opened her door.

"Thank you for a lovely evening," she said.

"Don't forget your present." He handed her the box. "I'll call you tomorrow."

She could still feel his eyes on her as she walked to the pub, felt the heat run up her spine again. She wanted Jim Thompson, but she realized she shouldn't. He was too young. Her life was different. Better to walk away from it now, before she got hurt again. She turned to look. He was still standing by the car, watching her. One final wave, and it was over.

chapter 25

Lysander's party was still going strong. They were in a private room at a club. Because Issy was underage, it was the first real club she had ever been to, though she would never have admitted that now. Anyhow she'd bet some of the other girls were under club-age too, even though they looked older and had fake IDs.

The deejay was a black girl who Issy thought looked great, with her hair twisted into about a thousand thin braids. She was wearing denim cutoffs and a black turtleneck and looked really cool. All the other girls were in skinny jeans or really short skirts and clingy tops. In her blue dress from Zara, even without the little black mesh shrug her mother had insisted on, she did not feel "cool" at all.

Lysander gave her another drag on his cigarette. She hated it but it made her look "cooler," and she choked on a glass of what he told her was champagne. "It's mixed with something else," she said.

"Brandy," Lysander told her.

"Mmm." Issy eyed it doubtfully, but she decided she liked it, and when they got up to dance she felt wonderful; she was one of *them*, and she was Lysander's special date. His girl.

It was after four when they returned to the house. Lysander kissed her all the way home in the big chauffeur-driven car, with Miranda, the model who had met her at the door, being felt up next to her by a much older man she'd picked up somewhere en route and who she'd told them was a famous photographer.

Issy didn't even protest when Lysander slid his hand under her skirt. Miranda was doing the same thing so it must be all right. In fact, Miranda's legs were parted and out of the corner of her eye, while Issy was being kissed by Lysander, she saw the famous photographer's hand reach all the way up under Miranda's skirt. Miranda wiggled a bit and moaned and Issy tried not to look, though Lysander was laughing.

At the house, Lysander put an arm round her waist as he walked her up the stairs. She snuggled into him, stopping outside her bedroom door.

"It was all so lovely, thank you, thank you . . ." she murmured, dissolving under another kiss.

Without warning, he pushed her backwards into her room, kicked the door shut and threw her onto the bed. Before she knew it, he was on top of her, his hands were up her skirt, tugging at her thong; his mouth was clamped over hers, she couldn't even protest or scream and then oh God, oh God, his fingers were inside her. Pushing. Spreading. Hurting. Oh God he was going to rape her . . . She needed to scream but he slapped her face . . . he was hurting her . . . she had to get away. This could not be happening. Anger gave her sudden strength. She got one knee up from under him twisted round and gave him an almighty crack in the balls that sent him gasping off the bed.

"*Little bitch*," he snarled, lying there with his pants down and his thing hanging out.

For a second or two, Issy just stared horrified, at him, then she leaned over the edge of the bed and threw up all over the floor.

"*Jesus*," she heard Lysander yell, then the door slammed and she was alone.

It seemed like ages, but was probably only minutes before she got to her feet and walked, still wobbly, into the bathroom, where she threw up some more. Then she took off her dress and the torn thong and washed herself down there.

She found her duffel and put on clean underwear and the cardi and the old sweatpants she'd brought for when she would be alone. She searched for her purse but it had gone. Somebody must have taken it. She flung on her mother's nice trench coat, stuffed everything else into her duffel and walked down the stairs, past the furious party sounds still coming from the drawing room, and let herself out of the house.

At the end of the street she caught a taxi to Paddington and paid with the money she'd stuffed into her pocket earlier, along with her ticket. Half an hour later she was on a train, on her way home.

Her hands still trembled, and her voice shook when she called Sam's mobile.

"*What?*" Sam was instantly awake.

"You were right, I should never have gone." Issy burst into tears. "*He practically raped me.*"

There was a shocked silence, then Sam said, "I'm calling your mom."

"No! No, don't!" She didn't want her mother even to know.

"But she'll have to come to the station to get you. Wait, though, maybe I should get *my* mom instead?"

Issy thought it would be better. "Okay," she agreed. "But it's too early, they'll know something must have happened, and I can't tell them, Sam, I just can't. Wait til nine o'clock at least. Let's tell Maggie I hated the party, they were all older, and I just wanted to come home. And *please*—please Sam, don't tell my mother."

Sam promised. "Don't worry," she said, "she'll never know the truth."

And of course, she never would know because Issy would never, ever, tell.

chapter 26

Caroline emerged from a haze of sleep, saw her clock said twelve and for a minute couldn't decide whether it was day or night. Then she realized it must be noon and leaped out of bed.

She took a quick and gaspingly cold shower to wake herself up, smoothed lotion over her arms and legs and a dab of Clinique moisturizer on her face.

Peering in the mirror she took a closer look at *that* face. At those *lips* that had been kissed, *so very nicely kissed,* only hours ago. Oh my God, what had she been *thinking*!

She went back to her room and got into a pair of gray sweatpants, old and comfy, and a red cashmere sweater the moths had had a go at, leaving a couple of wounds that she'd stitched together in little puckers, around the neckline. It was still good though, and it was the softest, most comfortable garment she owned, and that included the yellow that was now too tight.

When she thought about it, which she did now, she hadn't looked half bad last night, despite the fact that she'd worn a short dress while everybody else wore long. She picked up the small wooden box. It was as beautiful as she'd thought it was. She would show it to Issy when she got home. *Oh Lord, Issy! The party!* She was expected home this afternoon; she had to find out the train time and go meet her.

She tapped in Issy's mobile number but her phone was off. Worried, she ran downstairs and saw Issy sitting at the kitchen table.

"What are *you* doing here?" she asked, flabbergasted. "I just called you to find out what train you were taking."

"I came home a bit earlier."

Issy was holding Blind Brenda to her face but even so Caroline could see she'd been crying.

Something was wrong. She went and sat next to her. She didn't touch or kiss her or ask any questions.

"They were all too grown up for her," Sam explained, buttering a piece of toast and handing it to Issy, who removed Blind Brenda long enough to take a bite, then allowed the kitten to lick the butter until Maggie told her sharply to stop that.

"I just didn't like it there," Issy said, deliberately talking with her mouth full, because it was easier to fake-out her mother that way.

"Then you did right to come home," Caroline agreed.

Issy said, "I think I'll just take a bath. Then maybe I'll lie down. I'm really tired."

Sam said, "I'll come and run your bath for you."

"No need," Caroline said. "I'll do it." She went upstairs and turned on the taps, throwing in half a bottle of the gardenia-scented oil she'd been saving for ages. Steam wreathed round her. Jim and the dinner party seemed a lifetime away. She was back in her role of single mom wondering how to deal with a daughter she knew was in trouble, and not daring to ask why. She hoped at least Issy would talk to Sam.

She went back downstairs and told Issy the bath was ready. Then, because her head was fuzzy and there was too much going on to think about, she put on sneakers and went out for a run.

The early afternoon was crisp with wavery sun behind silhouettes of black trees.

Of course she had been wrong to allow Issy to go to the party. She had allowed her daughter to tell *her* it would be all right to go, when she had known in her gut it would not, and should have said so. She had made a mistake. Now, something terrible had happened.

Her phone was in her pocket and now it vibrated. It must be Issy. It wasn't. It was Jim.

"I'll bet you're wearing the yellow sweater and drinking too much coffee," he said by way of an opening shot.

"You're right." Caroline laughed. "Actually, I'm running along the lane that leads to your house. And I'm wearing old sweatpants and a red sweater with moth holes."

"I wish I could see it."

She could tell he was smiling too when he said, "I wanted to ask you out for a bite, tonight, but now I'm afraid I can't. I have to deliver the staircase, all the way down in Sussex. I'll finish it there, then install it. I'll be gone at least a week."

A week without him! Though she'd promised herself not to see him again, the thought upset her. She said, offhandedly, "Okay. I guess I'll manage the move without you."

"I'm really sorry, Caroline, there's nothing I can do about it. It's work."

"Don't worry," she reassured him, softening. "I've got the student body arriving to do the move. Young and strong and hopefully capable."

"Great." There was a small silence then he said, "Tell me, how did Issy get on, at her party. I know you were worried."

"I was right to be worried."

"What's up?"

"I don't know, and I have the feeling I never will." Then, remembering she shouldn't be unburdening herself on this man who was practically a stranger, she said, "See you when you get back. I had a lovely time, last night. And thank you again for the box. It's on my bedside table so I can see it before I go to sleep, and when I wake up."

"Wish it were me you were seeing," he said, laughing as he said goodbye.

chapter 27

Issy perched on the edge of Sam's bed, knees under her chin, fingers laced tightly over them, long brown hair falling over her face. She was crying. "*Bastard,*" she muttered.

"*Prick,*" Sam agreed, then could have kicked herself. "Sorry, wrong choice of word."

"I know what you mean." In spite of her despair, Issy gave a sniffly little giggle. "Sam, do you think I'm still a virgin? I mean, like well, he didn't actually *do* it, just, you know . . . tried."

Sam ran her hand worriedly through her blond hair. "Well, if you're not, you can always say you lost it riding a horse. Lots of girls blame that."

Issy managed to laugh. "It still hurts," she whispered. "Y'know what, Sam? I thought sex was supposed to be lovely, but he was so fierce and so angry and . . . ugly."

"He was a brute." Sam patted her shoulder. "Are you going to tell your mom now?"

"Never!" Issy recoiled in horror at the thought.

"Well, look at it this way, at least you can't be pregnant."

"*Oh my God,*" Issy said. "But Sam, if I didn't knee him in the balls he would have done it to me and I might have been."

"Trust me," Sam said. "He'll be hurting too."

Then Caroline's mom came in with a tray of chocolate milk and a plate of Cadbury's chocolate fingers, their favorite.

"Talking over the terrible party, I'll bet," she said. "Anyhow, this'll taste better than party food, whatever it was."

"They should have hired you to cater it, Mom." Issy felt a sudden surge of love for her mother; she was always there when she needed her, and she needed her now, even though she couldn't tell her why.

"Thanks," she said, biting into a chocolate finger. Then as Caroline walked back out the door, "Mom?"

Caroline poked her head back in again.

"I'll help you move into the barn."

"Great," Caroline said. But Issy saw she was smiling as she closed the door behind her.

The moving day weather forecast was fine with no rain expected. Issy had still refused to move and would be staying on at the Star & Plough until the "relocation" problems were worked out. Such as, for instance, the store delivering her new bed and the electricity actually working, which Caroline discovered when she arrived at six that morning, it certainly was not.

Then Georgki barreled up the drive crouched over the wheel of his beat-up third-hand Hummer, waving as he drew up in a cloud of dust.

He reached in back for an enormous cellophane-wrapped fern which he presented with a courtly bow. "For your new home," he said, giving Caroline that wondrous smile that made him look like an aging, innocent choirboy.

She kissed him and said pleased, "My first housewarming present," then caught sight of the decrepit student moving van wobbling along the lane. It missed the turnoff and drove past, then someone spotted her waving, and it backed slowly up her drive, trembling to a stop with a terrifying screech of brakes.

Georgki knew how to turn on the electricity, while the students hauled and lifted, tackling the spiraling stone stairs to the mezzanine without complaint.

They took a coffee break at eight when Caroline broke out the bacon sandwiches she'd prepared earlier that morning, and they all sat on the wall by the river, throwing bits of bread to the ducks.

By noon, they were finished. Looking round her new living room, Caroline realized how little furniture she really had; a couple of sofas and an armchair newly covered in heavy white cotton plus a small coffee table she'd found in the Oxford thrift shop, really just a Moroccan brass tray perched rather unsteadily on three legs. She'd said doubtfully she thought there should be a fourth, but the woman at the shop, who seemed to know about such things, told her no, in Morocco, it was always three.

There was a tall lamp with a base that looked like printed concrete, with a wide gold-speckled shade that Caroline had fallen in love with at a local auction, plus a couple of side tables topped with classic blue-and-white Chinese lamps. She'd bought a square of cream carpet to put in front of the fireplace, and had placed Georgki's plant under the tall windows where she was sure it would get enough light.

Her own bed had been delivered, but she had to put her lamp on the floor because she didn't yet have a nightstand, and had to hang her clothes on a rack until she could afford built-ins. She piled her books next to the bed, put her stuff in the bathroom, admired her newly installed and very expensive Jacuzzi tub, then called the store about Issy's bed which they told her would be delivered the next day for sure. She paid off the students, who shook her hand then kissed her anyway, just for the fun of it, then Georgki said he was taking her to Pangbourne for dinner, so she tidied herself up as best she could, called Maggie, said all was well and she would be home later. "Home" still meant the pub, and she called Issy and left a message saying she wouldn't be needing her help that evening after all.

Then, even though she didn't feel like it, she got in the Land Rover and followed Georgki along the twisting country roads to Pangbourne.

He was right, the pub was directly on a big swathe of the River Thames where it sloshed noisily over a weir. There were swans, and though the place was crowded it was a lovely evening and they found a free table outside. Georgki held her chair, like the gentleman he was, and she sank gratefully into it. It had been a long day. She thought it might also have been one of the best days of her life. She had her own home, and her new place of business. And best of all, Issy might even be coming around to the idea.

Georgki emerged from the pub, carrying two foaming beers. "Wine after," he said, settling comfortably opposite. "Now, you need to cool off."

Caroline grinned at him. "You mean I look hot and exhausted?"

He gazed at her with such deep affection, she was touched. She reached out and took his hand. "You'll always be my friend," she said. "You know that, don't you?"

He nodded. "I know that."

She held her breath hoping he was not going to declare his love; not right now, *please,* she prayed, but instead he clinked his glass with hers, "Good luck, Caroline," he said, then tilted back his head and drained the beer in one long swallow.

"Did you even taste it?" she marveled.

"It is the sensation, not just the taste. All that cold bubbling, is wonderful."

He was so simple and so nice and easy to be with, somehow it put her problems in perspective. Sitting there in the evening sunshine she remembered driving through Oxfordshire on that rainy cold evening with Issy slumped next to her, wanting to be anywhere else but there. She remembered stepping through the Star & Plough's door and Maggie taking them in, like the wet huddled sheep they had seen in the meadows.

"You've come a long way," Georgki said, as the waitress arrived with plastic baskets of chicken and chips.

It was true. Now, she could get on with her life. She had her place in the country. She was finally home.

chapter 28

The following night, in the bar with Maggie she said she wanted to spend the night, alone, at the barn. "A test run," she said, "just to see how it feels."

Maggie put down her glass and gave her a long searching look. Folding her arms, she said, "You're having second thoughts."

Caroline hesitated. "Not *exactly* . . ."

"Then exactly—*what*?"

Caroline gave her an under-the-lashes-indirect look that said she was worried.

"Afraid you'll be lonely, out there?" Maggie asked. "Alone?"

"It's the 'alone,'" she admitted. "I mean, Mags, Issy still doesn't really want to come, and now I'm thinking how much I'm going to miss you all, here, at the pub. You know what I mean . . ."

"It's like leaving home the first time." Maggie understood.

"There's always so much going on here, the work and the company, the customers, and Winter-White Sarah and Little Billy . . ."

"Don't forget Clumsy Lily."

"How could I possibly?"

They laughed and Maggie opened a bottle of Italian red and poured each of them a glass. "We're going to drink a toast to your barn," she said. "To your new home. To Issy's new home—she'll come round, eventually, I know she will. And to your future restaurant, when you'll be so rushed off your feet you'll wonder why you didn't just stay here and work for us anyway."

"I know," Caroline admitted, but still, she was filled with doubts. The barn was only a couple of miles away and she would continue working at the pub until she got her restaurant organized, but she was suddenly—and quite terribly—lonely.

"You should call your mom and dad," Maggie said. "Ask them to come and stay with you for a bit."

"But I don't have a guest room."

"Then let them stay in Issy's room, she's not going to be there any time soon."

Caroline thought of all the explanations she would need to make to her parents, about why Issy wasn't living with her, and she knew that would mean they would want to talk more about James. Who she hadn't heard from in weeks, nor had he sent any money.

Then the pub doors pushed open and a slew of Oxford's finest strode up to the bar. Before she knew it, she was back behind the Aga, and Sarah had sent word Little Billy had a cough so she wasn't going to be in that night, and Lily couldn't make it either, so Caroline and Maggie had to tackle it alone.

By ten thirty she was exhausted. The girls had gone to bed long before. Maggie told her she would drive them to school the following morning so Caroline threw on her coat, said goodnight and walked round the corner and got into her car.

It was raining. Again. And the wipers were sluggish. It was like driving in a mist. She chugged slowly along, thanking God there was no traffic and telling herself she would have to take the car in tomorrow and get it fixed. She drove even slower as she passed the gates to the Thompson Manor house. No lights showed. She had not heard from Jim since he'd left, not so much as a phone call. She shrugged. So much for that little episode. Out-of-sight-out-of-mind was true in this case.

She turned into her own drive, hearing the satisfying crunch of the new gravel deposited and raked by her just yesterday. At least she wouldn't step ankle-deep into mud this time. She pulled up in front of the barn doors.

And then she saw the car.

It was parked off to the side, and there was a man standing there, smoking a cigarette. Its tip glowed in the dark, then arced as it was tossed to the ground and stamped out.

Frozen with fear, Caroline saw him walk toward her. Then she came to her senses, turned on the engine, slammed into reverse . . .

"Caroline!"

She *knew* that voice. She took her foot off the gas, jerked to a stop, turned to look.

It was her ex-husband. James.

chapter 29

She felt him watching as she got out of the car. She slammed the door and waited, not trusting her legs to get her as far as her own front door. Her hands shook and she dropped the car keys.

"Caroline!" he said again.

She told herself to get over the shock, get her wits together, tell him to leave. What was he doing here, anyway? She hadn't heard a word from him in months, and now here he was, on her doorstep, soaked from standing out in the rain. His brown hair was plastered to his head, hands thrust in the pockets of his jacket, not even a raincoat . . . though there was a suitcase.

He walked toward her and instinctively she flattened herself against the side of the Land Rover.

He stopped in his tracks, shocked. He said, "You surely don't think I would hurt you?"

The sound of his voice sent shock waves through her. The rain was pelting down, her hair hung in strings and she could not even see him because her glasses were wet. She said, "What are you doing here, James?"

He said, "You're the only one I can talk to. Only you will believe me . . ."

She thought about Issy; James was her father, she couldn't just turn him away. "Better come in out of the rain," she said, gathering herself together and picking up her keys, hurrying past him to the door, which she unlocked and left open for him to follow.

She switched on the lamp and turned to look at him.

"What the hell are you doing here anyway?". "And what's with the suitcase? If you think you're moving back in with me, you can think again."

She had never heard her own voice sound like this, thick and ugly, a mixture of dead emotions and new ones; a result of all the things she had gone through; the struggles, the rejection, the humiliation.

"I know what's going through your mind." He put down his suitcase and stood under the light in the hall, looking at her.

Water puddled on the flagstones round his feet. She saw he was wearing sneakers and that his wet jeans clung to his thighs and his jacket was soaked. But his face was James's face, the face of the man she had fallen in love with, all those years ago in the Raffles bar.

She got that old feeling in the pit of her stomach and told herself quickly to stop. It wasn't right; he should not be here. "Better get out of those wet things," she said. "Come with me."

He followed her up the twisting stairs. She could feel the heat of his gaze on her even with her back to him. She spun round.

"Caroline, I need you," he said as their eyes met.

Not so long ago, she would have melted into his arms if he'd said he needed her. Now, though, she ignored what he'd said, merely handing him a fresh towel. She pointed him to a bathroom, went to her room, got quickly out of her own wet coat and into the old gray sweatpants and the red sweater. She definitely wasn't dressing up for any ex-husband, not even if he'd come here to beg on his knees . . .

She put chicken soup on the Aga to heat, opened a bottle of wine—the good red she had meant to save for a special occasion.

Was *this* a special occasion? *Why* was he here? Her hand shook. What was she *thinking*? What was she *doing*? What, anyway, did James *want*? Could he seriously think he was coming home again? To *her*?

She thought of how overjoyed Issy would be if she knew her father had come back. His return might solve their differences; she would no longer be blamed for the split-up. Anyhow, how had he known where to find her? Mark, she guessed.

She heard his footsteps and turned to look. He was walking toward her, wearing only a towel. *God, she knew that body, lean but muscled, browned from the sun . . . he seemed bigger than she remembered though; taller, towering over her as he came closer. Obviously he worked out.*

She turned quickly away, busied herself at the stove. "Still playing racquetball?" she asked. It was James's favorite sport, fast, immediate, and a little dangerous. Exactly like the man. "Better get some clothes on," she added, briskly.

She heard him pick up his suitcase and walk away. She hung his wet shirt and jeans on the Aga rail to dry, shook out his jacket and put it on the back of a chair then stood it next to the stove. She wiped off his sneakers and set them to dry too. She was acting like the wife again. Picking up after him.

She put two bowls on the table, got the pot of hot soup from the Aga and stood it on an iron trivet, found a ladle, poured red wine into two glasses. Yesterday's baguette would have to do. Butter, salt, pepper. She told herself she had to stop this welcome committee thing she was doing . . .

He came back in a clean white shirt and chinos, still barefoot, his wet hair neatly combed. She indicated the seat opposite, ladled out the chicken soup, tore chunks off the baguette and put it in a basket. Then she sat down and looked across the table at her ex-husband.

He took a sip of wine then said, "Caroline, I need you. Only you will believe me."

It was the second time tonight he'd said that. "Oh?" she said. "And here I was thinking perhaps you had come to see how your daughter was doing? Her so far from home, and almost, I might add, without her father's support." She glared at him.

"Remember the night we met?" He changed the subject back to her. "You in your short skirt and your glasses? How I loved you, Caroline." He reached across the table for her hand. "I was a man who thought he could have it all. And now I've found out no one can."

His touch sent tremors through her. She pulled away, took a sip of the wine, then a gulp. She topped up his glass, telling herself he couldn't just walk in here, into her home, waltz back into her life as though he had the right.

This man had dumped her, he had told her he didn't care anymore; he'd blackmailed her over Issy's custody. She remembered Gayle Lee saying that James "belonged" to her and always would and that she'd better not interfere . . .

"I'm in trouble," James said, sitting back and looking seriously at her.

"Then why not ask Miss Chen to get you out of it?"

She was hurting . . . James was so much a part of her life, so much of her past was with him, why didn't she simply say it's okay, don't worry, we'll be all right, you and me together again . . .

"I'm being accused of stealing," he said.

"Are you serious?" she asked, shocked. "*You? Stealing?*"

"I'm being accused of taking money meant to be invested. A kind of Ponzi scam. Some of that money has been traced to my personal accounts in Hong Kong and Singapore."

He got up and began to pace back and forth in front of the Aga, where his jeans and shirt still steamed gently. He came over and put a hand on her shoulder. "I came here to tell you first, before it hits the news, which it soon will. I needed you and Issy to know—to *believe*—I did not do this. Then I'll go back to Hong Kong and try to work it out."

Caroline remembered Mark telling her there was something strange going on in the business, money missing, James not always where he said he would be.

She didn't want to know all this . . . she pushed back her chair, picked up the pan of soup and carried it over to the stove. This scene couldn't be real. What he'd said could not be real. He had no right to be telling her his troubles. He should not be here, in this new home she had created. He did not belong in her Place in the Country. Yet he *was* Issy's father, and the financial scandal was going to break in the news, and of course he wanted his daughter to believe in him, despite the fact he seemed not to have thought of her in months.

Angry, she said, "Forget your own troubles for a minute. Why haven't you taken care of Issy? What's *wrong* with you?"

"It's simple. I couldn't get my hands on the money. Someone plundered my accounts."

She remembered Gayle Lee warning her not to interfere in their business and said, "I'm betting I know who."

James's face sagged. He looked haggard, a man at the end of his financial rope. Her heart melted just a little. "Of course you'll go to see Issy," she said.

He shook his head. "I can't face her. Later, when things work out and she can believe in me again. I *am* innocent, you must know that, Caroline."

Of course he must be innocent. He was still James. That's why she was letting him stand here, talk it out with her.

"The fraud squad will be looking for me," he was saying. "There'll be a big scandal. I want you to tell Issy it will be all right."

He walked over and put his hands on her shoulders. She gazed up into his eyes. Electricity sparked between them, the way it always had, and her body responded the way it always used to.

She stepped quickly back, told him she was sorry for his trouble, she hoped it would all work out.

He said, "Caroline, it's important you believe me."

"I do," she said. "Of course I do." And maybe she did. "And I promise I'll tell Issy that too, though I think it's a pity you can't tell her yourself."

She poured him another glass of wine, told him he could sleep on the sofa—she certainly wasn't going to put him in their daughter's room. Then she put the coffee on the timer for morning and said goodnight.

She turned her back on him and walked up the stairs to her room and locked the door. She leaned against it, wondering how this could have happened. He couldn't come back into her life, just like that.

She got undressed, got into bed and drew the white cotton duvet up over her head and cried until her pillow was soaked through. The tears were not because she wanted James back. They were for grief because she no longer loved him.

When she got up the next morning, he was gone.

chapter 30

She didn't even stop to work out the time difference, she called Mark in Hong Kong anyway. "James was here last night. Waiting for me outside the barn, in the rain."

There was a silence, then Mark said, "Wait a minute you're telling me *James* came to see you? Did he come to see *Issy*?"

"He didn't want to see her. He told me he's in financial trouble, said his accounts had been plundered, some sort of Ponzi scheme, stealing money that should have been invested."

"Wait just a minute," Mark said again. "*James* told you he was in *financial* trouble?"

"He said he'd come specially to tell me so I could explain to Issy that he was innocent. Before the fraud squad came and got him, was actually what he said. Before the scandal hit the world media."

"Listen, I believe I know where every cent is in my and James's business," Mark said. "Remember, when I saw you, I told you there were some discrepancies, but they'd seemed to right themselves. But James was also running his own business, another world entirely."

"You mean with Gayle Lee Chen."

"Exactly. I always believed it wasn't quite right, there's an underworld connection there, but James is so straight up, naive even . . ."

"He's also under that woman's spell."

"I'll get hold of him right away, find out what's happening. I'll do my best to protect him, Caroline, for your sake, but if he's guilty there's not much I can do. Or would want to."

She said, "James is a fool, he's weak, self-indulgent, but I'll never believe he's a thief."

She called Maggie, who had just dropped the girls off at school, told her what had happened. Maggie said she should get back to the pub immediately, they needed to talk. She would have coffee ready by the time she got there.

"Oh, Mags," Caroline said when the two of them were finally settled at the kitchen table, a mug in one hand, sticky-bun in the other. "The worst thing of all is, I can't tell Issy her father was here and that he didn't want to see her. How could I allow him to do that, I failed her, again." Tears rolled into her coffee.

"You must *never* tell her he was here," Maggie said. "This wasn't your doing, it was James. That man is so full of himself, he couldn't even face his child after what he's done."

"Maggie!" Caroline stared at her, stunned. "You don't think James *did it*?"

"Why else would he have the fraud squad on his tail? Now he expects you to make that all right with his daughter. She's having enough trouble coping with him deserting her without this."

Caroline couldn't even face the sticky-bun, and it was her favorite, straight out of the oven from Wright's Bakers down the street. "Mark doesn't think there's any money missing from his business. He says James is involved with Gayle Lee Chen."

"The Asian bitch." Maggie knew the story and recognized a whore when she heard about one.

"So, what do I do now?"

"We'll just have to wait and see what happens. Meanwhile, we'll carry on as normal, and you won't say one single word to Issy."

Caroline guessed she was right. She thought for a minute, then said, "Mags, it's finally over. Me and James. At least, *me,* anyway."

"Hallelujah! I knew. I saw it in your eyes when you said his name."

"I lost the spark."

"And did he?"

Caroline thought about the hot look James had given her, the way he'd spoken about the time they met and their first love. And she wondered.

chapter 31

James Evans flew back to Hong Kong and went straight to the Peninsula Hotel, where he called Mark and arranged to meet on the boat out at Lantau.

The island of Lantau could be reached via two stone bridges connecting it to Hong Kong, or by train or ferry. James took the ferry then a blue taxi, the only kind permitted on the island. He paid the driver, overtipping lavishly the way he always did, then stood, a hand over his eyes watching the cab disappear as though it was the last gasp of civilization as he knew it.

As always, he was immaculate in a white polo shirt and khakis with a bright red canvas belt some woman he'd met and wooed had bought for him. Women came and went in his life, always had. Except for Caroline. And Gayle Lee. And now Melanie. He carried a small Hermès shopping bag. If it were not for the frown between his brows and the hand stuffed uncharacteristically in his pockets as he walked toward the boat, you would have never guessed anything at all was wrong in James Evans's life.

Mark's boat was an immaculate thirty-eight-foot Hunter. Her black sails were neatly furled, her black hull freshly painted, her polished teak deck without so much as a single scratch.

Mark held the boat steady against the jetty as James leaped up the little gangway. James never climbed—he always *leaped,* always full of an all-consuming energy.

He followed Mark down the couple of steps into the cabin and flung himself onto the banquette, leaning back against the cushions, craning his neck to peer out of the porthole.

"Don't worry." Mark shoveled ice into a tumbler, topping it with Tanqueray and a spritz of soda. James had not changed his drinking habits since they were at business school together. He said, "I didn't call the police."

"Well, you wouldn't would you." James took the glass, raised it in a mock toast. "To better times, old buddy." He set the Hermès shopper on the banquette next to him and slumped forward, elbows on his knees, glass clutched in both hands. He said, "I want you to know I never robbed you. It was my business partner Gayle Lee. The Chinese gangsters she works for put pressure on her. I still don't understand why. Anyhow, she knew from my business records how to access my accounts. She told me she replaced it before any damage was done."

Mark laughed. "Have you never met Ms. Chen's underworld friends? The ones whose money she gave to you to be laundered? I'm guessing she took it and used it to finance her own grand lifestyle, the old Madoff pyramid trick, keep on paying them big dividends until someone calls you on it."

James was staring into his glass as though looking at icebergs in the North Pole.

Mark said, "You fucked me, James, I could have gone down in flames, still can if the truth ever comes out. You almost ruined me . . . and for no reason other than your infatuation . . ."

"Infatuation? You don't fuckin' get it," James said. "You never will. I loved her, Gayle Lee. She brought something special into my life.

She fuckin' *consumed* me," he added despairingly. "I would have done anything she wanted, no questions asked."

"She'll destroy you. She's already destroyed your family. You're her scapegoat, only you're too dumb to acknowledge it. That bitch doesn't love you, she owns you. And she's *using* you."

James got up and prowled the cabin.

"And what about the other woman?" Mark said. "The one you're keeping in an apartment in Macao?"

James groaned. He went and poured himself another gin. "Melanie's different." He stared unseeing out of the porthole. "She's the one I'm leaving Gayle for. She's from a different world, she's innocent, she makes me laugh again, makes me feel young. She'll help me, unlike . . ."

"Unlike Caroline."

James glanced at him. "You know everything don't you? You always did, Mark, that was your problem. You've always played the innocent. Now I wonder exactly how innocent you are? Maybe you and Gayle Lee were in cahoots, maybe *you* helped her get her hands on the money . . ." He downed the drink and pushed his way out.

"Where d'you think you're going?" Mark demanded.

"To get pissed."

He slammed unsteadily up the steps. He'd been drinking on the plane and had also hit the Peninsula bar before he'd even gotten as far as the boat. He swayed down the narrow little gangway, forgetting all about the Hermès bag with the present he'd bought for Gayle Lee, to sweeten the goodbye. She'd always liked Hermès.

Early the following morning, the Hong Kong Police Department received a call from Mark Santos, summoning them to his boat. He was waiting on deck and led Lieutenant Huang down to the cabin where James Evans was slumped on the banquette. A color-ful Hermès scarf was wrapped around his head. There was a small round hole in it where the bullet had entered. Blood from the exit wound drenched the cushions behind him. His sightless eyes stared up at the ceiling and there was a gun in his right hand.

"He was my friend as well as my business partner," Mark Santos was saying to Lieutenant Huang. "He came to tell me last night he was in big financial trouble. I offered to help but he said he would work it out. I believe there was also a woman involved, maybe a couple of women—and you know how much trouble that always causes. He'd recently lost his wife in divorce too and lost custody of his daughter. Obviously, it all became too much for him. He wasn't the James I knew. I'm afraid he just lost spirit for life, the will to go on."

Lieutenant Huang's shrewd eyes met his.

"James just gave up," Mark told him, meeting his gaze.

chapter 32

"*There's a man* from Hong Kong says he wants to speak with you," Winter-White Sarah said, tucking Little Billy under her other arm so she could pass Jesus the phone.

He looked at her, puzzled. "The *husband*?"

"Name of Mark Santos."

Puzzled, he took the phone.

"Mr. Gonzalez? I met you at the pub, that night with Caroline."

"I remember, of course."

"This is the hardest call I've ever had to make, and I'm making it to you because I can't tell Caroline cold, over the phone. You and Maggie are her friends and she's going to need you."

Jesus got the feeling he knew what was coming. "It's the husband?"

"The husband is dead." There was another long silence while Jesus took that in. "It gets worse. He shot himself."

Jesus crossed himself. "That's bad. Really bad."

Sarah, who had put Little Billy down in his carry-cot to sleep, glanced up alarmed.

Mark was saying, "I can't tell Caroline this over the phone. She'll need you and Maggie there."

"How could he do this to her?" Jesus was suddenly angry.

"I believe he saw no way out of his financial trouble."

Mark's tone became abrupt, and Jesus thought it was as though now he'd told him it was all his problem, and he'd have to deal with it.

"Maggie will tell her," he said. "We will be with her when she tells Issy. She will call you for the . . ."

"Details," Mark finished his sentence.

Jesus put down the phone and went in search of Maggie.

He found her in the bedroom. She could tell from his shocked face something was seriously wrong.

"It's not the girls," he quickly reassured her. He went and sat on the bed and she sat next to him. "It's Caroline's husband," he said. "He shot himself."

Maggie closed her eyes, not wanting to believe it. "But how could he do that? *How could he?* When his daughter loves him so much."

Jesus put his arm round her as they sat, wondering how best to deal with it.

"We'll tell Caroline together," he decided finally. "We'll have to get the girls out of school. You must call, explain there's been a tragedy."

"And then we'll have to tell Issy."

Jesus said, "No. Her mother will have to do that. God help her," he added.

chapter 33

Caroline was in her new kitchen, hanging a battered array of skillets on the overhead rack when she heard tires on the gravel, then car doors slamming. She glanced at the old wood-framed clock that took up most of one wall. It had been rescued years ago when a small local railway station had closed down, and rescued a second time by Caroline from a local junk shop. She saw it was not yet twelve. Too early for visitors. Was she expecting a delivery?

She hurried into the hall and poked her head out of the door, surprised to see both Jesus and Maggie. They stood there, just looking at her, not even saying hello. Jesus was holding Maggie's hand. A wave of foreboding swept through her.

"It's not the girls," Maggie told her quickly.

Relieved, Caroline sank onto the bottom step. "Thank God," she said.

Maggie came and sat beside her. "There's no way to pretend this isn't bad news," she said quietly. "It's terrible news, and I want you to try to be brave, for your daughter's sake."

Caroline knew it must be about James; she felt it in her bones. "It's James, isn't it?" she said.

Maggie put an arm round her shoulder and Jesus came and kneeled in front of her. He said, "He's dead, Caroline. Mark didn't want to break the news to you over the phone. He asked us to tell you, so we could be there for you."

Caroline closed her eyes, shutting herself into her own interior space. Her past was suddenly overlaid with a present so terrible it was hard to comprehend. She buried her head in her hands as tears sprang from her eyes, enormous tears, shooting through her fingers, trickling down her arms.

Maggie had tissues ready. She handed her a wad. "Cry," she said. "That's what you are supposed to do."

"I've cried so much over this man. *So much!* And now he's dead." She lifted her head and looked at them. "What happened?"

"It was suicide," Jesus said. "James shot himself."

Her face went slack with shock. "It's my fault," she said. "He came to me for help and I turned him away. Oh God, don't you see, *it's all my fault!*"

"It's nobody 'fault' when someone chooses to end their life," Maggie said firmly. "You have to remember that. James made his choice. It had nothing to do with you. It was all to do with him."

"I've heard," Jesus added, "that whenever something like this happens, those left behind suffer from guilt. You did not make that terrible decision, Caroline. James did."

She rocked backwards and forwards, her face buried in her hands again. "*Oh, God, oh, God,*" she wailed. "I have to tell Issy her father is dead . . . I have to tell her he killed himself."

The two of them looked at her, there was nothing they could do. James had left Caroline one last responsibility.

"I'll go to pick up the girls," Jesus told her. "I already called the school, they'll be expecting me."

"We'd better lock up here and get along home." Maggie stroked back Caroline's hair. "I'll help you, *amiga*, I'm here for you. Come, I will drive you home. You can call Mark later. Let him tell you exactly what happened. Meanwhile, you must simply tell Issy her father died. Later when you know exactly what happened you can tell her the truth."

Caroline got in the car with Maggie and they drove back to the pub. In the space of about five minutes, her whole world had changed. She thought that *not* loving someone anymore, did not mean you would not feel grief when they died, that you would not remember the good times when your love was new, and all the old regrets. And the guilt for not helping James out when he'd come to tell her he was in trouble. She had failed James. And now he was dead. How was she ever going to admit that to her daughter?

chapter 34

Caroline needed to speak to Mark, find out what really happened. When she called he answered on the first ring.

"I'm sorry to be the bearer of such terrible news," he said. "And I'm even more sorry not to be able to tell you in person. I had to break the news via the phone because I was sure it would hit the media before I could get to you."

He told her about James's visit and what he had said. "I should have realized how drunk he was, how much in despair. I know now, I shouldn't have let him go like that. He must have come back, later, looking for me."

"Tell me everything," she demanded, tearfully. "I have to know *everything.*"

So he told her how he had found James and called the police. "It was odd," he said. "James had tied a Hermès silk scarf around his head before he did it. He must have had it in the bag he'd brought on board. I think he was concerned he would mess up my boat and the scarf would stop the mess. You know how neat a man James was," he added. "Besides he knew how much I loved my boat. He was a decent man at heart, he'd just lost his way, that's all."

Caroline's brain was processing the images: the Hermès silk

scarf; the gun; the bloody mess. Oddly, she didn't remember James as being neat. He was a man who left his clothes where he'd stepped out of them, and always left the bathroom a wreck. Strange, he should become so neat when he was about to die.

"James told me he never stole clients' money," she told Mark. "He said he was innocent."

"I hope he was."

Caroline hoped so too, for her daughter's sake.

"Of course, Issy and I will come for the funeral," she said. The very word "funeral" almost choked her.

"There's to be an autopsy first, then I'll have James flown home to Singapore for burial."

Poor James, he's finally out of the hands of Gayle Lee, Caroline thought.

"It'll take a few days," Mark said. "And please, Caroline, tell Issy I love her."

"I will."

"And Caroline?"

"Yes?"

"Remember, I love you too."

"I will," she promised.

chapter 35

Issy was bored to tears in the middle of an algebra class, trying to make sense of the hieroglyphs. She was surprised when the Headmistress's assistant knocked on the door and went immediately to whisper in the ear of the math teacher, who nodded, then looked at her class.

"Sorry for the interruption," she said, "but will Isabel Evans and Samantha Gonzalez please go at once to the Head's study."

The two quickly gathered up their stuff, aware of the speculative whispering behind them.

"What have we done?" Issy whispered, worried, as they walked across the hall to the study. But then she saw Jesus standing there.

"Something terrible has happened," she said, grabbing Sam's hand.

"Everyone is fine," Jesus said, but he didn't tell them why he was there, and why he was taking them home.

The two of them sat silently in the back of the car. The drive home had never seemed so long. Caroline and Maggie were waiting for them in the kitchen.

"Your mother has something to tell you," Maggie said to Issy. "Come with me, Sam."

Caroline went and put her arms around Issy. "I'm afraid it's your father," she said.

Issy felt the blood drain from her face, her spine felt hot, her knees trembled. "What are you saying! He's dead, isn't he? You're telling me my dad is dead. *Why* is he dead? How could he go and die?" She was waving her arms in the air, screaming, she couldn't even catch her breath. The others heard and came running.

"He *can't* be dead. *He will not be dead*," she yelled. *"He's my father . . ."*

Her mother put her arms round her but she broke free. *"How* did it happen? *What* happened to him?"

"Sweetheart," Caroline said gently, "your father wanted to die. It was his choice."

Issy stopped yelling, staring at her mother, stunned. "Are you saying my father *killed himself?* My *father, James Evans?* How did *my father* do that, if you don't mind me asking? Did he hang himself? Drown? *What?"*

Caroline shook her head, numb, unable to say.

It was Jesus who finally told her, "Issy, your father decided it was time to go. He had a gun. It was what he wanted. You must remember that. And always remember, he loved you."

Issy stared at him, shocked, then she swung round and faced her mother again. "If you had not left him," she said, ominously, quietly. "If you had not taken me away, my father would still be alive. Anyway, I don't believe he killed himself." She was yelling again, angry now. "He would never, *ever,* kill himself. He would not have left me, all alone. He *really* loved me, you know that?"

"I do, oh, I do," Caroline said. "But he was in terrible, financial trouble. Money was missing, your father was suspected, he told me so himself . . ."

"Caroline!" Just in time Maggie stopped her from telling Issy her father had been there and had not gone to see her.

"Someone's blaming my dad for it then," Issy went on. "Someone took that money and said it was him. Someone who hates him, someone who's jealous of him because he's . . . oh, because of *who he is.*"

She looked at them all, standing there looking numbly back at her.

"Someone murdered my father," she said.

chapter 36

A few hours later, Caroline was in the kitchen with Maggie, Jesus, and Sarah. She had sunk two brandies and her hands had stopped shaking. The doctor had been called and Issy was now sleeping with the aid of a sedative. Sam and Blind Brenda were with her.

Maggie had taken charge of Caroline's laptop and any messages because Caroline had said she was no longer capable of thinking straight. All Caroline knew was they were going to James's funeral, and had to get to Singapore immediately.

Jesus had brewed his extra-strong coffee and now he served it in mugs dolloped with cream and thick with sugar, for energy. Sarah was at the sink rinsing dishes and piling them into the dishwasher, which she was reluctant to switch on because of the noise. Everything was very quiet. Nobody was speaking, everybody thinking. Then Little Billy gave a loud imperious squawk for attention making them all jump.

Little Billy's yelling seemed to bring Caroline back to life. She said, "She's quite wrong of course."

Jesus set another mug of coffee in front of her, wondering what she meant.

"Issy, I mean. She's wrong. James *did* do it. He *did* kill himself. He was in trouble and saw no way out. *He* told me so, and *Mark* told me so."

"Anyway, why would anybody else *want* to kill him?" Maggie asked.

"There's a woman involved."

"Jealousy." Jesus took the chair next to Caroline's and pushed the mug closer to her hand. "Drink," he said. "You'll feel stronger."

"You mean Gayle Lee Chen?" Maggie didn't sound too surprised. From what she'd heard the woman was a ruthless bitch and capable of anything.

Sarah picked up Little Billy and came and sat at the table. She was part of this little family; they worked together, they were chums, companions on the road of life. Little Billy, who was nine months old now, snuggled, still yelling into the crook of her skinny arm, and she shoved a bottle into his mouth, shutting him up instantly.

"Caroline," she said, and Caroline turned to look at her. "Are you sure you want Issy to go to the funeral?" Sarah had seen how hysterical Issy was, crazy enough even to think James had been murdered.

"She has to say goodbye to her father," Caroline said, wearily because she'd thought over the same problem endlessly in the past few hours.

"Issy must go to the funeral," Maggie said. "She has to see it all, maybe then she'll be able to let go." She glanced at the laptop as a message flashed onto the screen.

"It's Mark," she told them. "He's sending tickets, Singapore Air, leaving day after tomorrow. He's sending us *all* tickets, he wants Jesus and me and Sam to go with you."

Caroline thanked God—and Mark. The thought of all those hours on a plane with her distraught daughter had been worrying her.

"Of course I can't leave the pub," Jesus said.

"Yes you can." Sarah shifted Little Billy from one arm to the other, ruffling his silken blond hair. "I'll come in for you. I can do it, Lord knows I've been here long enough to know how. And there's always my mom to help."

The three of them looked at her, surprised.

"I have a family," she said defensively. "They just dumped me when I got pregnant without the benefit."

"Without what benefit?" Maggie asked.

"Of being married first, of course. Or even being married after." Sarah was comfortable with her single-mom status and no longer cared what anybody thought.

"I know you're a good mother," she said now to Caroline. "You shouldn't take to heart what your kid said. Lord knows, I've said a few things to my own mom that I wish I could take back. When you're upset that's just the way it is. Kids strike out at you. Little Billy's gonna do that to me, one day, I expect."

"Thank you, Sarah," Caroline said. "I know what you mean."

"Never mind about your mother, Sarah," Jesus said. "I'll call the pub company, tell them it's an emergency, they'll send someone over to supervise."

"The tickets are electronic, they're already here," Maggie told them. "And now here's another message."

Caroline tried the coffee, pulling a face, it was so bitter. Weary, she pushed back her hair and went and stood behind Maggie and looked at the message.

Caroline, I've been too busy even to think, but trust me I was thinking about you, subliminally, and our evening together. Will be back Saturday. Can we have a repeat episode, maybe Sunday night?

It was signed *Jim (Thompson, in case you'd forgotten)*.

Caroline's mind was so far from the world of Jim Thompson and dinner parties and real life as it had been only a few days ago, it seemed like a fantasy. "I can't deal with that," was all she said, so Maggie said *she* would, and sent a quick e-mail telling Jim that Caroline had been called back to Singapore and would be in touch when she got back. Maggie didn't think it her place to go into details. Later, if she wanted to, Caroline would tell him.

Weariness turned Caroline's limbs to liquid. The coffee had done nothing to offset the two brandies and for that she was thankful. All she wanted now was to lie down.

Jesus said he'd drive Sarah home, and Maggie walked Caroline up to her room. She waited while Caroline did the normal things everyone always does, even when they're dying inside from grief and anger. Normal things like brush her teeth and wash her face, take off her clothes, and hurl herself on the bed.

"Get under the covers." Maggie picked up her clothes and put them on the chair. "And try to get some sleep. Sam's with Issy; she'll wake me if there's any problem."

Caroline was glassy-eyed with fatigue and shock. *"Poor James,"* she said, still crying. *"Poor, poor James."*

chapter 37

Issy stared at the ceiling for a long time before she got up the next morning, thinking about her father. She knew it was true and he was dead. She would never see him again. She was not crazy though; there seemed to be no more tears left.

Sam, lying on the bed next to her, said, "It'll be better if we get up, fix breakfast for everyone. It's something to do." Issy put the kettle on while Sam burned the toast.

"It'll be okay, they'll never notice," she said, scraping off the black bits before slathering on the good yellow butter from Ireland Maggie preferred.

The water boiled and Issy dunked an Earl Grey teabag in a large flowery Wedgwood mug that Sam told her was only used on special occasions. They both figured this was "a special occasion." She put the tea and toast on a tray and carried it upstairs.

Caroline's door was open, as it always was, but Issy knocked anyway. "It's me," she said in a very quiet voice.

Caroline pushed hair out of her eyes. "Breakfast. Issy, how lovely."

Issy thought her mom looked terrible. She said, "I want to say I'm sorry."

"Me too," Caroline said.

"But I want you to know I meant what I said. I'll never believe
Dad . . . did *that*."

Caroline nodded, her heart was breaking all over again.

"I understand."

Issy put the tray on the floor and went and sat next to her.

"It's the second hardest thing you've had to face in your entire
life," Caroline said to her. She took Issy's hand and they both sat
looking straight ahead, not at each other.

"What now, then, Mom?" Issy asked, sounding resigned to her
fate.

"We have to go to Singapore for the funeral. To say 'goodbye.'
We're all going. Sam and Maggie and Jesus."

"We're finally going home," Issy said, and a sense of relief swept
over her.

Issy spent the entire flight watching movies and reading
magazines.

Looking at the others, she wondered how it was possible to feel so
completely alone when your best friend was reclining in the seat right
next to you, sketching on her iPad; and your mother was across the
aisle supposedly reading gossip in *People* magazine even though her
eyes were closed; and Maggie and Jesus played gin rummy silently. In
fact the only sounds were from the smooth throb of the engines, and
the movie on the screen set into the seat in front of her, and the quiet
voices of the attendants checking if anyone needed anything.

Her eyes felt like they were boring into the back of her head from
staring up at the ceiling, seeing nothing. Despair, she knew now, was
a physical presence. It was there, a dead weight pinning her to the
comfortable reclining seat, like heavy hands on her shoulders.

She told herself this was not her mother's fault. Caroline had done her best, she and Mark had dealt with everything, and Mark would be there to meet them. "Mark will take care of you," her mother had told her, even though both knew it wouldn't be the same as her father being there.

She wished Blind Brenda could be with her. Brenda was the love object in her suddenly loveless life. Also, though she had not yet told her mom, she had vowed never to set foot in that barn Caroline proposed to open as some kind of off-the-wall restaurant. She still believed if they had stayed in Singapore none of this would have happened; they would have had their same lovely home, her father would have talked over his problems; they would have found a way out. Her father would have told them he loved them, that he needed them. Then instead of shooting himself, which is what they told her he had done, he would have come home and they would have worked it all out. The three of them together. The family.

Why was she the only one who thought someone had killed James when it was clear as day to her. Her father hated guns, he never even kept one in the house, said they were weapons of war and violence and he would not permit them near his family.

"Family" had meant a lot to him, despite all the talk of the other woman. She remembered meeting "the other woman" that night in the hotel in Hong Kong. It occurred to her that a woman like that wouldn't think twice about murder because she had a heart made of ice. The Gayle Lee Chens of this world did *exactly* what they wanted. Still, there had to be a reason for murder; a "motive" they called it on the police procedurals she watched on TV. And she didn't know what that motive could be.

When they finally disembarked and stepped into the cool splendor of a spotless Changi Airport, Issy was just glad to feel she had legs again. First came immigration, then customs, and then there was a driver holding up a sign with their name.

A wall of humidity hit her as she climbed gratefully with the others into the white Rolls-Royce sent by the Raffles Hotel, where they were to stay.

Issy stared silently out the window, at the familiar city: at the river and the tall buildings with tiny gems of original colonial houses tucked between, at the streets of bungalows and open-front cafés and glitzy shopping malls; at the quays and bridges, the cricket field and the cathedral and the open markets. All Singapore's history and life was squashed into its less than 270 square miles. The faces on the streets were Malaysian and Indian and Thai and Chinese. If she opened the window she would breathe in the aromas of ethnic foods, hear the cries of the food hawkers and the seabirds, church bells and muezzins. All life seemed concentrated here, in her true home, Singapore. All except one.

Raffles was a cool white colonial-style haven set amongst courtyards and gardens. Its arched verandahs and covered walkways were dotted with high-backed rattan chairs and great swathes of brilliantly colored flowers. Issy had often been here, for Sunday brunch or sometimes for tea. She could almost believe her father would be waiting for them.

But of course he was not. This time it was Mark.

chapter 38

Caroline kissed Mark and said an awkward thank you. It was strange, she thought, she should feel this awkwardness with James's good friend, but somehow, now, everything was askew.

Mark hugged Issy and Sam and shook Maggie and Jesus's hands, said jokingly he'd remember to call him Heyzus and not *Jesus,* and thanked them too, for coming to support the family.

Caroline said, "In fact, James did not have 'a family,' except for us. He was an only son and both parents died early. They had never even got to meet me or their granddaughter." She thanked God silently, they had also not lived to see their son self-destruct.

Her own parents were expected later that evening. She had begged them not to make the long journey from France but they'd insisted. "We need to be there for you, and for our granddaughter," Cassandra Meriton, her mother, had said in that mind-made-up-so-don't-argue tone Caroline knew so well from her childhood. "We weren't there for your wedding," her father had said, getting on the phone. "At least we'll be here for James and you this time."

Mark had booked them into lavish suites with heavy silk curtains and plump brocaded sofas. A tray of fruit awaited and there were fresh flowers in heavy crystal vases. The bathrooms were sumptuous, all pale marble and Jacuzzi tubs and glass-doored showers, fluffy towels and perfumed soaps and lotions.

A waiter brought a tray with cool drinks, and Caroline told the girls to take them to their rooms and get some rest.

Mark was waiting by the window. Now he came over, sat beside her on the sofa and opened the waiting bottle of chilled champagne.

"This must be costing a fortune," Caroline said.

He shrugged. "The business will pay." He handed her the glass. She avoided his eyes, not really wanting to hear what she knew he was going to tell her, but she knew he had to tell her anyway.

"The coroner's verdict was suicide," Mark said. "The police were thorough, they even looked into James's finances." He lifted a shoulder in a shrug. "There's nothing more to be done."

Caroline said, "Issy thinks he was murdered."

He shrugged again, dismissively this time. "That's ridiculous. Anyway, the case is closed. It's over. Let James rest in peace."

He got up and began to pace the room. "I'll take care of everything," he said. "The business end, the apartment . . . I'll sort everything out. I'll put aside personal things you and Issy might want, old things, photos, his Montblanc pen, his watch, cuff links—like that."

"*Memento mori,*" Caroline said very sadly. She half-wanted to go back, see the place herself, but it would be too painful to take Issy there. "Don't they say you can never go home again?" she asked Mark wearily.

"There's nothing to be gained," he said quietly.

And everything lost, Caroline thought. The end of an era.

"James took out a second mortgage on the penthouse," Mark was saying. "I'll sell it for you, see what's left. There's not much from his part of our business. I'm afraid he gambled it away, took risks, gave it to that woman. Nothing I can do about it now."

Caroline drained her champagne and put down the glass.

He looked at her. "The funeral's at eleven thirty."

She sighed, thinking of the ordeal to come. "My parents arrive this evening."

"Then we'll have dinner together, try to keep things civilized."

Of course he was right. People had to be civilized when death entered the door. They had to behave, remember the good things, drink a toast to the deceased.

She felt Mark's eyes on her. "You going to be all right?" he asked.

She said, "I'm sadder for Issy than for James. She's the one who's really suffering."

"I'll do what I can to help," Mark said, and of course, Caroline believed he would.

chapter 39

Cassandra Meriton, Caroline's mother, had always hated her own name. What were her parents thinking, calling her after a legendary Greek prophetess who had refused to submit to Apollo's advances? "I mean," she'd said to her own daughter years later, "if they thought I might turn out to be a goddess they could have gone for Diana the Huntress, or Artemis, Apollo's twin sister, who seems to me to have spent her time lounging around with the girls and enjoying herself. That's why," she added, "I called you Caroline, plain and simple. And why I always shortened my name to Cassie. And now Isabel—such a lovely name—has become Issy. We sound like a couple of martinis, a Cassie and an Issy, please . . ."

Her mother always made Caroline laugh. She brought joy into the room. Even now, arriving at the Raffles in a whirl of garment bags and gifts, Cassie Meriton brought smiles with her.

"Sweetie," she said, dropping her parcels onto the floor and grabbing Caroline in her arms, squeezing her until she laughed in protest. "How wonderful to see you, though I'd prefer it wasn't here, like this." She took in the luxurious sitting room. "Either Mark is doing you proud, or you've come into money," she said, then looked sharply at her daughter. "James didn't leave you a fortune, did he?"

"I don't believe he did. Not with all the trouble he was in."

Her father, tall, broad, the Panama hat he gardened in still clamped to his head, stepped in for his hug. He took off the hat first though.

"He wouldn't leave that damn Panama behind," Cassie sighed. "It's become part of his bone structure by now."

She went and sat on the sofa, patting the place next to her. "Come, sit by me, let's talk," she said.

"Yes, tell us what's what, why don't you," her father said.

Caroline went through James's story, telling exactly how he had died and the silk scarf tied around his head before he pulled the trigger.

"Mark believes he didn't want to mess up the boat. He was so neat, Mark said. Funny, but I don't remember him like that. James was never *neat*."

She looked, puzzled, at her mother, who told her that when people were disturbed, as James was, they did strange things, and she just wished, for her granddaughter's sake he had made a different choice. Then quite suddenly she began to cry.

Cassandra Meriton almost never cried. She had complained about only two things in her life: being short in stature and being burdened with a name like Cassandra. She was five-two and always wore heels, kitten heels maybe but still they gave her a lift and, she believed, made her walk taller. She had blond hair that was frizzing in Singapore's humidity, cut in a short bob, blue eyes, and a pert nose. She always said if one more person called her "cute" she was going to sock them. "In my soul," she complained, "I am definitely not 'cute.'" And nor was she. She had a BA in literature from Oxford and a PhD she'd earned, when her husband was traveling so much and she had time on her hands.

"I couldn't just sit there and watch TV," she told her family. "I was never a lady who lunched." Yet for Caroline, she had always been a proper mom, cooking, keeping their world together. Her family and her dozens of friends adored her.

As did her husband, Henry Meriton. Henry was certain everyone thought he was the backbone of the family, but really it was his wife. He told them that, at every opportunity, until Cassie made him stop, they were all getting sick of hearing about how wonderful she was. Now, he was feeling desperately sorry for his daughter, and for his granddaughter.

They were to have dinner in the Grill at eight, so Caroline showed her parents to their room, then went back to check on her own daughter, who thank God, was sleeping.

Four hours to go 'til eight o'clock, she thought. *Four hours of peace.* She called Maggie, told her about dinner and arranged to meet. Then she took a long, hot bath, doused in some prettily scented oil. When she was soaked, and shriveled, she got out and went and washed her hair in the shower, then turned on the cold to wake herself up. She put on the soft white bathrobe and went to unpack. She hung up the black linen dress she planned to wear the next day. It was a dress from her past. She remembered wearing it with pearls and red lipstick, to dinner with James right here, in Singapore. She remembered how he had liked her in it.

She called reception and asked to be woken at seven—she never trusted in-room alarms—then lay back against the pillows and closed her eyes.

Mark was waiting for them at eight. Everybody showed up on time though the two girls were still sleepy, and everyone was weary from travel. They were in the Grill, which was next to the bar where Caroline had first met James.

"Remember the story?" she asked Issy.

"Stories," Issy corrected her. "I never heard the same one twice."

Then they went to the table and drank a little wine. Everyone managed to eat a little and made conversation and nobody spoke about tomorrow.

The funeral morning was sunny, but purplish clouds hung on the horizon. Caroline knew it would rain; it rained every day in Singapore, you couldn't go anywhere without your umbrella. You simply had to wait for the sun to come out again, which it always did.

A metaphor for life, Caroline thought, eyeing herself in the mirror in the black linen dress. Her legs looked very pale, and despite the heat, she had to wear stockings. She put on the black suede heels that were at least five years old; in fact, she had bought them right here in the Orchard Road shopping mall, where she'd also bought the dress.

Maggie and Jesus were waiting in the sitting room, Jesus wore a dark suit and Maggie was in a black skirt and jacket she'd picked up in Oxford just before they left. Sam stood next to them, solemn-faced, her blond hair tied neatly back.

Caroline had not wanted Issy to wear black. She knew James would not have wanted it either, so they had decided on a pink cotton skirt and a white shirt. Issy's skinny legs were still streaked with the golden-tan-in-a-tube bought from Boots, not so long ago. She was very quiet. Caroline thought she looked desperate, and forlorn, holding everything back.

Cassandra was wearing black and Henry had on a suit he hadn't worn since he retired and that was now too tight. Of course he also wore the Panama.

They went down to the lobby where Mark was waiting for them, and were driven to the church. Caroline took Issy's hand as they walked down the aisle. James's coffin rested in front of the altar. Issy's hand gripped hers. An organist began to play "Jesu Joy of Man's Desiring." The sound echoed from the rafters. Surprised, she saw that quite a few people had come to pay their respects.

She also saw Mark checking with the security guards he'd told her he'd hired in case Gayle Lee Chen decided to put in an appearance. If she did they had instructions to remove her from the premises, forcibly if necessary.

Caroline took her seat in the front row. She sat, staring at James's coffin, wondering why he had done it, and wishing she could turn back the clock and start all over again. The two of them in the bar of the Raffles Hotel, where it had all begun.

Issy sat between her mother and her grandmother, staring at the box that contained what remained of her father. The scent of the flowers covering it filled the air with sweetness. She understood her father was not there. That he would never be there again. She did not cry, though.

The service seemed to go on forever; she stood for hymns and knelt for the prayers. Then after the final blessing, everyone just got up and walked out, leaving her father there alone. They stood saying hello to people who gave Issy a sad smile and said how she had grown. And then it was over.

"I still believe he was murdered," she whispered to Sam as they walked to the car. But Sam said no use her even thinking about that, there was nothing she could do about it.

Issy knew she was right. She was only a fifteen-year-old girl, after all.

As she got into their car, from the corner of her eye she spotted Gayle Lee Chen stepping out of her limo, half a block away. She was wearing a white cheongsam. Issy knew white was the Chinese color of mourning. She hated her.

Mark saw her too and got everyone quickly into the car, then sent the driver on his way.

Issy looked out the back window and saw Gayle Lee walking into the church and felt a moment of triumph. She smiled. This time she was too late.

chapter 40

Cassandra Meriton had been through all the events and struggles and pleasures of bringing up a daughter, and there had been times, when things had been particularly difficult, she had asked herself—and her husband—if it was friggin' worth it. Of course it was. She had simply gone through the same frustrations and feelings of helplessness as everybody else who had ever brought up a daughter. Or a son, Cassie supposed, but then sons were supposed to be easier. Fathers took care of that, took them to football games, told them the "facts of life" as it used to be called in her day and to always use a condom, get a good job, marry a nice girl, buy a house and have two babies who their grandparents could spoil and pick up and leave whenever they wanted. After all, they had earned that right.

Now, though, Cassie was worried about her granddaughter. She saw the desolation in her eyes, and heard from Caroline that Issy had the strange belief her father had been murdered. She could understand why she would not want to believe James had killed himself. The very concept was alien. Fathers did not do that. Now, though, she knew Issy was lost in a sea of adult emotions that were in direct conflict with her teenage self. All she should be thinking about was school and clothes, school and boys, school and dancing, flirting and having fun. While working hard, of course, because sixth form loomed, and then, hopefully, university. Right now she wasn't thinking of anything beyond getting through the next day, and then the next. Her granddaughter was in despair. She needed help, normality, a change. In fact Cassie knew exactly what she needed. Her grandparents.

They were having dinner and Cassie squeezed Issy's hand under the table. She said, "Why don't you come to France with us for a while? You can help Grandpa pick tomatoes; he grows the best tiny little ones and we must get them before the birds do. Then we have to clean up all the figs that fall off the trees, too many to even be bothered with making jam and all that. Your room is ready, it's small but pretty and we finally got rid of the old Mickey duvet you've had since you were little and got a real 'girl' one."

"I'll bet it's white." Issy smiled.

"Do not mistake me for your mother," Cassie said. "It's black."

"Wow!" Issy said, astonished.

"Suede," Cassandra added.

"Jesus!" she was even more astonished. "Really? *Black suede?*"

"Well, it's probably called suedette, but it looks like suede. I knew you would love it, soon as I saw it."

"Wow," Issy said again, intrigued. "I don't know about the tomatoes, though."

Cassandra squeezed her hand again and whispered, conspiratorially, "Forgot the tomatoes, we'll go shopping in Bordeaux, get you some cute French clothes." *And I'll also scrounge round my friends for some boys,* she was thinking.

Issy looked at her mother. "Could I go, Mom?"

"If you would like to."

"Sammy's invited too," Cassandra said, but Maggie said Sam had to get back to school.

Looking at her granddaughter, Cassie saw that for all of a few minutes she had forgotten the reason she was in Singapore, and she was glad. She squeezed her hand again. "It will be okay," she said softly. "It may take time, darling girl, but you will get past this. I promise."

Issy looked longingly at her. "How do you know that?"

Her eyes were so like her father's, it took Cassie's breath away. "Old age and experience, child," she said. "Isn't that what all grandparents say?"

Part Two

chapter 41

A few days later, back in Oxfordshire, at the Star & Plough, Caroline was tidying up her kitchen, restacking pots and pans the way she liked them, and not the way Sarah and her band of helpers had while she was gone, mixing up the sizes so she had to search for the cast-iron frying pan she needed. Finally she found it stashed under a load of others.

"Sorry," Sarah muttered. For once, she had left Little Billy home with a sitter and now she was chopping Vidalia onions that Caroline needed caramelized to serve on top of the flat-iron steak which was to be the night's "special." It wasn't the onions that were making Sarah cry though. Quite suddenly, she stopped chopping and put her head down and began to sob.

Caroline heard her. She quickly got a clean kitchen towel and soaked it under the cold tap and gave it to Sarah. "Hold this over your eyes," she said, "or you're going to look like a snowman, with your white skin."

"Pokey little red eyes." Sarah managed a small laugh that turned into a hiccup.

Caroline pulled out a chair for her and went and sat next to her.

Blind Brenda was sprawled on the table in front of them. Of course it was unhygienic, but what the hell. "Man trouble?" she asked.

"Not that kind of man. It's my landlord." Sarah sniffed, holding the wet cloth over her eyes. "It's nothing really, not compared with what you just went through," she added. "It's just that, well, he's chucking me out. I'm only on a month-to-month and he says he's got somebody else, and maybe they'll buy the place."

"Weekenders," Caroline said. There were plenty of those around in the Cotswolds, buying up cottages to escape the city's rat race.

"So, what will you do?"

"I've no option. I'll just have to go back to my mom."

Caroline remembered she'd said the mum was not happy about her having a baby "without the benefit." "Doesn't sound like the perfect answer to me," she said. Then she suddenly had a brain wave, the kind she often seemed to be having when she thought about the future.

"There's a cottage out at my barn," she said. "It's small, *really* small, but it's all been redone, new plumbing, electricity—the works. Let me tell you what *I* think, Sarah. I am going to need help in my kitchen. Why not you? You could work for me and you and Little Billy could have the cottage, rent free. I'll still pay you the going rate."

Sarah lowered the towel, and looked at her. "I can't," she said. "I can't just leave Maggie in the lurch, first you leaving, then me."

"I'll never leave Maggie and Jesus in the lurch," Caroline said. "I'm not opening until I've got a good replacement here in the pub. Meanwhile, you and Little Billy will have a roof over your heads. You can move in, whether you come work for me or not."

Sarah's sigh seemed to come all the way from her black boots which, Caroline noticed, were worn down at the heel. She knew all

Sarah's money went on keeping that roof over their heads, and on the baby she adored.

"See, good does sometimes come out of bad," Sarah exclaimed, delightedly. "You've just proven it."

chapter 42

It was not until after the pub closed that Caroline found time to check her e-mail. She was sitting up in bed, with Blind Brenda squeezed under her pillow, her hair scrunched into a stubby pony-tail, and Clinique Repairwear hopefully doing its job. She had on a too-tight pink tee. She could have sworn she'd lost weight the last couple of weeks, she'd hardly eaten what with all the worry. Sighing, she guessed it must have shrunk in the wash. Laptop balanced on her knees she pressed Gmail and got her mother's message.

Isabel doing well (I refuse to call her Issy anymore, she says she does not like it anyway, and is too grown-up for baby names.) I told her she can call me Cassandra if she likes. She's slept a lot since we got back. She's very quiet and has not mentioned her father once. Nor does she mention that word "murder" anymore. Let's hope that sleeping dog will lie (as they say). She has agreed to go rescue the tomatoes with Grandpa tomorrow, and is currently feeding the fish in the pond at the far end of the property. Your father drives her there, perched on the back of the John Deere, he with his Panama, she with a baseball cap that says Upperthorpe Hockey on it. I didn't know our girl played hockey. Caroline, trust me, this is a good space

for her, away from the reality of life and death. She'll never forget it,
but one day, as we all must, she will be reconciled to it. As you must
too, darling daughter of mine, pig-headed though you always were,
plus you always had bad taste in men. Remember the long-haired
one with the yellow teeth? Played in a rock band? And how about the
marathon runner in obscenely short shorts who ate macrobiotic and
totally ruined my dinner party? Always thought you should have
married Mark. A much better bet. Love you anyway, and we will
take care of your girl.

There was a smile on Caroline's face as she finished reading her
mother's missive. Typical, she thought. Her mom never gave up. Still,
she was taking good care of Issy—Isabel, she wanted to be called
now. Yet "Isabel" had not called her. She supposed she must give her
time, let her settle in. Meanwhile, she would just text quickly, tell
her she was missing her, loved her, say have a good time in France . . .

There was a second message, though this one, surprisingly, was
from Jim Thompson:

I heard the news—everybody has. I think the whole village sends
their sympathy, along with mine. I hope your daughter is okay, this
must be really hard for her. I know that's an understatement, but
I'm a clumsy man with words. Much better with my hands. Call me,
when you can. Jim

Caroline glanced at the beautiful little box he had made for her.
The lamplight deepened the colors of the different woods, and she
traced its sinuous curves with a finger. He was good with his hands;
she could still remember the feel of them against the small of her back
as he kissed her goodnight. But that was then, before all this happened. *Goodbye good times, hello trouble,* though she had not known

that night of the dinner party what was to come. Now, she inhabited a whole different world. Thanks to James.

A third message popped up as she looked at the screen. This time it was Mark.

Not wonderful news but you should know the penthouse was mort-gaged to the hilt, so there will be no money accruing there. I went back and packed the things I thought were special, to you and Issy, as I mentioned before, plus some pieces of furniture, antiques that I smuggled out before the auctioneers could put claimers on them. The hell with the creditors, these were really yours and not James's anyway. There's a couple of wonderful console tables, elmwood, from the best antique shop on Hong Kong's Hollywood Road— you'll remember them, of course, plus some chairs. I'm getting the permits and having them sent to you at the barn. I guess it will take about a month but I feel you should have them. Caroline, please do not allow them to bring back sad memories. You had good times, too.

Now, about James's will. Of course you know he left "everything" to his daughter. Quite properly, I suppose, since he had already made a financial settlement, unfair though it was, with you. As far as I can tell, there might be enough to put Issy through school and then university. That should be a help.

About the business, forensic accountants are still sorting through it but it seems clear James did do a bit of plundering, though my own investors will be okay. I believe most of James's customers pulled out some time ago, when, I guess, he began drifting off course. Not all "Madoffs" get away with it. Personally I am lucky to get away with my reputation intact.

I have to tell you that I sold my boat, for more than I expected. I'm not sure I shall get another, or if I do, then I will keep it any-

where but in Hong Kong. No news of the "other woman." Thank God for that.

　I just needed to tell you all this, Caroline. And to tell you I love you. And I always have, since the day I first saw you, marrying my best friend.

She closed the laptop and put it on the bedside table. She turned out the light, then got up and opened the curtains, and the window. It was early summer but the breeze still held a bit of the nearby river's chill. She got back into bed and pulled up the duvet, thinking.

Fatigue quite suddenly got the better of her. She seemed to have been running on spare for the past couple of weeks. Now, she sank into a deep sleep, dreaming, guiltily, she thought later, not about James but of how to arrange the Hong Kong Hollywood Road antiques in her new home.

chapter 43

A few days later, Georgki called.

"Caroline?" He said her name as a question, as though he were expecting someone else.

"Yes, it's me," she replied. "And of course I know it's you. How could it be anybody else with that Serbian accent?"

"Russian," Georgki said. "From Estonia."

"Right." She would agree to any story he chose to weave for her. "How are you, anyway?"

"I call to say sorry for your troubles. It hurts me that you are hurting."

She said, "Thank you, Georgki, I appreciate you taking the time to tell me, to *feel* for me."

"And the daughter?"

"She will be okay. One day."

"I have surprise for you," he told her now, his voice rising to a different level. She could hear a definite pleasure factor in there.

"I love surprises," she said, hoping it wasn't another trip to Pangbourne and the swans and the chicken-in-a-basket.

"Me and Jim Thompson have surprise for you. At the barn, or however you call the place now."

"The Place," she said, laughing. "That's exactly how I call it now."

"Meet us there at four." He was giving her an order. "Surprise will be ready then."

"Ohh, but . . ." Caroline had like a million things to do, to catch up . . .

"No 'buts,'" he said to her, sounding so forceful she had to laugh again.

She promised to be there and went to tell Maggie about "the surprise."

Maggie was in the living room with the windows wide open, her shoes off, feet on the ottoman. The cat had found a nesting place in her lap and was contentedly licking its left paw then stroking the paw over its face, washing its whiskers.

"This cat is anybody's," Maggie said, taking a sip of her coffee.

"Any lap in a storm," Caroline misquoted and they both laughed. "I kind of feel like that myself," she added. She poured coffee into a mug and went and sat next to her friend on the sofa. "If you know what I mean."

Maggie looked shrewdly at her. "Mark."

"It would be too easy, Mags." Caroline slumped forward, stroking the cat absently with one hand. Affronted at having its freshly cleaned fur disturbed, it commenced licking furiously at the spot she had touched. "Oh, sorry, Brenda," she said. Then, "I mean, Mags, he's so *there* for me, so . . . *right*."

"The last thing you need in your life now is a man. *Any* man. And that includes Mark, *and* Jim Thompson."

Caroline looked at her, surprised. "What do you know about Jim Thompson anyway?"

"I bumped into his sister at Wright's bakery. She told me Jim was worried sick about you, and all your troubles."

"I suppose everybody knows," Caroline realized.

"A village is a small world. They also know Sarah's getting kicked out of her cottage."

"I've offered her mine. It's tiny but it'll be okay for them."

"Better than where she's living now. Anyway, she'll be good company for you out there. And the baby."

Caroline laughed. "I won't make a good babysitter. Too old. I've lost the knack."

"What that kid needs is a grandmother, but no chance of that, so we'll have to fill in." Maggie knew her role in life was earth mother to all struggling women and children.

"Thank God for you, Maggie," Caroline said, patting her friend's hand affectionately. "Whatever would we do without you?"

"Get me a new chef and a new assistant," Maggie said. "And teach them how to make the crust on those chicken pot pies."

"Easy," Caroline said. "So you'll let Sarah come with me?"

Maggie put down her cup and shifted the cat onto Caroline's knee. "I think it's a great opportunity for Sarah to make something of herself. She needs to get on in this world, think of a future for her boy. And you as well," she added. "Besides, I always find two is better than one."

Caroline dumped the cat on the sofa and went and kissed her friend. "Anyway, now I have to go to the barn. Georgki says he has a surprise for me."

"I'm sure this time it will be a good one," Maggie reassured her.

chapter 44

Isabel—as she had now chosen to be known—was sitting on the terrace of her grandparents' house, with pale purple wisteria petals drifting down on her head from the old blossoming vine. She was thinking about taking a walk through the well-mowed grounds. Her grandpa never got off his bloody tractor, he just buzzed around smiling and cursing the bugs which took huge bites out of him, threatening them with DDT spray that of course he would never use. He just put Neosporin on the welts and hoped for the best.

"The bugs were there before you," she'd heard her grandmother telling him calmly. "They resent being disturbed."

She walked down to the pond—more like a lake really. It was so quiet she could hear the whirr of the dragonflies' wings as they hovered, iridescent green and turquoise and coral over the water, snapping down every now and then onto the surface without so much as a ripple or a plop.

Her grandpa had created this lake, he had personally hauled the rocks that lined two sides, laid the springy turf that sloped directly down to it; he had even made the wooden bench from a couple of trees felled in a major storm a couple of years ago. Just two stumps and a plank across, but perfectly suitable for the rustic surroundings, and very useful for an idle girl to dawdle away an afternoon, trying to think about nothing in particular, because thinking was too painful.

Isabel supposed she would "get over it." Everybody said she would. "Work through it," was an even worse phrase someone had used. As if it were a math test and not a death in the family. Her grandmother, though, had the right attitude.

"Fuck it, Isabel," she said, "if you'll pardon my French. Let's just go shopping. It's only a temporary solution, but you'll find out before too long, life is made up of temporary solutions."

"Temporary" was now Isabel's new philosophy in life. After all, nothing so far had turned out to be permanent. "Wise up to it," she told herself. "Life goes on, with or without some people in it."

Anyway, today she was wearing the dress her grandmother had bought her in Bordeaux: red, strapless, and too short. She suspected it was totally unsuitable but her grandmother had laughed and said, "Go for it. Just don't save it for a special occasion, you might have grown out of it before that happens."

That's why she was wearing it now, to feed the fish who came clustering round her dangling feet as she threw their special food into the water. She suspected she was overfeeding them. Her grandpa only did it once a day but she loved the feel of them swimming round her toes. Maybe they liked it too.

Her phone beeped. It was a text from Sam saying she missed her, and that Upperthorpe was in the swim meet against two other schools that weekend. "Have a good time," she texted. "I think about us, together in Singapore." She signed it, "love you . . ."

Isabel texted back immediately. "Tweet me, so I can know you're really there. I'll be at home tonight," she'd said. Like she was off to parties other nights or something. Actually, she had been out quite a lot, her grandparents had loads of friends who often invited them over and always included her. She'd sneaked quite a few neglected glasses of wine, left lying around, just for the taking. Wasn't sure she liked the taste yet though. She supposed that came with age.

Age. When oh when, did a girl stop being a mere girl and become a woman? How did you do that? She was totally sick of this teen thing. Yet, when she remembered that terrible party and Lysander shoving her onto the bed, groping her like she was there simply for his taking, she longed to be a child again. She did not want to have to deal with the reality of sex. Of course, over the previous year or so, she'd enjoyed kissing, knew what it felt like to experience "desire"— she supposed that's what they called that feeling. But "innocence" was a state of mind, not merely a physical impairment. And right now, she wanted very badly to be "innocent."

However, because of Lysander and her own bad judgment, she no longer was. She probably was no longer a virgin either. Other girls she knew had gone there, done that, laughed and giggled about it, though she guessed some of them lied to appear more popular, whereas she would have given anything to go back to what she had been.

It was like with her father, too. There was no going back.

Her grandmother's voice floated down through the garden, calling her. "Come on, Isabel. Let's go into Bergerac to the movies. It'll all be in French but we can pretend we understand. And we'll have popcorn and Cokes."

Isabel laughed. She liked her grandmother.

chapter 45

Gayle Lee was still in mourning white. She was wearing a bulky skirt that fell well below her knees and an oversized shirt with cheap flat cotton shoes that also looked a couple of sizes too big, and carried a large handbag bought on a Hong Kong street and not even a designer knockoff of the kind Kowloon was famous for. She also wore a western-style wig, black with waves and curls that drooped over her now-bulky-looking shoulders, and large glasses with gray-tinted lenses. With a shapeless jacket thrown over, she was unrecognizable as herself. Which was exactly the look she was aiming for.

She was in a vast casino on the island of Macao, once verdant and mosquito-ridden, now a gamblers' paradise. Unrecognized, she strode through the crowd oblivious to the rattle of slots and the roar of background music and the flashing TV screens promoting the games and the next hot act to hit the casino theater, making her way to a quieter area where the more serious gambling took place.

For a few minutes she stood contemplating the blackjack table and the tourists rapidly losing their money. She moved on to the pai gow rooms where frozen-faced Chinese were playing. Winning or losing, no one could tell. She made her way to the roulette. She checked the scene at every table before making her choice, then she had to wait for a space to become free. She was impatient but like the pai gow players, did not let it show.

Fifteen minutes later, bulky skirt settled around her, big white plastic handbag slung by its strap over her shoulder—there was nowhere to put it down and a big bag like that, on her knee, would have drawn attention and suspicions of cheating. She wished she could cheat here but even for a clever woman like her that was impossible. Besides, tonight she was not Gayle Lee Chen. She was some plain, anonymous, overweight, older woman, who gained no notice or respect from her fellow players, or from the croupier, and especially not from men. Ms. Chen no longer existed. She was just another lonely frump, lured to the casino and probably about to lose her life savings on a few turns of the wheel.

She checked the piles of chips in front of her fellow gamblers, assessed the odds and her luck and pushed a stack of five hundred forward.

"Nineteen. Black," she said, in a voice that had suddenly acquired a strong Cantonese lilt quite different from her usual educated Mandarin, because a country woman of her class would speak the language of her own district.

The croupier spun the wheel. It whirred and clattered. "Nineteen black," he intoned in that special croupier-monotony-speak. He shoved a pile of chips toward Gayle and she collected them. Her hands were innocent of nail polish and silk wraps and rings. They were a working woman's hands.

She played nineteen black a second time. It was her number. It had always done well for her. She saw no reason to change now.

It came up again. This time she collected her winnings and moved on, pushing through the crowd, still oblivious to the shrieks and gurgles and trills and the rattle of coins from the slots, heading for the pai gow table.

It was quieter in there, just the smooth slither of cards across the green baize tables and the clatter of ice in the complimentary drinks being served by young women wearing short skirts and tall heels with the smell of cologne coming from the high rollers and the sweat of fear from the losers. Pai gow was a Chinese game of stealth and bluff, of manipulation and bravado. Gayle had all of those qualities. This was a high-stakes game. She needed to win big. She was playing for her life.

Five hours passed. Her luck was holding but it was time to take a break, change tables. She would gamble all night but now she needed a drink and some food. First though, she took her chips to the office window and cashed them in. She asked for an electronic check rather than cash, which she immediately had transferred to a secret account in Hong Kong.

Then she went and sat alone in a booth in the steakhouse where she ordered a fillet steak and a martini. They did not have the Tanqueray gin she had learned to like with James, and she had to make do with Bombay, with a drop of French vermouth and a twist of lemon peel. It went down well and she ordered a second before the steak had even arrived. When it came, perfectly cooked, she toyed absently with it, nibbled at the salad, and drank a third martini, which for her, was very unusual. She was thinking about her winnings. It was still not enough to get her out of the mess. The gangsters whose money she had been laundering for years, investing through James and others like him, had finally caught on to her. Like all classic Ponzi schemes it was a house of cards, and now it collapsed. The walls were closing in on her, as they had on James. But poor James had had no way out, and maybe she did.

Toward dawn she collected her winnings and with a polite bow, departed the still crowded pai gow table and walked again through the now half-empty casino to the office where she cashed in her chips and had the money deposited electronically to her anonymous account in Hong Kong. Up in her room, exhausted, she kicked off the painful ugly shoes, so flat they made her calves ache, then, before she took the longed-for shower, she transferred all her winnings, plus more currency, from her Hong Kong account to that of her client in Beijing. That should keep him quiet for a while.

She was smiling as she took her shower. Her naked body was smooth, and meticulously waxed—there was not a hair on her arms or her legs, or anywhere else on Gayle Lee Chen. She was herself again. She missed James though. It was a great pity he'd had to die.

chapter 46

On her way to the barn Caroline couldn't help sneaking a glance at the Thompson Manor. Not that she expected to see Jim, nevertheless there was always that little schoolgirl-crush feeling she couldn't get past. Even though he was too young for her she wondered if Issy—*Isabel*—felt like that, sometimes. And anyhow what had happened to Lysander? He had not been mentioned since the party that Issy had told her was a gigantic dud and full of "old" people, "at least twenty." Where did that leave poor old Mom? Caroline asked herself with a grin.

When she pulled into her own freshly graveled drive though and saw Jim's giant white pickup parked alongside Georgki's old Hummer, she got that schoolgirl-crush feeling again; a little bit breathless, a touch flushed. Hot under the collar in fact. She checked herself in the mirror. She *had* put on lip balm but she had not thought to powder her nose and her hair looked flat . . . okay, so she would have to do . . . Anyhow, she had no right to be feeling like this about Jim Thompson after only one date, and that not even alone. Except after, in his studio, when he had given her the beautiful box.

The upstairs windows were open and she could see her bedroom curtains—cheap white cotton held up with metal rings that clattered when she closed them—fluttering in the just-up wind that brought with it a scent of grass and cows, and night-blooming jasmine that, oddly, flowered during the day, as well as the flat, cool scent of the river. She hadn't had time to order umbrellas and tables for her terrace yet. In fact her restaurant was no farther along than the planning stage and her brilliant ideas.

She climbed out of the Land Rover and pulled her short cotton skirt primly down. "Hi," she called.

"Hi yourself." Jim appeared in the doorway, smiling anxiously at her. "Hope you don't mind we 'broke in,'" he added. "Georgki still has a key and we needed to *gain access,* as the cops say."

"I don't know what the cops say, but I love surprises."

She leaned in to kiss him. He smelled good, of wood shavings and a citrusy aftershave. She must find out, buy him some for Christmas . . . *my God she was already thinking of Christmas, and all they'd had was one rather impersonal date.*

Georgki came out to greet her and she kissed his cheek too.

He said, "Now is okay to come in. Is ready."

She was told to close her eyes then taken by the hand and led forward. She could tell they were walking into the big empty room that was to be her restaurant.

"Open eyes. Look now," Georgki said, dramatically.

She did, and thought how pretty it looked with the sunlight streaming in.

"At the ceiling," Jim directed, and she looked up.

A cream canvas "sail" stretched from wall to wall. "Oh my God," she exclaimed. "It's wonderful." She had been right, it brought a feeling of intimacy to the big room. With the French doors standing open and the cool smell of the river, and the "sail" fluttering gently in the breeze, it was outdoors brought indoors, old with new, water and stone.

"I'm in a dream," she said, turning to smile at them. "It's my brilliant idea come true, thanks to you. It's wonderful."

"Thanks God you like it." Georgki crossed himself. He was in one of his more reflective moods. "I want for you to be happy," he said. "Sad times is over now. Right?"

"Right." Caroline hoped so anyhow. "After all, what else can go wrong?"

Jim said, "I was concerned about you, what with all the rumors going around."

"What rumors?" Did everybody know her business?

"You might as well know people have been talking. About maybe there was some kind of . . . well, y'know, rumors about your husband being killed. Sorry," he added quickly. "I didn't want you to be the last to know. And anyway, Georgki and I got the sail together, we thought maybe this would bring a bit of happiness back into your life, get you back on track."

So "everybody" knew her business. "Everybody" talked about it. "Everybody" was concerned for her. She was part of the village, one of them.

"Thank you, thank you so much," she said. "I'm on track now. It's just wonderful. Beautiful. I shall put up a brass plaque saying Jim and Georgki did this." She had to get back to the pub. "Drinks are on me tonight," she said, kissing them goodbye. "And anyhow," she whispered in Jim's ear, "I owe you a dinner. My treat, this time."

"Sorry," he said, and she felt her face drop. "I can't make it tonight. I'll call you later, though," he said as he waved her goodbye.

chapter 47

A few days later, the rains came back to Upper Amberley. Gutters overflowed and water swirled down the streets, carrying the usual detritus of discarded soda cans, plastic bags, and Styrofoam cups, slamming up against the walls in ugly little piles. Caroline had already swept the front of the pub twice, getting soaked in the process, even though she'd put a plastic bag over her head to protect her hair. She needn't have bothered; some people's hair frizzed in humidity; hers simply flattened out.

Now she had taken over bar-duty from Maggie and Jesus who were still in the back courtyard attempting to staunch the flow heading toward the kitchen door. Thunder made the glasses behind the bar rattle, while lightning lit the sky like Guy-Fawkes-Night fireworks, only without the bonfires and the lovely hot potatoes baked in the scarlet ashes. Sarah was on cooking duty though they were not expecting a crowd, not in this weather. Caroline thought anyone with any sense would stay home, light the fire, and turn on the telly. Of course there were two or three old faithfuls, the domino players who had been there the night Caroline and Issy had arrived in a rainstorm just like this one, and old Laddie Rice whose Border collie, Frisky, still showed no signs of living up to his name, and who anyhow was currently hiding under the table, scared witless—if he had any—by the thunder.

Soft-hearted Caroline scooted back into the kitchen, grabbed a piece of ham from the fridge, came back out, walked over to where Laddie sat nodding over his beer. She got down on her knees and coaxed Frisky out from under with the treat. The dog woofed it up in a split second and Laddie suddenly came back to life and ordered another half, which Caroline pulled, letting the foam subside before she carried it over to his table.

Back behind the bar she leaned on the counter, suddenly lonesome. She took out her phone and checked for messages. Nothing. At least Issy could have called to say hi, and so could Cassie. And what about Jim Thompson anyway? Who she had invited out to dinner and who, so far, had not gotten back to her. Not a word from him. Not one fuckin' peep! It could make a girl paranoid! She thought of the canvas "sail" soaring over her empty restaurant and told herself that instead of just *waiting* for him to call she should be more assertive, take charge. Trouble was she'd never really been a take-charge sort of woman. It was time she changed; she had put his number on speed dial. She heard it ring, then the click as it went into message mode. She decided it was better not to leave a message because it would look like she was chasing him, and remembered Maggie telling her to "get pushy." Was that only a few weeks ago? So much had happened since then, time seemed to have disappeared. The pub door swung open and she glanced up, smiling a welcome.

A young woman in an expensive Burberry trench coat was standing by the door. Her blond hair was wet, her blue eyes had a look of panic in them.

Caroline said, "Come on in and take off that wet coat. I'll get you a towel and we've got a good hot chicken soup brewing on the Aga. That and a glass of wine, or a brandy, will straighten you out, I'll bet."

The woman said nothing, just stood there, water dripping around her feet.

Caroline hurried to throw another log on the fire, poking at the embers to get it to flame, standing back as it roared into life. "There you are," she said with a cheerful smile. "That'll take the chill off you."

The woman seemed to come suddenly to life and walked over to her. "I'm Melanie Morton," she said.

"Welcome." Caroline shook her hand. It was freezing. "Quick, let me have your coat." She slid the Burberry off her shoulders. "It's a terrible night," she said, pulling a chair closer to the fire. "Now, what can I get you, Miss Morton?"

"You don't understand," the girl said, still standing rooted to the spot. *"I am Melanie Morton."*

Caroline eyed her warily. Something was wrong. "Right, Melanie," she said. "Pleased to meet you. I am Caroline."

"I know who you are."

Caroline was surprised but she supposed everybody did, around here anyway, though she had not seen this woman before. And she still had not sat down, nor made any attempt to dry herself with the bar-cloth Caroline now handed her.

"I'm James's lover," she said.

"Oh my God!" Caroline was the one who sat down, quite suddenly. *James's lover.* She wondered what she was supposed to do. Say, glad to meet you. Come on in, have a drink on me . . . let me nourish you with my home-cooked soup while you've been fucking my husband for years . . .

"Six years," Melanie told her, as though reading her mind.

"The bastard," Caroline said, stunned.

"Oh, yes . . ." Melanie Morton's voice was a breathy Marilyn Monroe whisper. "He was such a bastard, but you see I couldn't leave him even though I knew he was married and I was doing wrong. I was a nicely brought-up Catholic girl, and I knew you were not supposed to go with married men, but I couldn't resist him."

"Seems like nobody could," Caroline said. She went back behind the bar and poured herself a shot of brandy. She drank it in one gulp, choked, made a face, then poured a second glass for James's second mistress. Well anyway, the second one she knew about. Who knew, with James, there might be half a dozen. Some of whom, like this one, might just show up at the pub and expect her to explain James to them, or look after them. What was she doing here, anyway? The mistress seeking out the wife so she could confess her sins? Or maybe she was here simply to twist the knife in the wound.

Melanie Morton had leaned her elbows on the table and put her head in her hands. "I won't say I'm sorry because what I did had nothing to do with you," she explained. "It's James who should be sorry. And now he's left me with nothing. Not a cent." She looked up and held Caroline's eyes with her huge blue ones. "I have responsibilities, and so does he," she said. Then she got up suddenly and walked back to the door.

Caroline stared after her. Thank God she was leaving. "Don't forget your coat," she called, but she was already gone. Two minutes later she was back, this time with a child.

Melanie thrust the little girl forward and the light shone on her face. The child's brown eyes scrunched in the sudden glare.

Jesus Christ! Caroline said to herself. *Does Issy have a sister?*

chapter 48

The child was small and lanky-limbed, in a summer dress that was totally unsuitable for a rainy English night. The dress was pink, smocked in navy; the kind of old-fashioned outfit you might associate with royalty. It looked especially out-of-place on this girl, who had the look of a waif out of Charles Dickens. Thin no-color hair cut chin-length, clipped to one side with a pink barrette; a narrow face with no visible bones to it; a chin that appeared to sink in but that was probably because the girl was holding her head down, hiding in her neck and peering up at her with those big brown eyes. Dear God, could they really be *James's* eyes?

All Caroline's normal maternal instincts were canceled. She did not even want to look at this child. She didn't want anything to do with her mother. And anyhow, she could be quite wrong about James's involvement; any kid with brown eyes could pass as his.

She felt Melanie Morton watching for her reaction. Now she saw that the pub's three customers were taking in the little tableau, and the dog who never normally moved unless it was to snap up a morsel of food, even got up and wandered over, wagging its tail, like it lived here and was acting as host instead of her.

"Get out of here," Caroline snarled at the dog, and saw the girl shrivel into her mother's legs, obviously thinking she meant her.

"Sorry," she sighed, wondering how she ever got into these situations, when all she did was keep her head down and try to do her best. There had to be some special kind of doom hanging over her. She obviously must have been a very wicked woman in some previous life and now she was having to pay for it. Well, fuck it, she wasn't about to take on this responsibility.

The kitchen door swung open. Maggie came in. She saw the drowned-rat woman and the shivering child. She looked them up and down, took quick note of the mother's tears, the child's terrified expression.

She said, "Give that woman a brandy, Caroline, while I tell Sarah to fetch them some of your soup."

Maggie went back to the kitchen and Caroline got the brandy and an Orangina for the kid. She sat them both at the table near the fire, the very same table where Maggie had put her and Issy when they had wandered in out of the rain, on exactly a night like this, over a year ago.

Sarah, bursting with curiosity, bustled out of the kitchen with two steaming bowls of soup full of chunks of chicken, carrots, and potatoes. Maggie was behind her with a towel.

The woman thanked them. She dried off her child first, though the little girl wasn't nearly as wet as she was. Maggie said the kid could use a sweater and went off to get her one. She also got a gray sweatshirt that said STAR & PLOUGH UPPER AMBERLEY in red for the mom.

The woman thanked her. "I'm Melanie Morton," she said.

"Yes?" Maggie looked at the small girl, obediently sipping Orangina through a straw.

"And this is Asia." Melanie indicated the child and they all looked at her.

"*Asia?*" Maggie said.

"It's where she was conceived."

Sarah laughed. "Then maybe instead of Little Billy I should have called him 'Ford.' Back seat of," she explained when they switched their glances to her.

"Jesus," Caroline said. Then, "Sorry Mags. This seems to be getting very complicated."

"Oh, no, I don't think so." Maggie took charge. "I don't think it's complicated at all. In fact I'll bet I could tell you the story without any prompting, but why don't we allow Miss Morton to tell us instead."

They stood around the table, waiting. Asia spooned up a little of the hot soup, looking up at them. She was missing two front teeth.

"Fell off her bike," her mother said hastily, in case they were assuming child abuse. "Anyway, long and short of it is, I was James's mistress. We lived together, in Macao and Singapore for six years."

Caroline waited a minute for it to sink in, for her to feel the stab wounds again, the humiliation, the pride wiped in the dust. She wondered how James had managed his complicated love life while still being married to her. And having a second family.

"Means nothing to me," she said, in a clipped voice that sounded nothing like her. But of course it did. She still bore the scars of a betrayed woman.

"That bastard," Sarah said, amazed. Her own boyfriend dumping her when she'd told him she was pregnant was nothing compared with this.

"Asia is James's daughter," Melanie told them. Then she swigged down the brandy, slammed the glass back on the table and looked Caroline in the eye, as though daring her to dispute it.

Not knowing quite what to say, finally Caroline came up with, "So why are you here?"

"We had nowhere else to go. James left us with nothing, not a penny. I maxed out my credit cards just to get us here. I thought since you are Asia's only living relative you would . . . you know you'd . . ."

"Look after you," Maggie said, looking at Caroline to see what she was thinking.

Caroline heaved a dead kind of sigh. She met Maggie's eyes, then Sarah's, then the little girl's, who gazed solemnly back at her with those eyes, so like James's. *Like Issy's.*

Melanie said, "I'm also here because I want you to know I don't believe James killed himself. He would never have done that, never have left me penniless, left his daughter with nothing."

Caroline thought oh yes he might. He did it to us, after all.

"He loved me," Melanie said. "He would never have left me—us—alone."

"What do you mean?" Maggie asked, and Sarah held her breath, waiting for the answer.

"I think somebody killed him. James was set up, he was murdered." Seeming shocked at what she had just said, Melanie put a hand over her mouth and turned to look at her daughter, who slurped the last of the Orangina through her straw then glanced innocently up.

It was the innocence that did it. Caroline knew that look, understood it from her experience as a mom. Somebody had to look after this kid.

"Okay," she said, in her normal more kindly voice. "I guess you'll have to come and stay at the barn with me tonight. Eat up your dinner first. What do you say, Mags? Shall we have a bottle of wine? We can sit here, let Melanie tell her story. Then tomorrow . . ." She shrugged. "I may be misquoting Scarlett O'Hara, and to tell you the truth I'm feeling a bit like her, but anyhow, tomorrow is another day. We'll think about it tomorrow."

chapter 49

Asia fell asleep in the back of Caroline's car.

"It's been a long day," Melanie told her.

Caroline thought it certainly must have been. And now she was going to have to put James's lover and child in Issy's room and she was not happy about it. After all, Issy had not even slept in her own room yet, not even broken it in, so to speak. And what's more, she still did not know whether she ever would.

Good thing she had bought twin beds so there was room for both of them. This kid was too old to sleep in a drawer, the way Issy had when she was tiny, when they'd visited the grandparents and Caroline had forgotten the traveling crib. Padded with a cushion and a folded baby blanket it had done the trick. Infants were so much more portable than "children," who tended to want to run around on a plane, speak to total strangers, race down hotel corridors. She had been a mom a long time. Sixteen years next week. She wondered exactly how old Asia was but for the moment did not ask. She'd had enough for one day.

Gravel spurted satisfyingly under her tires as she stopped the Land Rover in front of the barn. All was in darkness; she must have forgotten to leave the outside light on. She got out and opened the back door and Melanie eased herself out, still clutching the sleeping child.

Melanie stared worriedly into the pitch-black night. Nearby, the river gurgled and rippled. The wind flung rain against windows. Trees rustled and fretted. "This is scary," she whispered, as though afraid somebody might be lurking. "You really live here?"

"It's my home." Caroline had no time for nerves, she was fed up with the whole deal. She was tired and emotionally wrung out and all she wanted was to go to bed and not have this woman—this *responsibility* here. As she unlocked the door and switched on a light she asked herself if she was going to be picking up the pieces of James's other lives forever. What more could he have done? Except get himself murdered. And if so, by whom? And for God's sake, why?

Asia woke as her mother carried her up the stairs but she did not speak. In fact so far, Caroline had not heard a single word out of her. Not even a whimper.

"Oh," Melanie said, when Caroline showed them Isabel's room. "I forgot all about my rental car. I left it at the pub. All our stuff is in it."

Caroline sorted out a bathrobe for Melanie and a T-shirt for Asia. She found one new toothbrush—they would have to share, Asia was missing a couple of teeth anyway; gave them extra blankets because she thought they might be feeling the cold after Singapore's heat and humidity; found fresh soap, said there was shampoo if they wanted it and Melanie said thanks but she was too tired. Caroline went to the kitchen, made a pot of tea, carried it upstairs with some biscuits, knocked on Melanie's door, said it was outside and to sleep well, they would talk in the morning.

Then she went and locked herself in her bathroom and contemplated crying. She decided it wouldn't do her any good so she washed her face instead. Despite all the trauma she remembered to put on the recovery cream. "Just in case," she told herself with a weary grin, "your face falls off overnight." Which it just might, with all this . . . this *what*? Stress was an underwhelming word for it. She sighed, climbed into bed and checked her e-mails.

Mom, Isabel had written.

Grandma is so funny, she makes us laugh all the time. Grandpa mows a lot. The bugs are terrible. Can we come and live here?

Caroline slammed shut the laptop and sank lower into the pillows. She had just gotten them, by hook or by crook and a hell of a lot of debt into this bloody converted barn, a proper home, a business for the future, and now her kid wanted to go and live in France near the grandparents. Hadn't she *asked* her, for fuck's sake . . . Hadn't she said, "Shall we go try France?" And hadn't Issy said, "NO . . . ?"

Her mobile was blinking. Two messages. The first was Maggie. *"We'll work it out, do not worry, amiga. Plus, that child may have brown eyes but are we sure they are James's? Think about it very carefully and we'll talk tomorrow."*

Caroline thought about it very carefully *now*. After all, Melanie had just shown up, she had not offered proof of her relationship with James, which she claimed was a six-year deal. She had not offered proof of little Asia's fatherhood. Could she be playing her for the fool? Showing up broke, with a kid, saying James left me with nothing, now I'm your responsibility? Where's the money?

This would take a lot of thought.

The second message was from Jim Thompson. *"Terrible weather. How about a cozy candlelit dinner? Chez vous? I heard you were some kind of great chef. Just let me know when. I'll bring the wine."*

Caroline turned out the light and slithered deeper into the pillows. Great. Even if she'd allowed herself to, now she couldn't even have the remotest beginnings of a love affair—after seventeen bloody long years—because she was stuck with James's leftovers. She thought about James and wanted to cry for him, but she didn't. It was over. Except because of Melanie and Asia, it was beginning all over again.

chapter 50

In France, over breakfast Cassandra Meriton said to her grand-daughter, "It's time you went home, y'know."

Isabel lifted her nose out of the bowl of coffee into which she had just stirred vanilla sugar and gazed silently back at her grandmother.

"Well?" Cassandra awaited the reply she knew was to come.

"What home?"

Cassandra sighed. Teenagers were nothing if not predictable. They were sitting at the painted metal table under the gnarly old wisteria vine, whose blossoms were rapidly turning into seed pods that exploded with a little pop every now and then, sending seeds flying. She thought propagation was easy when all you had to consider was another flower or two. With humans—especially girls—it was quite a different matter.

"So? When did you last see a doctor?" She swiped homemade fig jam over a segment of croissant, carefully not looking at Issy.

"What d'you mean?"

"You know perfectly well what I mean. You'll be sixteen in a couple of weeks. And that's grown up enough, these days anyway, to have to take care of yourself. Just in case."

"In case I want to go to bed with somebody you mean?" Isabel wanted to say "fuck somebody," not go to bed with, but somehow it didn't seem appropriate over the breakfast table, with her grandmother.

Cassandra looked her in the eye, anyway. "And do you?"

"You mean *have* I?"

"You don't have to answer if you don't want. Privacy is necessary, but sometimes we women need to talk. About things like the curse and should you wax pubic hair or have a bush, and should you spray perfume where you want to be kissed . . . and where is that place anyhow. You are a normal and very attractive girl. What you feel is normal. Sex is a good thing, in the right way."

"The right place, the right time." Isabel finished Cassandra's thought. "Just so you'll know, I have not," she said. Then added, "Yet."

Cassandra looked steadily at her. She'd heard what her granddaughter had said but knew she was keeping something back. "But?" she prompted.

And over the crumbled croissant crumbs and the popping wisteria pods, Isabel found herself telling her about Lysander Tsornin's assault on her body.

"Bastard," Cassandra said, when she had finished and sat staring sadly into the bowl of coffee. "Here, have some more." She topped it up, put the pot down next to her on the table. "He was drunk, I suppose. Men are men and when drunk they can't think straight, about who you are and what they are. It certainly doesn't excuse him, and let me assure you, Isabel, he won't be the last to try. The trouble comes when you *want* him to try."

She stirred her coffee and thought some more. God, it was so long since she had been through all this, how could she remember the first time a boy had put his hand between her legs and she had almost fainted in rapture.

"I probably shouldn't be telling you this—in fact your mother should . . ."

"God, I couldn't possibly tell her!" Isabel blushed at the thought.

Cassandra said, "Nobody can. That's what grandmothers are for, as well as best friends, and other girls going through the same thing. Look, Issy." She forgot for a moment she was supposed to call her Isabel, having called her Issy for going on sixteen years. "Sex is good. With the right man, it can be fantastic. Sublime, I would call it," she said, suddenly remembering her past and thinking even women in their sixties, like her, and probably older, enjoyed sex as one of the great benefits of the world.

"How will I know?" her granddaughter asked.

"Hmmnn . . . that, my dear, is tricky. You can be fooled by your own body jumping like a trout on the line, into thinking this is it, this is all I want, all I need. But I'll tell you something I found, after a couple of those little episodes—in my long-ago youth, of course." She smiled at her granddaughter, who laughed. "It's *afterwards* that you know. When you're lying in his arms and you know that's where you want to be and exactly where he wants you to be. Then, my little Issy, you will understand what the sex act means."

"True love?"

"Sometimes. Sometimes not. Life can be cruel that way. But should you ever achieve that emotion do not ignore it. It might be called love."

"Wow." Issy gazed admiringly at her grandmother who she now called Cassandra, trying to imagine her as a petite blond sixteen-year-old, dancing up a storm in her kitten heels, challenging those young guys with her blue eyes. She'd bet she'd been really cute, and sexy. "I could never talk like this to mom," she said, wistfully.

"Nor could I to mine. But there, now you've done it. And you're a little bit wiser, a little bit more cautious."

"And I know what's what," Issy said, positive she did now.

Her grandmother shook her head. "Oh no you don't." She smiled. "But you will."

chapter 51

Caroline woke suddenly in the middle of the night. Her spine prickled and her hair stood on end. Had she really heard somebody going downstairs? Was the stranger absconding with her silver? Pathetic bits and pieces though they were, bought at auction, tied up in bundles with bits of string. There, she heard it again. But it wasn't footsteps, it was the muffled sound of a child crying.

"Oh, God! Oh, Jesus!" The poor little drowned rat was crying! She sat up, clutching the quilt to her pink-T-shirted chest, wondering what to do. She heard no soft voice saying it was all right, they would be okay, not to cry . . . all that motherly stuff she herself had done, that she'd gone through with Issy.

Bloody Melanie Morton. Bloody James. Now, what should she do? *Call your mother,* the voice in her head told her, clear as any church bell. Of course, she should call Cassandra. Wasn't that what any daughter in trouble would do? Well, maybe not *would* but certainly *should.* Mothers, as she now knew, were a fount of knowledge and experience. Mothers knew everything. At least they were expected to and now she was about to put her own to the test. Besides, Issy—Isabel—was due home in the next couple of days and if she was coming here to meet a sister she knew nothing about, who knew what might happen?

She got up, pulled on her old chenille bathrobe and unlocked the bedroom door, asking herself why she had locked it anyway. *Because the woman was a stranger and she had brought her into her home. She was sleeping next door and child or no child, she did not know her, and you never knew* . . .

She opened her door cautiously. She had left the landing light on, just in case. In case *what*? They wanted to go down and fix sandwiches? Or make phone calls? Or watch TV? Their door was firmly shut and, standing, listening, Caroline heard nothing. The child had stopped crying.

Thanking God, she crept barefoot down the wooden stairs through the darkened living room and into the kitchen, thinking to make a cup of tea and check how early she could call her mother. She switched on the kitchen light and jumped about a mile. Melanie was standing by the window.

God knows how long she'd been standing there, in the dark, staring out into nothing! *And* she was wearing practically nothing . . . black lacy underpants and a T-shirt with no bra, that showed off her breasts. "Taut" was the word that came into Caroline's mind and she wondered for a split second whether the same could be said of her own. Probably not. Anyhow, why wasn't the woman wearing the robe she'd lent her?

"You made me jump," she said.

"Sorry if I startled you. I couldn't sleep. Asia was crying, she's a little 'disturbed.'"

"I heard. Is she okay now?"

"Sleeping. Exhausted."

Caroline filled the kettle and put it on the Aga. "Like some tea?"

"I'd really like a double vodka."

Caroline nodded and went to the sideboard to get it. Nothing would surprise her anymore. Certainly not double vodkas at three in the morning. She poured one for herself, set the glasses on the table, offered tonic, cranberry juice, lime? She topped the glasses up with ice cubes and went and made the tea. She couldn't face another biscuit and got out a bag of pistachio nuts instead. She scraped back the chair next to Melanie, sat down and put the bag of nuts between them.

"Cheers," Melanie said, lifting her glass.

"Cheers," Caroline replied, wondering where all this was going.

"I didn't tell you everything," Melanie said, after a large gulp of the vodka. It didn't even make her cough which it would Caroline.

"I guessed that." She sipped her own drink more delicately.

"It's just that . . . well, I'm scared." Melanie slumped in the chair and put her head in her hands, a position Caroline remembered taking herself when she was filled with the kind of despair she now felt from this woman. This *stranger*.

"I'm so sorry. There's nothing to be scared about here. You're just not used to the quiet of the countryside, that's all."

"No. It's not that. I ran away from Singapore because I was afraid that woman was gunning for me, after what happened to James . . ."

Caroline knew Melanie must mean Gayle Lee Chen. She spilled some of the pistachios onto the table and cracked one open. "And exactly why would you be afraid of 'that woman?'" No need to mention her name.

"Because she killed James." Melanie lifted her head and looked directly into Caroline's eyes. "You realize that don't you?"

"I hadn't actually thought about it," Caroline said carefully, because in fact it had crossed her mind, though there was as far as she could tell no "motive." And from all those TV programs she knew a motive was what you must have before you killed somebody. The thought also crossed her mind now that when Issy was told James had killed himself, she had said the same thing. Immediately. She'd said somebody killed him. Somebody wanted him dead.

"But why?" Caroline asked.

"Gayle Lee was in bad financial trouble. James never really knew exactly where she got her money. Never asked either. Just thought she was fabulously rich. Until later, when he found out she was working for the Chinese mobsters. That man was under her spell for so long it was a miracle he ever ended up with me."

"And without *me*," Caroline added, with a sudden thrust of anger.

"Well, yes . . . But I came after you."

"You did not."

Melanie's eyes rounded in surprise. "You're *kidding*? James told me it was over, that you hadn't even made love in years . . ."

"That's what all men say about their wives when they're chasing after another woman."

Melanie looked bewildered. "He said you were cold, calculating, all you wanted was his money and the good life."

"I ended up with neither. So much for the 'calculating.'" Caroline thought about it. "Was I cold?" she asked out loud. "Maybe, when I realized I wasn't the only woman on the scene, that I was only 'the wife.'"

"Jesus." Melanie cast her eyes down, staring unseeing at the pistachios which had rolled out of the bag and lay scattered across the scrubbed pine table. "I swear I didn't know that, I told you I'm a good Catholic girl, I wouldn't . . ."

"I'll bet you *would*," Caroline said. "Women like you always do."

"Ohhh. I see what you mean. From your point of view of course."

"Who else's point of view should I have? Yours? James's? Shit, Melanie Morton, you stole part of my life and now you're here with the kid you claim is my ex-husband's—he was in fact *still* my husband at the time you gave birth, I'll have you know. And how old is Asia, *exactly,* anyway?"

"Five. Going on six."

"And my daughter is fifteen going on sixteen."

"I shouldn't have come here." Melanie looked warily at Caroline. "It was a mistake. I'm sorry. But I meant what I said. I was frightened. I *am* frightened. That woman will get me because she knows I know what happened. And she believes I might tell."

"*Who* will you tell?"

"You." Melanie seemed to pull herself together, sitting up straighter, folding her arms over her very attractive chest, stopping for a moment to think about what to say next.

She finally said, "You should know this too, not because I want the Chen woman to go after you, but because you should know about James and her. He told me the whole story, how he met her at some social event years ago, held on a *junk,* one of those old wooden Chinese boats with the black sails that you can rent out for parties and sail across the harbor, thinking you're a big shot. Anyhow, that's the way James described it to me."

Caroline remembered James using those exact words years ago when he had described that same party to her, though he had not mentioned Ms. Chen.

"He said she was gorgeous, different, exotic. And very sexy."

"Not the way she came off to me." Caroline was remembering the ice-maiden act in the Peninsula Hotel suite.

"James was working with his partner, Mark Santos. I never met him," Melanie added quickly. "Just so you know. Anyhow James was instantly smitten, bowled over . . . all that . . . and she was clever too, told him she could help him, she had money to invest. Of course James was thrilled. He told me she had an endless financial supply, that she practically floated his business in the beginning, but she wanted her name kept out of it. She wanted it to be secret. He was worried that maybe it wasn't legal, worried about tax dodges and things like that, but she was a woman of importance, of good standing in the Chinese community. And she was so sexy he was crazy about her. It went on like that for years, him seeing her, investing for her, making a lot of money for her, and for himself. Then he met me. And things changed."

"For me, too," Caroline couldn't help saying.

"Yeah. Well. Right . . ."

"Go on." Caroline wanted to hear the truth, finally.

"Gayle Lee started to threaten. She worked for powerful men, laundered their drug money, arms deals money. She was their front, though James didn't know that then. But she was a gambler and she was gambling with their money. Like Madoff, she kept sending back profits on deals she never made. She lived big, spectacularly. It was a house of cards. One investor got suspicious, others followed. They wanted their money back. *Or else . . .* Gayle Lee became desperate. James suggested she sell the Hockney or the Matisse or something, but she said she would lose face, everybody would know she was finished financially. Anyway the paintings were fakes, done by a little man in Canton who could fake any artist, and did, for anybody. They weren't cheap, either, she said.

"She had James crazy, said he had to help her. She knew everything about James's business with Mark. She'd accessed the accounts, taken money, but James caught her. He managed to put the money back in the account just in time."

Caroline remembered Mark's story about that.

"James told me finally, he couldn't take it," Melanie went on. "He couldn't stand her threats, her demands, the emotional drain, the lies and cheating. When we met he told me he'd been finished romantically with her for years but he was still in business with her and couldn't get out. But he loved me, and what with Asia and our life together he had to get out. He told me he was through.

"He went to Hong Kong to see Mark. He was going to confess everything, tell him he would get out of their business, out of Mark's way, that he was sorry. Then he was going to the police, tell them about Ms. Chen and what he had done and that it was finally finished. At least, that's what he told me."

Melanie poured more vodka into her glass. Caroline replenished the ice. She made another pot of tea they probably wouldn't drink, poured a cup anyway. She was nervous and it gave her something to do. She wasn't sure she wanted to hear the rest of this story. It was becoming too real.

Melanie said, "James wanted to buy Gayle Lee a parting gift, to 'sweeten the blow,' he said, even though he hated her for all the destruction she'd wrought. He even asked me what he should get. I told him Hermès, of course, for a woman like that. A scarf, nothing too extravagant, especially since he was broke. I drove him to Changi Airport. Asia was with me. They were already calling the Hong Kong flight, we were late, hardly had time to say goodbye."

Caroline's head was filled with the tragic image of the little girl waving goodbye to the father she would never see again.

"I have no idea of what really happened after that," Melanie said. "I heard the details from the police, read it in the newspapers. They said it was suicide. Of course, I knew they were wrong but there was nothing I could do. And then Gayle Lee Chen found me, at our apartment in Singapore. She didn't phone, she just showed up, said she was James's partner, she demanded all his papers from his office, the details of where the secret bank accounts were.

"She mowed me down like a steamroller. I was wounded, dazed, didn't know what to say, except there was no money, no secret bank accounts. She didn't believe me, said she would haunt me 'til my dying day until she found the truth. And that day would come sooner than I thought. 'Take care of your child,' she warned me, standing at the door of the apartment I'd shared with James. 'Children are always vulnerable.'"

Melanie stopped. The silence of the country night settled around them, not a bird, not an insect, not even the kettle boiling on the hob.

"And that's when I knew I had to get away," Melanie said finally. "I had to protect Asia. That woman is a killer and she will kill me to get her hands on James's money."

"Money he didn't have," Caroline said.

"Money she said she had given him, that he had stolen."

"Poor James." Caroline reached out and patted Melanie's hand. It was very cold, she'd been clutching the iced vodka for so long.

"Poor me," Melanie replied.

"Poor Asia," Caroline said, then realized in fact they were all in trouble. Gayle Lee was a loose cannon. She sipped the now cold tea, thinking about what to do. She wondered how early she could call her mother.

"But you must have the money," Melanie said. "James told me so."

It was eight A.M. when Cassandra got the call. Caroline knew her mother well enough not to wake her earlier.

Cassandra heard the story to the end. To her credit she did not tell her daughter one more time that she had married the wrong man. Instead, she said they'd be there later that day, they would bring Issy home and sort things out.

Then she went to find her husband who was buzzing around on

his tractor, told him to shut that noise off for just a minute so she could hear herself speak and they were off to England to meet Issy's new sister. "And decide whether Caroline is about to be murdered for money she doesn't have," she added.

chapter 52

Jim was on his computer drawing a set of library shelves to scale, intended for a real live castle up in Northumbria. The "library" would take up three walls, continuing over the top of the double doors leading into the room with shelves of different heights and levels, to keep it visually interesting. The job was an expensive and meticulous one, a slight error could ruin the whole thing, which was why he was concentrating, calculating and recalculating to the merest millimeter. He had already ordered the woods, expensive, Brazilian zebra-wood, with rare tulip and Macassar ebony for the facings.

His client who was in his eighties and had so far lived his life without a "library" was now going the whole hog. It was nothing but the best, though Jim had told him at his age he would be better off installing good central heating and taking a world cruise and using the local library for all the reading he did nowadays.

Still, there was no deterring him though Jim guessed his heirs, who no doubt were waiting in the wings, would rather have inherited the money than a library.

His concentration was broken intermittently by thoughts of Caroline. Why had she not replied to his e-mail? His texts? His phone calls? Could she be avoiding him? If so, she couldn't keep it up for long. Upper Amberley was a tough village to avoid anyone in. Like it or not you bumped into people on the high street or in the post office, or the bakers'—actually the "bakers" preferred to be known as "confectioners," because of their fancy cakes, particularly the éclairs which had the habit of melting all too quickly in the mouth, compelling Jim to buy another at once. He did not have a sweet tooth but he loved those éclairs.

He put down his slide rule and his calculator, switched off the computer and sat staring into space, his mind on the éclairs and Caroline; thinking perhaps she might enjoy one, or even two with her morning cup of coffee, which he was sure she must have around elevenish. And that if he went to the confectioners and bought them then simply showed up she couldn't possibly turn him away. Good manners would force her to invite him in and then she'd have to explain why she was avoiding him when what he wanted was a repeat of the evening they had spent together. It wasn't that he was obsessed with Caroline, it was that he simply could not get her out of his mind.

Ten minutes later, spruced up a little, which meant he had changed his shirt and combed his hair, he was saying good morning to Belinda Wright who he had known since childhood, and who was behind the counter in Wright's Bakers and Confectioners and ordering a dozen éclairs.

"My, a dozen," Belinda marveled, eyes widening behind her specs. "You having a party tonight?"

"Just a craving," Jim said, and it was true, but the craving was not for sweets; it was for the woman.

With the paper bag oozing chocolaty-custard-cream on the seat beside him, he sped down the lanes, grumbling when he had to follow a flock of loudly bleating sheep the farmer was relocating to the field next to the barn, where the cows used to graze. Time now for the hard-nibblers who would mow the grass down to the earth with their gnawing little teeth, instead of the ruminants who curled great swathes of it into their mouths, and produced milk and cow pats in equal quantities at the other end.

Finally, the sheep were all in, the gate closed, the farmer, who of course Jim knew, waved his thanks. Gravel spurted under his wheels as he drove up to the barn, stopped the truck and picked up his bag of éclairs.

A small girl was sitting on the doorstep, staring at him. She was wearing a crumpled pink cotton dress and a scared expression. Grabbing his bag of oozing éclairs he jumped out of the truck and waved hello.

"No need to be frightened," he called, walking toward her. "I'm a friend of Caroline's. I've brought you some éclairs."

He held out the bag to show her. She turned her head away.

Caroline appeared in the doorway. "She hasn't spoken a word since she arrived," she said.

"Oh? And when was that?"

"Last night. At the pub. In the thunderstorm."

Their eyes met over the top of the child, who continued to sit there as though nothing would ever persuade her to get out of the way, so Caroline was forced to lift her up, tuck her under her arm and carry her back into the kitchen.

"Let me introduce you." She set the child down on her own two feet. "This is my ex-husband's child. Her name is Asia."

The thought had crossed Jim's mind that this must be another of Caroline's daughters, but was quickly removed when he considered the way she had introduced her. "My ex-husband's child," she had said. Not "*my*" child.

"The mother's taking a shower," Caroline explained. "It's a long story," she added.

"I brought éclairs."

"Just what I feel like." She grabbed the bag, took a yellow plate from the sideboard and arranged the éclairs on it. "A dozen," she exclaimed. "How extravagant."

"What's extravagant?"

Jim glanced up and saw a sexy vision with long yellow hair still wet from the shower. The vision had huge round blue eyes and stork-like legs that went on forever under the very creased skirt she was wearing, and that also looked, when he thought about it, as if she had worn it for at least a week.

"I'm Melanie, Asia's mother," the vision introduced herself, and Jim shook her hand and was given another, but a very different kind of dazzling smile. Flirty, if he was not mistaken, and he rarely was. He pointed out the éclairs.

"They go well with double vodkas," Melanie said, darting her eyes maliciously at Caroline. "Sugar is what a girl needs right now."

Caroline tore off a piece of paper towel, wrapped an éclair in it and handed it to Asia, who bit eagerly into it.

Jim sat back in his chair. They all looked wrecked, he decided.

Caroline caught his eye as she took a second éclair. "It's a long story," she said again.

Jim shrugged. "Go ahead. I've got all day."

chapter 53

All the éclairs had been eaten with a second batch of hot coffee by the time Caroline and Melanie finished their story, just as Jesus, Maggie, and Sam arrived in the black pickup.

"What's going on?" Jesus nodded hello to Jim and gave Melanie a hard stare.

"Oh, just the usual drama," Caroline said. "Sorry, Sam," she added, getting up and hugging the girl. "We ate all the éclairs."

"Wow." Samantha went and sat next to Asia, who shriveled in her seat, hands squashed between her knees, head down. "Too bad. I love éclairs. Were they from Wright's?" Jim nodded and she said, "They're the best ever." She glanced sideways at Asia who was obviously trying not to look at her, or have any physical contact. "Did you have one?" she asked, but the child still said nothing.

"She's scared," Melanie told Maggie, when she looked at her for an explanation, since in Maggie's experience children did not normally behave like that.

"Did Asia ever meet that Chen woman?" Maggie asked, and Melanie nodded.

"Once. She came to the apartment, after James . . . after . . ."

"Let's not go there." Jesus jutted his chin in the children's direction. "It is not appropriate."

"Right," Melanie agreed.

"So, now we all know the story, where do we stand?" Jesus asked.

He took the chair next to Caroline, who poured coffee, then put up another pot while she was at it, thinking this was a coffee day if ever there was one, and to hell with the caffeine count.

"There's cookies," she told Sam, who shook her head, looking again at Asia, who this time sneaked a look back.

"There, I knew we'd get to know each other," Sam cried, delighted.

Asia put her head down, but her tight hands had unraveled and she smoothed her pink dress and sneaked a second look.

"To answer your question," Caroline said to Jesus, "my parents are arriving this evening. They're bringing Issy—Isabel back. They're going to sort everything out."

"Right," Maggie said, already recalculating accommodations. "Issy—sorry I can't remember to call her Isabel—can bunk in with Sam. Melanie and Asia can have Caroline's old room at the pub, and the grandparents can stay here, with you, Caroline." She did not add "for safety's sake," but that was what she was thinking. She did not trust Melanie one inch. "Bring them for dinner," she added. "I'll get Sarah to cook tonight. We'll have a meeting, decide what to do."

"Does anybody really have a clue?" Jim asked. "I mean, are we talking *for real* here, you think there's a killer on the loose?"

"It's serious." Melanie fixed him with a glare. "I was there. I know."

"I believe it," Caroline said.

Nobody wanted to put into words that the Chinese woman had murdered James, not in front of the children, but everybody got the implication. Including now, Jim.

"I'm there for you," he said to Caroline. "I'll bring Georgki, we can stand guard in case she shows up."

They all laughed and Caroline said there was no need to go that far, and anyhow a glamorous Chinese woman like Ms. Chen would stand out in Upper Amberley like a Hollywood movie star.

"A cat amongst the pigeons," Sam said, and they all looked at her and laughed.

She hadn't quite got the correct simile, but she was right.

"Anyhow," Maggie, ever practical, said, "however are we going to tell Issy she has a new sister?"

chapter 54

If it were not for the brown eyes, Caroline thought, that child could be *anybody's*. And anyhow, they were not the same brown as James's. This child had dark eyes, Spanish eyes, Caroline would call them. And come to think about it, she also had that lovely Mediterranean-color skin. Almost *olive,* whereas James had very white skin under the year-round tan he'd maintained.

The Gonzalez family and Jim had left and now Melanie was standing by the door, smoking a cigarette. Caroline thought she was a very attractive woman and had no doubt James had fallen for her. But if she'd come here, broke, looking for a financial fix, claiming James was her child's father, she was knocking on the wrong door. As far as Caroline knew, there was no more money.

Jim was still there, leaning against the kitchen sink, arms folded over his chest, one ankle crossed over the other. Caroline caught Melanie looking at him.

"You two an item?" Melanie asked, with that lowered-chin, catlike smile Caroline noticed she was using now she wasn't crying anymore.

An item! What movie era was she coming from! "Certainly not," Caroline said, and Jim grinned.

"Okay. I think I'll take Asia for a walk, get some sun while it lasts." She plucked Asia from her chair and wandered out into the courtyard, heading toward the field which Caroline noticed now had sheep in it.

"What happened to my cows?" she asked indignantly. She had become attached to them and their goofy lowing, looked forward to them peering over the hedge at her as she drove by. It was silly but she always waved and could swear they knew her.

"I guess the farmer decided a change of scenery would be good for them," Jim said. "Fresh fields and pastures new," he added.

She knew he must be quoting something but after a sleepless night her brain wasn't up to remembering exactly what.

"Less flies with sheep," he mentioned, still leaning casually against the sink.

Caroline didn't want to think about flies. She definitely needed something to wake her up and it was not vodka, and definitely no more coffee. She had Issy to deal with and she was afraid her daughter was going to be hurt. She looked at Jim. "I don't know how to explain it to Issy," she said helplessly.

"I've found truth is always the best way, one painful thrust and then let the healing begin."

"She's had so many 'thrusts' recently." She met his eyes and thought how brown they were.

Jim unfolded his arms and held them wide. "Get over here, sweetheart," he said, and she moved into them as though it was the most natural thing in the world.

Wrapped close to his chest, her head under his shoulder, Caroline could hear his heart thudding. She had just time enough to remember she was in her old chenille bathrobe, unshowered and unclothed beneath it. His hand pressed into the small of her back, urging her closer, the other held her head as his mouth lingered over hers.

"I've been wanting to do this again but you've been avoiding me," he murmured, dropping kisses across her uncombed hair. "You know you have the prettiest hair, soft and swingy and that fringe, always in your eyes." He stopped for a second, puzzled. "Where are your glasses, anyway?"

"I forgot all about them." Caroline couldn't even remember where she had left them after last night's vodka.

"Good. Now I can see your eyes." He kissed her eyelids then ran his tongue over them. It made her shiver.

This was getting too heady, too out of hand, too wonderful . . . she had not felt like this in . . . oh, forget how long, she was feeling it now . . .

"Your eyes are green." He held her away, to look at her. "Tell me something, do you take your glasses off when you're in bed?"

She was laughing and so was he. "Depends who I'm in bed with," she said, and then she took his face in both her hands and began kissing him. Seriously.

After quite a while she pulled herself away. "This can't go on," she said shakily.

"Tell me why not?" He wasn't about to let her go so easily. Not after this kind of progress.

"I have things to do, Issy's coming home, my parents."

"Ah. The parents. Am I going to be introduced?" He was grinning at her. "You know, hey, Mom, Dad, here's my new boyfriend." He paused to think for a second. "No, even better, here's my new *lover*."

"You are not my lover," she cried indignantly. "And I've never had a 'lover.'"

"Then it's about time."

They could hear Melanie calling to Asia. They were coming back. "Well, maybe not now. Unless you want to come back to my place."

Caroline thought he looked so cute, so full of himself, so full of sexual attraction, of heat and affection and . . . oh, she didn't know. She only knew it was everything she wanted right now, this minute.

Melanie strode back into the kitchen. She seemed to have acquired a new confidence since arriving in a puddle at the pub. Could that really be only last night?

"Oh!" Melanie said, looking at them pretending to be embarrassed. "We can always go out again, if you'd rather . . ."

"Don't bother on my account," Caroline said. "I have things to take care of." Her parents and Issy would be arriving soon. "And since you and Asia are going to be staying at the pub, *temporarily,*" she added, "perhaps Jim will give you a lift. I know your car is still parked there, with all your stuff. I'm sure you'll be more comfortable."

"Right." Melanie picked up Asia, told her to say goodbye to the nice lady and thank you. Asia said nothing.

"I must say thank you, too," she said, looking directly at Caroline who wondered if she had been wrong. She was like the child in the nursery rhyme: *There was a little girl who had a little curl right in the middle of her forehead, when she was good she was very, very good, and when she was bad she was horrid.*

"See you later," Melanie said.

Jim said, "Am I asked to this meeting tonight?"

"If you promise to be good," Caroline told him.

"I'll try," he called over his shoulder.

Caroline watched them go, then went to call Mark, to tell him about Melanie. And about Asia.

chapter 55

Isabel sprawled on the backseat of the rental car behind Cassandra and her grandpa, who was driving. They had flown into Gatwick and it was a long slow haul up the M25 past Oxford to Upper Amberley. Conversation had long since dwindled into tiredness.

"You've still got your seat belt on I hope?" Cassandra's voice seemed to float somewhere over Issy's head. She replied automatically that of course she did, then slipped back into silence. She really did not want to go to the place her mother was now calling by the totally wrong word "home." That wreck of a chilly old barn by the sluggish cold brown river could never be her "home." That word would only ever mean the apartment in Singapore where they'd lived as a family; the place they had not even gone back to, after her father's funeral because Caroline—*everybody* said—"you can't go home again."

They'd all thought that, but no one had taken her feelings into account. That she might want to. *Need* to. Even Cassandra had agreed, the one time in Issy's view her grandmother had ever put a foot wrong.

"Closure" was a stupid word she'd heard too often on TV programs when people meant they could finish with a certain emotion. But in a way death finished *you* as well as the person who died because a little part of you died with them. Call it memories, or *nostalgie de la vie*, or maybe she was clinging on when she should let go, but that was the way she felt.

Anyhow, it was over. And so was her small escape in France. Now it was back to real life again, complete with *nostalgie de la vie,* which really meant a longing for life as it used to be.

She switched her thoughts to the Star & Plough, the place she now considered "home." And to Sam and of course Blind Brenda. Would that skinny darling little runt of a cat even have missed her? Or by now would she have switched allegiance to Sam? Would Blind Brenda even *remember* her and that it was she who had saved her life? Who knew with cats, they were so single-minded, able to cut out the unpleasant and live for the moment. If any cat had proved that it was Blind Brenda who'd overcome her physical disability, to say nothing of her appearance, though of course the cat wouldn't know that she didn't look like other cats, with her blank pale eyes and thin fur and spindly legs.

Issy wished she was a cat. How much easier life would be, not having to sort anything out, handle emotions that sometimes raged out of control; deal with the mother who drove you crazy; and now having to deal with leaving her grandmother who understood her better than anyone.

"You'll be okay, Isabel." Cassandra's voice floated to the backseat again. "We're almost there, but I should tell you we're going to the barn first. The Place in the Country your mother calls it."

Isabel sat up. "Why aren't we going to the pub? I'm not staying at that place. It's *her* home. It has nothing to do with me."

"Stop that, Isabel." Cassandra turned to look over her shoulder at her. "It does have something to do with you. For once, put your feelings aside and think of your mother."

Cassandra turned back with a weary sigh. Sometimes the young could demand too much, get on one's nerves. She contemplated with pleasure the glass of wine her daughter would certainly have waiting. Perhaps with some squares of cheese, a nice Wensleydale or a cheddar to accompany it. It was silly she knew, living in France, but she missed those good old-fashioned English cheeses. She thought of the trouble also awaiting them and sighed again.

Issy heard her. "What's up?" She sat bolt upright. Something was going on. She felt it.

Cassandra decided there was no point in hiding things, they were already making the right turn off the A40 into Burford. Ten more minutes and they would be there.

"You might as well know there's a bit of trouble. Well, not 'trouble' exactly. Let's say a 'quandary.'"

"I'll bet it's about my father again, Mom's going to tell me something bad about him. Jesus! What more can they say that they haven't already!"

"It *is* about your father. But nothing that can't be worked out, if you—*we*—all keep our heads and think it through."

"Make our own judgments," Henry said, tilting his Panama back so he could cast a quick look at Issy. "Ooops, shouldn't take my eyes off this road," he muttered, as a big white truck pulled out in front of him. Of course he did not recognize it was Jim who was driving because he had not yet met him. "Silly bugger," he said.

Cassandra, who did not like cursing unless she was doing it herself, let him get away with it this time. "Here we go," she said, as they bumped over the narrow stone bridge and continued on, passing the sign that said they were now entering Upper Amberley designated one of the prettiest villages in Oxfordshire.

Staring out the window Cassandra thought they were right; all those stone cottages, walls abloom with roses and herbaceous borders overflowing with delphinium and hollyhock and other old-fashioned flowers. White iceberg roses seemed to have taken a hold of every fence and even the Star & Plough which they were now passing had window boxes of coral geraniums with blue verbena and white phlox.

"Why don't we just stop here?" Issy asked with such longing in her voice her grandmother felt bad for her. Little did the poor girl know what was to come. Wait just a minute, she thought, spotting a tall blond walking down the street, tottering on the cobbles in her towering heels and looking very out of place for the countryside. She was holding a small girl by the hand. The child was dressed like minor royalty in a white smocked dress tied with a big bow. She had on Mary Janes and white socks. Cassandra wondered, amazed, whatever happened to shorts, a T-shirt, and sneakers?

She got the sinking feeling this was James's woman and his supposed daughter. She cast a quick glance back at Issy (Cassandra still called her Issy), who seemed not to have noticed anything. Then Henry made the turn into the lane that led to the Place in the Country. "Nice old manor house," Cassandra said approvingly as they passed the Thompsons'. "You'll have good neighbors."

"You mean my *mother* will," Issy said pointedly, slumping back in the seat as her grandpa stopped the car in a swirl of gravel. (Issy noticed the gravel was new and thought at least there was no more mud.) He gave a little honk on the horn to say they were here, and her mother appeared in the doorway, a big smile on her face, her red glasses sliding down her nose as usual so she had to peek over the top. Issy knew she couldn't see like that but anyhow she suddenly felt the need to be clasped in her arms. She was out of the car in a flash, streaking toward Caroline who held her arms open, the way she always had and said, "Hello, sweetie, glad to have you back. You must be speaking French like a native by now."

"She knows how to order a Fanta Orange and a *croque monsieur*," Cassandra said, delighted to see her own daughter looking so well. She was wearing a decent skirt for once *and* heels, and a nice white shirt with a tiny silver brooch, a bird on the wing, pinned in front. Her black hair swung in a smooth perfectly cut bob to her shoulders and she had even brushed out that wayward fringe. *And* she was wearing lipstick.

She and Henry glanced approvingly at the freshly graveled drive and at the stone building glowing in the evening sun with the river curling gently in the background. The sheep bleated as if on cue and hidden in the now dense foliage of the chestnut tree, a bird sang.

Inside, they exclaimed admiringly while Issy took a cursory glance round. It really wasn't too bad, not at all what she had expected.

"First a drink then I'll show you the rest of it," Caroline was saying. "This is where it's really at," she added, leading the way through the French doors onto the flagged terrace.

She had placed a tray with glasses, wine, and the cheeses (she knew her mother's preferences) on the low stone wall overlooking the river, and put a few striped-yellow-and-blue outdoor cushions there too so they could sit comfortably and enjoy the view.

Issy stood near the French doors, taking it in suspiciously. It was not supposed to look like this. It was supposed to be bleak, like some sort of Charles Dickens orphanage. Now even the bloody ducks were trolling by, she could see their orange feet paddling like mad as they hurried toward the prospect of a few scraps of food. Stupid ducks, she thought, allowing her misery to return. She didn't understand why she felt miserable—why she *wanted* to be miserable—she only knew she did. Things would get better when she saw Sam she told herself.

Caroline said, "We're to have dinner at the pub. Seven sharp. Sarah's doing the cooking tonight. She's my assistant," she informed her parents. "She's a single mom and her landlord's chucking her out so she'll be moving into my cottage in a couple of days. And when I open the restaurant she'll come and work for me. We'll make a good team."

"And when will that be?" Caroline's father asked, and was answered with a sigh and a shrug.

"Soon as I can get it together; furniture's ordered, suppliers are at the ready, I even have my menus partly worked out. And of course, I'll only open Friday and Saturday nights at first."

"Until you get going," he answered, lifting his glass of red wine in a toast.

Issy said, "I'll go get the bags out of the car. Not mine, of course," she added hastily.

"You're staying at the pub then?" Caroline called after her.

"Thank God, yes," Issy said over her shoulder.

Cassandra sighed. "She's determined to be a bitch. Better get what you have to say over with before we have to leave."

"And face the consequences," her husband said.

Caroline thought, it wasn't going to be easy. And somehow she knew it was all going to be her fault.

chapter 56

Henry drained his glass and went off to help Issy with the bags. Cassandra looked anxiously at Caroline. "So? What are you going to say?"

"Tell her the plain unadorned truth. I've been told that's the best thing."

"Hmm." Cassandra thought about it. "Better soften it just a little, y'know . . . *this might come as a lovely surprise* . . . that sort of thing."

"But I know Issy and I know it won't," Caroline said. "No, I'm just going to give her the facts and then . . ."

"Wait for the blow to fall. We mothers always have to take the hit. After the shock wears off she'll get around to thinking about it and understand it had nothing to do with you, it was all James."

"*Mom,*" Caroline said, wearily, "it's *always* me. That's the way it is with moms and teenagers. Don't you remember? I blamed you for everything, including my shortsightedness *and* the fact I could never wear contacts, and that you wore a bikini for chrissakes on the beach in Ibiza, causing me endless shame."

Cassandra burst out laughing. "I still wear a bikini in Ibiza," she said. "So you'd better not come with me."

Caroline laughed too. "Now I'd join you in my own middle-aged bikini."

"What are you two laughing about?" Issy was back. She stood framed in the open French doors, looking accusingly at them as if it was wrong of them to laugh when she was feeling miserable.

"Issy," Caroline said, "come and sit here, by me. I have something to tell you."

"You're not getting married again!" Issy thought with her mother anything could happen.

"*Of course not!* Nothing like that."

Issy noticed her grandmother holding her mom's hand. "What's up anyway?"

Caroline said, "I had a visitor last night. There was a big storm here, lightning, thunder, sheets of rain . . ."

"I know all about the weather in Oxfordshire," her daughter reminded her impatiently.

"Anyway, this woman came into the pub, soaked through just the way we were that first night. Remember?"

"Of course I remember. We'd found Blind Brenda only we didn't know then she was blind."

"No . . . well anyhow, this woman, nice-looking, tall, blond . . . anyway, she had a child with her, about five years old. They both looked frozen and tired, they had flown all the way from Singapore . . ."

"*Singapore?*" Issy gave Caroline a hard what-are-you-talking-about stare.

"It's like this, Issy." Caroline began again. "You know some of what happened between me and your father. Well, the truth is he fell out of love with me and he fell in love with this woman."

Issy walked away. She heard what her mother was saying but did not *want* to hear it.

Her grandmother called her back sharply. "Stay where you are," she commanded. "Listen!"

Issy stopped, but stood, half-turned away from her mother.

Caroline said, "Your father was living with this woman at the same time he was living with us."

Issy looked, despairing, at her grandmother, the rock she could always depend on to understand, she had to stop her mom from saying these things she didn't want to hear.

"Please listen to what your mother has to say," Cassandra said gently. "It's important."

"I thought Dad was with the glamorous ice-age Chinese woman," Issy said.

"Her as well," Caroline said.

Issy looked down at the flagstones. She didn't want to hear all this but knew she had to, and that it was going to be very important. She scraped her shoe along the line of greenish lichen. "She's here now?"

"She is. And there's a daughter."

The sudden clench in Issy's stomach was like an iron fist. That's all she could compare it to . . . This couldn't be true, it wasn't real. *She* was her father's daughter . . . *only her. All these years . . .*

"How old is she?" she finally managed to ask.

"She's five and her name is Asia. The woman claims your father is also her father."

Now Issy understood what devastation meant. *"It's not true,"* she yelled. *"It can't be. He wouldn't do that to me."*

Caroline remembered her saying those exact same words when she'd been told her father had killed himself. *He wouldn't do that to me.* She wondered if Melanie's story was true and James had been murdered.

She said, "We don't know for certain. That's why we're all meeting tonight. They say the truth will out."

"Who said that?" Cassandra asked.

Caroline shrugged. "Doesn't somebody always say that? I'm just hoping they're right."

Issy turned on her, filled with anger. "If you had not left my father this would not have happened."

Caroline's eyes met Cassandra's with a resigned expression. Somehow she'd known she would get the blame. She said, "Darling, this happened *before* I left your father. He was living with this other woman at the same time, they had an apartment together, right there in Singapore."

"In *Singapore*?" For the first time Issy took in what her mother was really saying, rather than what she wanted to believe. She kicked silently at the lichened flagstone.

"The little girl seemed very frightened," Caroline told her. "She's so small, she's come such a long way and here she is with strangers in a strange place."

"And no father," Issy said. "Like me."

"Yes," Caroline agreed.

"Do I have to meet her?"

"Tonight. At the pub."

"Oh. Right. Dinner."

Beaten, Issy looked at them, sitting on the river wall with the ducks still paddling hopefully behind them. "It'll be just one of those family reunions," she said coldly. "Let's hope I remember my manners the way you always taught me," she warned, flinging an icy look at Caroline.

"I certainly hope so," her grandmother said. "And since Melanie and her child are rooming at the pub I'm giving you the option of staying here at home, with your mother. Your grandfather and I can stay at the pub instead. Or you can go there and take your chance with 'the other family.'"

"I'll take my chances," Issy said, without hesitation, not looking at her mother.

chapter 57

Looking at them, Cassandra melted between being sorry for Issy and sorry for Caroline. She walked over and put an arm round Issy's shoulders.

"Do you even think of how your mother has been hurt by all this?" she asked.

"I do think about Mom, I do, *I do* . . ." Even as she said it, Issy knew it wasn't true. She had not for one instant considered her mother. Anyway, this only went to prove how much her father had loved another woman. "He's a bastard," she said turning to Caroline, verging on tears. "How could he do this to *you?*"

"It's okay," Caroline said, though inside she was shriveling with humiliation at her husband's betrayal. It was more than mere humiliation, if "humiliation" could ever be referred to as "mere" as if it were a temporary event, a moment in time when you were exposed as worthless in the eyes of everyone who ever knew you, and even those who did not. This was *betrayal* and that was far worse. *Betrayed* brought the same kind of grief as death, because the loss was horrific. The one you loved, the one you trusted, who you thought would be with you forever, was gone. By his own choice. And he'd left for someone he'd chosen over you. No woman ever got over that.

"Anyhow, I'm only behaving the way teenagers are supposed to behave," Issy appealed to her grandmother. "The way I guess my mom did with you."

"Not quite." Cassandra was not letting her off the hook.

"Well?" Henry asked finally, fed up with the delays. In his view the only thing to do was get on with it. "Let's just see which way the cards fall," he suggested, making Caroline smile, recognizing where she got her habit of misquoting.

Issy was frowning. Her jeans and the retro Johnny Hallyday T-shirt were creased from the long journey. She said, "I have to change. I'll go get my bag." She hurried to the door then turned to look at her mother. "Not that I'm staying here, I'll take my chances at the pub, thank you. At least Blind Brenda will be there."

Sighing, Caroline's eyes met her mother's.

Cassandra shrugged. "Teenagers behave like this, but then some-times they can be sweet as sugar and more loving than any faithful old Labrador. Remember, I speak from experience," she added.

"Never one like this," Caroline said, because new five-year-old sisters did not usually appear out of the blue.

While they waited Caroline showed them the rest of the house. "Showing you where your money went," she told them.

"It's your money now." Her father shrugged it off.

"It's quite beautiful," Cassandra said, taking in the charming liv-ing room, sunlight streaming over the newly polished chestnut floors. But she remembered Caroline's lavish Singapore penthouse, and her elegant lifestyle and felt sorry for her, with the junky furni-ture collected, from auctions and would-be antique shops. She prom-ised herself to speak with her husband about at least getting Caroline a decent sofa and a nice vase because an old teapot was not exactly a thing of beauty even when filled with blossoms picked from a hedgerow.

"Isn't it lovely?" Caroline asked, proudly fluffing up the flowers that had slipped down a bit in the pot. "I do love this old blue and white teapot. It's made of tin you know. It's a wonder the Victorians didn't poison themselves, pouring boiling water into it."

"The boiling water was probably what saved them," her father said. "You've done a lovely job, Caroline, and I particularly love the sail over the restaurant's ceiling."

"Jim did that," Caroline said, even more proudly. "He and Georgki. They worked on the barn with me. They're my friends," she added. Then she left them in Issy's room to freshen up and went back to the kitchen to wait.

Issy was getting changed in the downstairs guest bathroom, meant for the restaurant. She'd expected crumbling walls, a rickety toilet, and basic washing facilities, but this was lovely. Her mom had even put nice soap instead of that liquid stuff, small individual paper-wrapped slivers that smelled divine. She sluiced her face, patted it dry with one of the good paper hand towels, wished she had some moisturizer, maybe she would tell Mom about that . . . Wait a minute what was she *thinking*? Recommending things for the restaurant bathroom when she hated the very idea of it anyway.

She went through her duffel, dragged off the tee and the jeans and pulled on the red dress bought in Bordeaux, wiggling it up over her boobs so they didn't show too much, but which had the unfortunate effect of making the short skirt even shorter. She slipped on the black suede heels bought for rotten Lysander's party, decided against combing her hair because she liked the just-out-of-bed look, found the Bourjois lip gloss bought in France and gave it a swirl across her lips. She thought it was a bit purply for the red dress but now it would have to do.

She stood for a while, staring in the mirror, trying to imagine what it would feel like to have a little sister. She had always been her father's "little girl," his "baby doll." That was what he called her when he wasn't calling her his "heart's delight." "Asia Evans." Issy said the name out loud to see how it sounded. She scowled. One thing she knew for certain, her father would never have called any child of his *Asia*.

She zipped up the duffel, took one last glance in the mirror, thought she looked sufficiently grown up and woman-of-the-world to take on any woman who considered herself closer to her father than she had been, then she went to join her family who were waiting in the kitchen where everybody always waited. Nobody she knew ever sat in their sitting rooms; it was always the kitchen and she would bet it would be the same tonight.

"Okay, so I'm ready." She posed near the door, enjoying the effect her outrageous appearance was having on them. She wished she'd put on the big shoulder-skimming chandelier earrings, it would have been the last straw. The thought made her smile.

They were all looking at her, stunned until finally her grandpa said, "All set then? Well, time to go."

As they left, Caroline was wondering where she got a grown-up daughter like that when just last week she had been a mere child.

chapter 58

Jim had already driven to the pub once that day, to drop off Melanie Morton and her daughter. Now he was driving to the pub again. It was seven o'clock and he was going to the big meeting where, he guessed, all was to be revealed. He wondered if Melanie Morton had really been coming on to him when he'd dropped her off earlier that afternoon. Jim was twenty-seven years old and had been flirted with and had flirted back with plenty of girls since the ripe old age of thirteen when a friend of his sister's had pinned him down in the mud room (the small hallway where everybody dumped their wellies and wet boots before coming into the kitchen at Thompson Manor) and told him breathily he was cute and didn't he think she had nice breasts. She'd lifted her shirt obligingly so he could make a judgment and he'd looked—obligingly—at the twin spheres pointing aggressively at him and agreed that indeed she had.

The fact that she was all of seventeen and he was thirteen had only increased his liking for "older" women, since they knew a lot more about things than he did. That was then.

He had learned more in the intervening years and whenever they met could even smile unembarrassed and say "how are you" to the girl who'd attempted to seduce him as a boy, and who was now married with twin sons the same age Jim had been then. Unblushing, she would smile and always say, "Better for seeing you, Jim, and I'll bet you say the same about me."

Cheeky, but she was fun.

Melanie was another matter. When he'd driven her to the pub earlier, she had strapped her child into the backseat and then come and sat next to him, and lit a cigarette. She didn't ask him about the cigarette though Jim did not smoke and disliked the smell of it in his car. Anyhow he thought she shouldn't smoke around children. He opened his window and let the air blow in instead.

"Sorry," she'd said, glancing sideways at him under her lashes. She'd cracked open her window and blown out the smoke and thrown out the cigarette. "I just can't break the habit. A lifetime of smoking, you know."

Jim had told her she was crazy to throw a lit cigarette out. Didn't she know she could start a fire? He opened the ashtray and said would she use that in future.

"You mean you and I have a future, Jim?" She'd turned to look at him. "I know we've only just met and I shouldn't be saying this because of Caroline, but I find you so sexy. Most men adore me," she murmured in his ear. "They always like naughty girls."

Jim thought stunned, either she was insane or he was. He was driving her to the pub, and later that night they were going to a meeting to settle the parentage and future of her child. And discuss James's supposed murder! And now she was sex-talking him?

He'd removed her hand from his arm as he made the turn into the village, and said coldly, "You've got the wrong man, I'm afraid."

She laughed and said, "Oh, please, Jim, don't be afraid. I won't hurt you."

He brought the car to a stop, tires squealing, then turned to look at her. He said, "Did you kill James Evans?"

She looked into his eyes for a long moment then she'd flung herself back against her seat. "You're mad after all, just like all the others," she'd said. Then she'd slammed out of the car, unhitched her child from the back and marched off into the pub.

Jim had not told Caroline about this. If he had to, though, he would.

Now, he parked in front of the pub again. It was exactly seven P.M. Showtime.

chapter 59

While her parents waited in the Land Rover Caroline called Georgki. She filled him in quickly on what was happening and he told her Jim had been in touch and he knew all about it. "Except not the truth," he added.

"Me either," Caroline said. "We're kind of hoping to find that out, or at least some of it, tonight. Can you come, Georgki? I really want you there."

"I will come. I always there for you, you remember this."

"I do," Caroline said. "And remember I thank you for it. Seven, then? At the pub?"

"You will see me."

Caroline got behind the wheel, they were in her Land Rover. Her father flung Isabel's duffel in the back then climbed in beside her. Cassandra sat next to her granddaughter.

"Well," Cassandra said pleasantly, "isn't it a lovely evening. One of those grand English nights when you wonder why you ever left the place anyway."

"The midges," her husband remembered. "The midges always get you on nights like this."

Issy said nothing. She crouched in her seat, hauling on her skirt to make it longer.

"It won't," her grandmother told her. "It's short-short and you bought it that way and you have to live with it and be proud of it."

Issy met her grandmother's eye and they both laughed.

Caroline spotted Jim's white truck already parked in his favorite spot, round the corner under the trees near the church even though he got irritated by all the bird droppings on his roof. She also saw Georgki's Hummer cresting the hill at the top of the village street, and Melanie's black rental car parked dead-in-front of the pub where nobody ever parked because it blocked the entrance.

"Looks like we're all here," she said, climbing out from behind the steering wheel managing to smack her shoulder as she turned. *Bad omen,* she thought opening the door for Cassandra. *Clumsy is never good. I must remember to be cool, careful, watch what I say and always ask the right questions.* She only wished she knew what they were.

She had parked behind Jim and now Georgki trundled round the corner seeking a spot. "Over there, after the church gate." Caroline waved him on. She waited while he'd parked and came walking past the church toward them.

"My goodness," Cassandra said mildly. "What a big man."

"You should see him in his canvas overalls with a plastic visor and an electric drill in his hands," Caroline told her.

"Is pleasure," Georgki said, bowing formally over Cassandra's hand, which she thought charming. Then Caroline introduced her father and her daughter.

"This is Issy," she said, putting an arm round the girl's shoulder.

"I have heard," Georgki said, giving her a smoldering Russian look that made Issy wonder uneasily what *exactly* he had heard.

She threw her mother a suspicious glance but they were already walking up the street to the pub, where Sammy was waiting, blond and plump in denim cutoffs and a Duran Duran tee.

"Ohh, Sammy, Sam." Issy ran to her and Sam ran to her. They met in the middle, hugging frantically, jumping up and down, saying how they'd missed each other. Then Issy pulled back. "Have you seen *her* yet?" she asked.

"No. I get the feeling she's being kept as a sort of surprise."

They didn't have time to say more because by then the grandparents were there. Cassandra hugged Sam and told her she knew all about her, there were absolutely no secrets, which made Sam blush, wondering what she meant.

They pushed through the pub doors and were instantly engulfed in the familiar smell of old log fires and chicken pot pies, beer and wine and food.

"I'll bet Sarah's already cooking," Issy said, and Sam told her she was right and that Clumsy Lily was skipping homework tonight to help, which Maggie did not approve of but had no say in the matter; it was up to Lily's mom. Besides she knew Sarah and Lily were dying of curiosity and couldn't wait to see what happened.

Jesus was standing by the door leading into the kitchen. "We're in here tonight," he said, when the introductions were over. He smiled admiringly when he met Cassandra, shook her hand and told her he hadn't known Caroline had such a "cute" mom. Cassandra held her breath and counted to ten then smiled and said people always said that about her.

They followed Jesus into the kitchen where Maggie was waiting. Sarah was already hovering over the stove with Little Billy right there in his swing chair, busily booting himself back and forth with his little socked feet. Lily was washing up and seemed suddenly overcome with shyness and true to form dropped a plate, said oh shit then sorry and hastily swept it up. Maggie welcomed everybody, full of smiles, while Jim waited in the background not quite part of the family.

Caroline spotted him though. "Mom, I'd like you to meet Jim," she said, taking his hand and hauling him forward. "I warned him I was going to introduce him as my lover, except that wouldn't be true."

Jim threw her an exasperated look; it was not the way one wanted to be introduced to one's girlfriend's mother. And Caroline was now his girlfriend, or would be by tomorrow anyway, if he could ever get her alone again.

Issy looked round for the cat. Of course it was sprawled in the middle of the kitchen table but sat up when Issy said, "Oh, look, there's Blind Brenda." The cat managed its weird little buzz that was meant to be a purr when she picked her up and hugged her.

"She remembered me," Issy said thankfully.

But Caroline was looking around. There was no sign of Melanie.

chapter 60

Jim was looking round too. He made a quick mental inventory of those present: Jesus and Maggie; Sam and Issy. Caroline with Cassandra and Henry; then there was Georgki and himself; plus in the background Sarah and Lily. Maybe he should count Little Billy in on the proceedings too; he might be able to be used as a witness in later years. That made eleven of them, well eleven and a bit (Billy), and the "stars" of the "show" had yet to make an appearance.

"There's only one person missing," Caroline said, thinking of Mark.

"Two," Issy said, thinking of James.

"If we were in an Agatha Christie novel this would be taking place in the library," Jim said, accepting half a bitter from Jesus. He took a grateful swig wiping the foam from his upper lip. "All the suspects and participants assembled so Poirot can tell them who did it."

"Isn't it always the butler?" Cassandra asked, thanking Maggie for the martini, with two olives, a rare find in an English pub.

Caroline said, "I wish Poirot were here now, he always knew what to do." She had refused a drink; she wanted to keep a clear head. A great deal was at stake both from her and Issy's points of view, to say nothing of the other child involved. Poor little thing, being hauled fatherless halfway round the world to be presented by her mother like a . . . like a what? A human fait accompli? She looked at her own daughter, clutching the cat to her chest, looking tired and quite ridiculous in that awful red dress (*What had Cassandra been thinking?*) with her boobs hanging out. Caroline caught her eye and frowning, motioned Issy to hitch it up. Scowling back, Issy did so.

Issy said to Sam, "I almost forgot, I have a present for you. I'll give it to you now, before they come in." She meant before *they* came and *ruined* everything.

"How lovely," Sam said, admiring the tiny dark blue bottle of perfume called Evening in Paris. "Thank you for thinking of me, especially."

Issy shrugged it was okay. "It's kind of antique, that perfume. Like from the forties or fifties, or something. It was quite glamorous then."

"Smells wonderful," Cassandra said nostalgically. "And I'm old enough to remember it."

"No!" both girls said, disbelieving, just as the door opened and shrinking little Asia Evans walked in. Was *pushed* in, more like it.

For a second Caroline was frozen. Then she was on her feet and so were Cassandra and Maggie. They were all hurrying toward the child who simply stood there, looking at them, fist in her mouth, eyes bigger and darker than blackberries.

"Come with me, darling," Maggie said, picking her up. "Come, sit at the table with all of us, we'll have some supper together. I'll bet you'll like an Orangina, then you can tell me where your mommy is."

Asia's body went rigid. She refused so much as to bend her knees to sit.

"Very well then," Maggie said. "You may stand right here, between Caroline and me."

Asia stood, eyes now cast down, fist back in her mouth.

Caroline could see tension gripping her small body. Again, pity overwhelmed her. She looked across the table at her own daughter, who looked back at her over the top of Blind Brenda's head. She clutched the cat close to her face as though, Caroline thought, she didn't want Asia to even see her.

"Sweetie, where is your mommy?" Caroline asked Asia, but Asia only hung her head further.

"That bitch shoved her in here to face the music alone," Cassandra said.

"And she knew perfectly well what she was doing," Jim agreed, getting up and walking to the door. As he had expected Melanie was standing outside listening.

"Might as well come in now you've got an audience," Jim said, holding it open and giving a theatrical wave of his arm. "The stage is all yours," he added as she stalked past him in a waft of Versace.

Then all of a sudden Melanie seemed to lose her nerve, or her head, or maybe it was her heart, because she just crumpled to her knees and began to weep.

"You don't know how hard this is," she murmured, hands covering her face. "You can't possibly understand what it means to be so completely alone, just me and Asia. James should not have left us like that, he shouldn't . . ."

"He didn't leave you," Caroline said coldly. "You told me yourself he had been murdered."

"I don't know that for sure," Melanie said indignantly, raising her face to them for a moment.

Was she going back on what she'd already told her? Caroline wondered.

"I think he was murdered," Issy said, eying Melanie, who was scrambling ungracefully to her feet, hampered by her tight black skirt. With it she wore a black chiffon blouse with a big pussycat bow. With pale makeup and no lipstick, she was all innocent blue eyes and long blond hair.

Caroline thought it odd though, her child bore absolutely no resemblance to her; no blue eyes and pale skin. "Mark also believes James was killed," she said. "And the matter is now being investigated by the police."

Melanie smoothed her skirt over her curvy hips. She looked suddenly nervous. "Yes, well they can't call me as a witness at the trial," she said defensively, "I wasn't even in Hong Kong when . . ."

"When it happened," Issy finished for her. The two eyed each other across the table. Then Issy turned to look at her "supposed" sister.

"Who is your *real* mother anyway?" she said.

Everyone turned to look at Asia, who hung her head and said nothing.

"You'd better have some proof of all this," Henry said, and this time to Melanie, but Melanie just cried some more. Jesus got up and handed her a box of tissues. She took one and dabbed her eyes. There was the sound of a dropped plate in the background and then Sarah swearing at Lily who apologized loudly to anyone who was listening.

"You can't be Asia's mother." Issy turned to look at Melanie. "Dad would never have had anything to do with a woman like you. He knew about classy women, just look at my mother. I know he *knew* how to love, what he wanted from that love and that he loved me."

There was a sudden hiccupping sob from Asia who Melanie seemed to have forgotten. Issy went over and put her arm protectively round Asia's shoulder. She just couldn't bear to hear her cry.

chapter 61

Melanie turned and went into the bar. A minute later she came back holding what looked like a double vodka. It certainly wasn't water.

Henry walked round the table and pulled out a chair for her. "Sit here, Melanie, why don't you," he said. "Opposite me."

She threw him a wary glance. "Thank you," she said, obviously wondering why he was suddenly being nice to her. She took a gulp of the vodka and put the glass on the table.

Then Jesus went to the bar and came back with another round of bitters for James and himself, and a second martini for Cassandra. He sat down again and they all looked silently at Melanie.

"First thing Melanie," Henry said. "Since you came here to prove that James is Asia's father and that you are her mother, you will have brought Asia's birth certificate. We would like to see that."

Melanie said triumphantly, "Hah! I knew you would ask that. Just you wait!" She took another gulp of vodka, pushed back her chair, got up and walked out.

They heard her heels clacking up the stairs, then clacking back down again. She was holding a piece of paper. She took another sip of the vodka.

"Well, here you are then. *The evidence.*" She slid the paper across the table.

Henry read it, then passed it to Cassandra, who also read it then passed it on to Caroline.

Henry said, "Everyone, this is Asia's valid birth certificate. It says James Evans is the father and Melanie Morton the mother. It's signed by both parents and properly notarized."

Caroline read it again, still not quite believing. *How could James have had a child with this crude vulgar woman with her snaggly overshot teeth and predatory blue eyes? How could he possibly have loved her?* Memories of how she and James had loved each other, him so beautiful (if you could ever call a man beautiful, James was) and she so young and passionately in love. Theirs had been a wondrous relationship. It had not lasted but now she felt lucky to have had it, and to remember James as he used to be and not the man he'd become.

Melanie leaned back in her chair and lit a cigarette. "Now what?"

Jim got up and removed the cigarette from between her fingers. "This is a no-smoking zone." He doused it in the sink.

"Good for you," Clumsy Lily whispered to him. "She's a right bitch, ain't she?"

Sarah shook her head at Lily, she should not interfere. "Sorry," Lily muttered. "Got a bit caught up." Then both girls leaned back against the sink, arms folded, dying to see what would happen.

Relaxed, Melanie sat back. "So, now you'll want to know why I am here? With James's daughter!" There was a fresh note of triumph in her voice which had risen a couple of notches with the vodka. Jesus motioned Maggie to get her another double. Booze unlocked many a tongue and drunks talked truth.

"My daughter . . . *me and* my daughter need help. Financial. James gave me nothing. I am broke. Of course I can't work with a little kid like that to look after, I mean it's all too much, the least the man could have done was take care of his child. And me, of course. *Asia's mother,*" she added with a smile at Caroline. "*You* know how it is, don't you? Except I'll bet James made sure to take good care of Issy. He told me there was plenty of money."

Caroline thought of her meager divorce settlement. Now of course she knew James had been in severe financial trouble, otherwise he would have been sure to take care of Issy. "He didn't have it to leave to anyone," she said. "That's the truth of the matter, Melanie. There is no money."

"Oh yes there is." Melanie was on the second double. Her eyes narrowed. "It's in a Hong Kong bank account. A big trust fund for Isabel Evans, to be accessed when she is sixteen years old."

"*Sixteen!*" Cassandra exclaimed. "But that's next week."

"What *trust fund*?" Caroline demanded. "I know nothing about any big trust fund, there's only the one meant to pay her school fees."

Melanie shrugged. "James told me so himself. He said there was lots of money and it was for Asia. And I'm her mom so that means it goes to me."

"*You are not my mommy,*" Asia said.

Stunned, everyone looked at her and she began to cry again, howling, head thrown back, tears gushing.

Issy grabbed her and Sam hurried her out of there. They put her on the bed in Sam's room. Asia howled some more.

"Oh my God, she wants Melanie," Issy said. "I think she really must be my sister."

In the kitchen, still sitting round the table, Henry knew Melanie was lying. He said, "I'd like to see your passport Melanie please."

She jerked suddenly upright, obviously frightened. "I only show my passport to immigration. You've no right to ask . . ."

"I think I do."

"Well you can't and that's that." She downed the rest of the vodka and sat there, glaring at him.

Maggie got up and left the room.

"It would be better if you just showed it to us," Henry told Melanie. "Then I won't have to call the police."

"What're you *talking* about, *cops . . .*"

Maggie came back with the passport. "People always hide things in their underwear drawer," she said, handing it to Henry.

He flipped it open, looked at the picture, then checked the name.

"This is interesting," he said. His glance took in the people sitting round the table. "May I introduce you to Jacqueline Ferris. Single woman. Age thirty-eight. Resident of *Singapore*. No children."

Caroline sagged with relief. Melanie was not Asia's mother after all. Maybe her whole story was an invention, a ploy to get money. Her eyes met Cassandra's. *"Thank God,"* her mother mouthed silently.

Melanie was staring down at the table, twiddling the vodka glass with its melting ice.

Henry took out the piece of paper folded into the passport. He read it and said, "This is a note from the real Melanie Morton, giving this woman, whose name is Jacqueline Ferris, permission to take her daughter, Asia Morton Evans, out of the country for the period of one month. It seems Asia's real mother was in cahoots to try to extort money."

"Bravo, *Hercule*," Jim said, seeing the game was up.

Jesus opened some wine. Maggie got glasses from the shelf. Sarah sprang to life and brought over a platter of fried chicken nuggets, overdone to a crisp and not anything Maggie or Caroline would ever serve, but needs must and it was all she had time for, what with all that was going on.

Henry looked at his daughter. He thought about his granddaughter upstairs with that little girl, James's other daughter. "Well, Caroline," he said, "now I think we have the truth."

Caroline wasn't so sure. Was Asia James's daughter, or wasn't she?

chapter 62

In Hong Kong, Gayle Lee Chen knew something was wrong the moment the elevator doors slid open and she stepped into her elegant apartment. No white-jacketed white-gloved houseboy was there to greet her. No maid in a black dress and ruffled apron came to attend to her. She stood for a moment listening to the silence, then she walked over to the bank of floor-to-ceiling windows with their faint golden tint that kept out the glare. The view of Repulse Bay was what had drawn her in the first place. By day it showed a jumbled over-crowded city with the gunmetal sea beyond, so often in monsoon season capped with white-frothed waves that sent boats spinning and capsizing. Nighttime was her favorite though. Then it turned into a neon bejeweled city, rubies and sapphires, emeralds, and a million diamonds, reminding her of the ones she had collected and had often worn around her neck, on her wrists and fingers.

She stood for a long time looking at her jewel box, as she called the city, before turning back to the table in the entrance. She had noticed the casket placed there as soon as she walked in but had chosen to ignore it. Now, she no longer could. That gilded casket contained her future.

Opening it, she looked at the gun that had killed James.

The night it happened she had followed James to the boat, then to the bars, she'd waited in her car, until James returned alone to the boat again. He was drunk; passed out on the banquette. She had hoped to blame him for the missing millions, get off the hook from her mobster investors.

She saw the Hermès bag with the scarf, knew somehow this was meant to be her own farewell gift, as though all those years together had meant nothing. Still, she could not bear to see James's blood spilled, and she'd wrapped the scarf carefully round his head. He'd opened his eyes, looked at her, surprised.

Had he recognized her? She hoped not. She would not have liked his final memory of her to be the moment she pulled the trigger.

No one heard. No one saw. Or if they did, they took no notice. And James, *her beloved James,* was gone. No one else would ever have him. Only she knew his last moments. It was her final secret.

Now, the apartment was deserted. She kicked off her shoes and padded barefoot into her bedroom. The missing servants had always hated her anyway, hated her arrogance, her demands for perfection, her lack of interest in who they were, only in what they could do for her. Humanity was not part of Gayle Lee Chen's allure, yet it was that very coldness that had drawn James to her. She knew he'd wanted to conquer her, make her his own; for years he had fought her, challenged her, left Caroline for her, but he'd always come back. She had enthralled him, with his lust for her and the money. Until he had finally fallen in love with someone else and she had proven powerless against that emotion. She'd found she was an ordinary mortal, after all.

A quick glance at the small gold Cartier clock on her bedside table told her time was passing. She must hurry.

The casket with the gun had been placed on the table in her home by the man she worked for; the man whose money she had taken to invest, whose money she had stolen. She'd gotten away with it all these years, sometimes she'd invested, giving him grand financial returns. And sometimes not. Somehow it had always worked out, walking that tightrope. Now, like all classic Ponzi scams, it was over. And his answer faced her in that casket. He knew about James. He knew everything, and he knew how to exact his revenge. He'd given her a choice. The gun? Or the police?

Gayle took a quick shower then went and sat at her vanity table, properly named she thought because she was the most vain of women. She looked at herself in the Venetian mirror that dated from the seventeenth century and was framed in golden twirls and leaves. The short platinum bob was her trademark. Walk into any room, everyone knew her. Now, she put up her hands and lifted off the wig. No one knew about that, well, only the man who made it for her in India of the finest European hair. "A virgin's hair," he used to say, cackling with laughter.

Gayle looked at the different woman she saw in that beautiful mirror. It was the same Chinese woman who played the gambling tables in her old-style dark blue jacket and wide-legged pants. In one moment she had turned herself from urban sophisticate to traditional peasant.

She wiped off her makeup and went and put on the dark blue jacket and pants. She put on the cotton slippers and buttoned the strap over her instep.

She wasted no time now. One quick glance around the splendor of her master suite where only she had ever been the true "master." Then she walked back into the hall, took the gun from the casket, checked that it was loaded, put it in her pocket next to the small packet of dollar bills held together by an elastic band.

One last glance in the mirror. It showed a small, aging Chinese woman who might be anybody from anywhere in that vast country. In just twenty minutes she had turned back the calendar a hundred years. She looked exactly the way her mother and her mother's mother had, when they rolled up their pants legs and worked, backs bent, up to their knees in water in the rice fields. She had achieved nothing, after all.

She took the service elevator down because she no longer merited the luxurious private wood-paneled one she usually entered her apartment by. No one noticed her go. No one even looked. No one cared.

Less than half an hour later, Lieutenant Huang rode that smart elevator up to Ms. Chen's apartment. He had a warrant to arrest her for the murder of James Evans. She was not there. No one was. He was too late. Hong Kong was a big city. China a very big country. It was possible to remain anonymous there. Forever.

chapter 63

Henry said to Melanie at the pub, "Better tell us the whole story. It's us or the cops."

"Jesus! No need to go *that* far." Melanie sniffed into her tissue.

"Yes there is," Cassandra said. "There's a child involved."

Melanie glanced up through the soggy tissue. Realizing she was outplayed she sat up straight, knees together for once. She adjusted her chiffon pussycat bow and said, "Well, okay then, so Asia is not my daughter. I was only doing this to help someone out. She wouldn't do it herself and she needed help. I mean this *is James's daughter.*"

Caroline felt the sigh that escaped her had been held in from the moment she had first seen Asia, with her blackberry eyes and olive skin, and her "lostness." "Poor baby," she murmured.

Cassandra said, "Well, at least now we know that truth."

"If Melanie ever speaks the truth," Jim reminded them.

She gave him an indignant glare. "I am not a liar. I only did this to help."

"You mean you only *lied* to help." Cassandra never let anybody off the hook.

Caroline was thinking oh my God this means Issy really has a little sister—well a half sister. What will she think? What will she do? Things are tough enough as it is, between us . . . now what? And what, she also wondered suddenly, *would* she *do about Asia anyway?*

"Get on with it, Melanie," Henry said. "Or I suppose we should call you Jacqueline, now."

"Jackie. Like Kennedy, y'know."

"Only without the pearls," Cassandra said; thinking, *and also without the class.*

"So. Okay. It's like this. I live in Singapore, been there a long time now. I work in a cocktail bar, hostess I suppose you'd call me, a nice place though, no hanky panky, no showing your female assets for the customers."

She glanced round the table. She had their attention.

"Yes, well, then," she went on hastily. "There was this young woman. She worked at the boutique opposite, selling clothes, nice stuff, not upmarket but not down either. Actually, that's where I got this blouse." She fingered the bow again and there was a collective impatient sigh.

"Right, well, we used to pass each other on the street, she'd be opening up the shop and we'd say hello, stop to chat a while . . . After a bit we met up for lunch, told each other our stories. She said she was madly in love, his name was James and he loved her so much it made her feel she was walking on air, or in a dream."

Caroline felt a shaft of pain right in the place where she could swear she once had a heart. James, oh James. How? Why? Where did it go, our love, our walking-on-air dream?

"Asia's mother's name really is Melanie Morton. She's a nice girl." Jackie threw Caroline a long shafting look, checking her reaction but Caroline's eyes were closed, her face blank.

"Anyway, then Melanie got pregnant. James said he couldn't marry her. 'Yet' he said." Jackie laughed. "Haven't you noticed there's always a 'yet' in cases like this?

"Anyhow, Melanie had the baby. James wasn't around when it was born, he was off on his travels so she named her Asia—for the place she was conceived. By the way, Melanie is half-Thai, half-Vietnamese.

"Anyhow," Jackie said again. "Like so many other people I've met in my travels, Melanie had no family. She was okay though, earned her living at the shop until the baby came and James kept her in a nice apartment nearby. Then he started not showing up, money got tight, he'd send some, then not . . ."

A familiar story, thought Caroline, the same thing had happened to her, probably at the same time.

"When James did come to see Melanie though, he really showed how much he loved that little girl. He spoiled both of them rotten, buying them clothes, presents, taking them places. Melanie told me he wouldn't so much as go out to dinner without Asia so that kid got to go to some pretty fancy restaurants. When James was in funds that is, because after a couple of years it was clear, even to Melanie, blinded to reality about him, though she was—I mean him not marrying her and all that; it became clear James was in financial difficulties. Working in a bar I heard rumors, asked a few questions. Nobody really knew anything except James seemed to have a couple of different lives going, and of course they all knew about you, Caroline, and your daughter and the divorce. They also knew about Gayle Lee Ching . . ."

"Chen," Caroline corrected her automatically.

"Yeah, Chen. Well, then James got murdered . . ."

"How do you know he was murdered?" Henry asked.

"I didn't, but the real Melanie did. She said James loved his child too much to kill himself, he would never leave her, and never leave them un-provided for. But that's exactly what he did. And that's why I am here, with Asia, to try and get money for the real Melanie out of you cheap bastards because the real Melanie sure as hell wouldn't do it. She's in that boutique, seven days a week, putting the kid in preschool, working her butt off . . . so I suggested I come here with Asia. I suggested I'd be the 'mother,' I'd get the money that's due her from James."

"And exactly how much were *you* planning on making from the deal?" Henry asked.

"What d'you mean? I was doing Melanie a favor, a good turn. Doing what she should have done herself."

"But Melanie had too much pride," Caroline said, because she understood completely. She had been there herself.

"I'll bet you wanted fifty percent of whatever settlement you made," Henry said to Jackie.

She stared defiantly back into his eyes. "So what?" she said with a shrug. "Without me, they would have had nothing."

Caroline said to her father, "Whatever the story is, obviously we now have to take care of the real mother and Asia."

They agreed and Cassandra nodded. "Of course. And 'Jackie' has to leave right away."

"What!" Jackie was indignant. "But I have to look after that child."

"No you don't," Caroline said. "I'll do that. Meanwhile, I'm calling Mark, in Singapore. I'm telling him the whole situation and that I'm keeping James's child here with me until we can decide what to do."

"If we find the real mother is 'unsuitable,' we might even have to go to the authorities," Henry warned.

Caroline understood he meant then she would be left in complete charge of James's daughter. She sighed, thinking of Issy and their already tense relationship, wondering where all of this would lead.

"First, I'll call the airlines," Henry said. "We'll get Jackie out of here."

"*Asap*," Maggie agreed. "And then we'll deal with the real mother."

Behind her Sarah put the kettle on the hob and Lily put the Darjeeling in the pot and organized mugs without breaking anything, silenced for once.

chapter 64

Mark was not in Singapore when Caroline called. He was in a teahouse in Hong Kong, in an area where tourists never ventured. Old men with dusty feet came in for their dim sum breakfast, some carrying little wicker cages containing pet birds. These were placed carefully on the seat beside them and allowed to watch the proceedings. Occasionally, they were fed a live cricket. Mark wondered if when the birds were at home they were freed from their tiny wicker prisons and sang for joy. He certainly hoped so.

A hawk-eyed waiter trundled past with the dim sum cart and Mark chose a steamed shrimp wonton and a sweet-bean bun. More tea was poured into his small cup, a fresh pot placed by his hand, another chit flung onto the table.

"Glad to see you're enjoying Hong Kong's best breakfast." Lieutenant Huang settled himself in the chair opposite.

The waiter knew him and backpedaled to their table. Huang made his choice, far more exotic than Mark's: steamed buns containing gelatinous fishy substances and eel and egg and rice. Another teapot appeared, a fresh cup.

"I thought it best to meet here, anonymously," Huang said, after he had demolished the eel dim sum and two gulps of boiling-hot green tea. "There are bad characters around who you might not want to know. And also because I have news for you."

"I hope that means good news? If any news could be good in this situation."

"*Good.* And *bad.* I'm not sure which way you'll take it. First, we know she killed James."

Mark did not have to ask *who,* but he did ask *how* they knew.

"Somebody turned her in, a witness. Says he saw her go on the boat, heard the shot, saw her run off again, says she almost tripped on your little gangway she was hurrying so fast. 'In those heels,' was what he said. That was kinda one of the things that made us believe he was speaking the truth. Besides, he corroborated the time, and described her perfectly."

"How did he know her?"

Huang shrugged. "Everybody knows her, or more like knows of her."

"And exactly *who* is your witness?"

Huang laughed. "Nobody you would trust with your life. Ms. Chen was set up. One of her own kind turned her in; works for an undesirable who makes too much illegal money and has kept Ms. Chen in splendor for years. More splendor than he knew about until recently, when he found out about her Ponzi scam. He had two choices. Kill her or get her another way. This way was tidier, and besides Chen had done the job for him. He didn't even have to get his hands dirty."

"So? What next?" Mark didn't trust Ms. Chen not to have already hired the best lawyers or to have come up with the perfect alibi, or to be able to prove she was somewhere else at the time of the murder. A woman like that could do anything.

"She killed him," Lieutenant Huang said. "Make no mistake about it. Her prints were not on the gun but we were given evidence that she bought that gun the week before the murder. She was seen at the boat when the shot was fired, seen running away after . . ."

"And that's enough?"

"Don't you want it to be?

Mark remembered James, good-natured, weak, emotional, torn between two lives, between women, between trust and wrongdoing. "It's enough," he agreed.

"When are you going to arrest her?" he asked Huang who was already on his feet, about to leave.

"We're doing the paperwork, getting the evidence together, then we'll get the warrant. We'll go there tonight." He was smiling as he patted Mark's shoulder and said goodbye. "Then watch what happens," he said, heading past the birdcages for the door.

Mark's global mobile rang. It was Caroline. "Caroline," he said. "Good news."

"Shall I tell you mine first? Or do you want to tell me."

"Okay, you first," he said.

He did not interrupt while she told her story. "I'll be back in Singapore tomorrow, first thing," he said. "I'll find the woman. Of course I will Caroline. It's a sad tale though."

"And a sad little girl," Caroline said.

It was only after Mark had rung off he remembered he had not told her Ms. Chen was to be arrested for James's murder. He sat for a while, sipping his tea. Where, he wondered, did this leave Caroline? He knew the answer, of course. Where James had always left her. Responsible.

chapter 65

Back in Singapore, he went immediately to the boutique where Asia's mother, the real Melanie Morton, worked in the busy Orchard Road mall. It was evening and crowded.

Orchard Road was definitely not a place Mark usually found himself and he had to ask the way. The boutique seemed quite well known and when he got there it was larger than he'd expected, and busy.

From Caroline's description of the child, he knew her mother immediately; small, dark-haired, with delicate bones and blackberry eyes that tilted slightly upwards.

He went up to her.

"Melanie Morton?" he asked.

"Yes," she said, glancing up at him.

"It's about your daughter," Mark said.

She clutched a hand to her heart, looking terrified and he told her Asia was safe. "She's with James's ex-wife," he said. "They found Jackie Ferris was pretending to be you."

The real Melanie Morton's face folded into tears and she said, "I knew I should never have agreed to it but Jackie said it was the right thing to do. I couldn't bring myself to go to James's family and ask for charity. I'll always work for my child . . . but Jackie said Asia was *entitled*. It was her *right*. I mean I can put food on our table but that's about all. I can't guarantee Asia a good education and a better life and I wanted her to have a better chance than me. Her father loved her, you know, he really did."

Mark said, "We need to talk. Tell the store you'll take a break." He was finally going to hear the truth.

Much later, he called Caroline back and told her he'd met Asia's mother, that she'd believed Jackie only wanted to help her. Now she was ashamed and knew it was wrong. She did not want Jackie to have anything more to do with Asia, and he was faxing a certified document handing custody of the girl to Caroline.

"Temporarily, of course," Mark said. "Until we get this finally sorted."

"How, *sorted*?" Caroline asked, knowing she was stuck with a despairing child who only wanted her real mother. "Of course I know we'll have to take care of her, but James didn't leave her any money."

"Melanie's a nice woman," Mark said. "James did not do the right thing by her," he added, knowing that James never did; he simply played the game by ear, or by the moment, shrugging at whatever happened until finally the game had caught up with him. But this wasn't only about Asia.

"There's something else," Mark remembered. "I almost forgot about James."

Caroline said, "I don't see how any of us can forget him, especially now."

"You'll be seeing this in the media. Go online now, Caroline, it's all there. The Hong Kong police have a warrant for the arrest of Gayle Lee Chen for James's murder."

"*Oh my God.* Then they believe she really did it . . . ?"

"Lieutenant Huang told me they have evidence. There's a witness who saw her go on the boat, heard the shot, saw her running down the gangplank again."

"Out of the blue, just like that, there's a *witness?*"

"Caroline, *she did it.* That's all the cops are worried about now. Anyhow, Ms. Chen has disappeared. China's a big country. I doubt we'll hear from her again."

Caroline remembered the elegant ice-woman at the Peninsula Hotel, platinum-haired and ruby-ringed . . . James's fantasy woman.

Overwhelmed, she handed the phone to her mother, asked her please to talk to Mark, he would explain everything. Then she went and sat on one of the cushions on the river wall because her knees had suddenly buckled.

"How ever am I going to tell Issy?" she asked out loud.

Henry heard her. He did not know exactly what had happened though he was getting the gist of it from the one-sided conversation his wife was having with Mark.

"You'll find a way," he said. "You always will, you and Issy."

chapter 66

Asia woke with the first light. She turned her head to look at the girls lying one on either side of her. Both were sleeping, mouths slightly open, eyes tightly shut. They were still holding her hands and she lifted her head to look at this miracle, then lay back again, careful not to wake them. She wanted this moment to go on forever.

When Issy finally opened her eyes she found herself looking directly into Asia's unflinching stare.

"*Jesus!*" she said, startled. "What are you doing?"

"Waiting for you to wake up," Asia said truthfully. "I'm hungry."

Issy remembered they'd had no dinner the previous night. She leaned over and gave Sam a nudge. "Get up," she said. "Asia and I are starving."

Sam tried to lift the fog of fatigue from her brain. "Who's Asia anyway?"

"It's me," Asia had found her voice. "Issy's sister."

"Oh my God," Issy said. "How do you *know* that?"

"My daddy told me."

"*James?* Your daddy?"

Asia nodded. "And yours."

Issy didn't want to question Asia *directly* about her mother but anyway asked her in a roundabout way, saying, "My mother is Caroline."

"And mine is Melanie Morton," Asia said proudly.

Sam caught Issy's eye and they both groaned.

"My mommy is waiting at home for me, in Singapore," Asia said. "She told me it would be all right to come here with Jackie. She said Jackie would look after me like a mommy, and I should behave myself and say nothing. So I did, except when I got scared and I didn't like it."

"It's okay now, though," Issy reassured her. "Come on, I'll bet you need to go to the bathroom, then we'll all wash our hands and comb our hair and go down and see what's happening."

Asia perched on the loo, hands politely folded in her lap, looking up at Issy who stood by the door waiting. "Is your mommy here?" she asked.

"No she's not." Issy remembered Caroline would be at the barn.

"My mom's here though," Sammy called from the bedroom where she was brushing her hair. "She'll fix you some cereal. I'll bet we've even got Froot Loops."

"Don't like those," Asia said. She went and washed her hands and Issy helped her dry them, thinking this was what it was like having a little sister.

They found Maggie alone in the kitchen. She had just gotten off the phone with Caroline and knew everything about Asia's real mother, and also that Gayle Lee Chen had shot James.

She gave Asia a kiss, told her that her real mother Melanie sent love and that she and Caroline would be looking after her until she went back to Singapore.

"I want Issy to look after me," Asia said, asserting herself and making Maggie smile.

The child even *looked* different this morning, swollen-eyed of course from all that crying, in fact Maggie had never heard a kid bawl like that before, but now her face was tinged with pink and her dark eyes glittered with pleasure instead of tears.

Maggie shook her head though at the drooping ankle socks and the very slept-in smocked dress, with its dangling sash. "Asia," she said, "don't you have a pair of shorts, or jeans, or something? You know, a little T-shirt?"

"At home I do. Jackie got me these." Asia smoothed down the frock. "Don't you like it?"

"It's a party dress." Issy sat her at the kitchen table while Sam made toast and Maggie brought glasses of juice. "She doesn't like Froot Loops."

"Then she'll have to have Rice Krispies," Maggie said, bringing a bowl and getting milk from the fridge and putting them in front of her.

Asia looked at the box, then under her lashes at Issy. "Don't like those either," she whispered.

"Well, now you'll have to because that's all we've got." Issy tipped cereal into the bowl and poured milk over it.

Sam managed not to burn the four slices of toast. She put them on the table and went to get the Tiptree Little Scarlet jam, her favorite. She buttered a piece of the toast, slathered on a layer of jam, and put it on Asia's plate next to the cereal bowl. Maggie poured her some juice and then they all just sat back and watched the child eat.

Asia devoured the cereal and the toast in five minutes, drank her juice then looked up at them and said, "Now what?"

"A shower," Issy said. "Come on." Being a big sister was becoming a habit.

Maggie drove into Burford, where she picked up a child-size tourist T-shirt that said COTSWOLDS on the front and had a picture of a sheep on the back. She also found a tiny pair of cotton jersey shorts and some flip-flops she hoped would fit. At least the kid would look normal now and not like some leftover from a royal event.

Issy's mobile beeped. It was her mother asking how she was.

"I'm okay," she said. "Asia's okay, she's had breakfast, now she's in the shower. I'll get Maggie to bring us over."

"No!" Caroline was sharp. "No, don't bring Asia with you. I need to see you alone first. Maggie will bring you over, as soon as she gets back. Then we can talk."

"What about?" Issy was wondering what else could go wrong.

"Ohh . . . we'll talk when you get here," Caroline said. "And Issy, thank you for taking care of Asia last night. You were absolutely right, she should not have been listening to all that."

"Asia's okay, Mom. She's a good kid."

"I'm glad to hear you think so." Caroline sounded amazed. "I'll see you in a bit then?"

"Okay," Issy said, still wondering why she shouldn't bring Asia because after all that woman Jackie was still here at the pub, sleeping in Caroline's old room. Nobody had seen her so far this morning and Issy hoped to get out of there before *she* did.

chapter 67

It was Jesus who finally drove Issy to the barn; Maggie had elected to stay with Asia and Sam, and await the emergence of Jackie. It was already almost noon and so far no sign of her. Asia didn't seem troubled though. She told them her real mom never slept late because she had to drop her off at preschool before she went to work.

Sam said she would take Asia for a walk and they ambled off together down the high street, Asia stumbling in the too-large flip-flops, happily clutching her hand. "Will there be ice cream?" Maggie heard her asking and Sam saying of course there would be.

Maggie thought it was time Jackie got up and went and knocked on her door. There was no reply and she knocked again then opened it and poked her head round. The curtains were closed, the bed unslept-in and Jackie's suitcase was gone. Maggie thought if Caroline were here she would have said Jackie had *flown the coop*! She ran back downstairs and went outside where Jackie's rental car was usually parked directly in front of the pub. Of course it was gone.

She immediately got on the phone and told Jesus who had just reached the barn.

"Good," he said. "Saves us the trouble of chucking her out."

. . .

It was a fine morning and Caroline was sitting with her parents on the terrace, enjoying the sun. Henry was reading the *Telegraph* and Cassandra was helping herself to more coffee from the drip-pot, thinking she really should tell Caroline to get herself one of those new Italian machines where you slotted in the little container of the flavor of your choice, and out came the perfect cup of coffee, with frothed milk on the side. She had one at home and it was so good she often drank two cups. She either had to make the change to decaf or she'd be up dancing all night. She sighed. Those days were over, but at least she could dance the *early* part of the night. She looked affectionately at Henry whose eyes were closed, dozing over the newspaper as he did every morning. She had loved him a long time and found herself wishing Caroline could find that kind of love, some way along life's too-short route.

Caroline was wearing sunglasses, watching the river uncurl itself onto the tiny weir in a flurry of foam, thinking about how she was going to have to tell Issy that her father had been murdered. *And* who the killer was. It wasn't fair. To know your father had died was one thing; to accept that he had killed himself quite another; and then to understand he had been murdered . . . It not only would be hard on Issy, it was hurting Caroline. She couldn't bear to think about James's final moments, what happened, what he must have gone through. She hoped he had not suffered. All she knew was he had not deserved it. James was never a *bad* man.

"It'll be all right, she'll understand," Cassandra said, watching her, knowing what was going on in her mind. "It's what Issy always thought anyway."

"It was the first thing she said when she heard about it. Somebody killed him."

Cassandra nodded; she knew. Jesus's truck was coming up the

drive. "Well, here she is. We had better leave you two alone." She nudged her husband who opened his eyes. "Time to go, Henry," she said, and realizing he got quickly to his feet.

"Good luck, darling," he said to Caroline. "Call if you need us."

Issy got out of the truck and waved goodbye to Jesus. She stood for a minute by the front door, remembering when she and her mom had stood in the pouring rain looking at the sign that said *Bar, Grill and Dancing*, like a roadhouse in an old American movie transplanted to a field in the Cotswolds. The sign was still there, a faded weather-beaten plank of wood that had triggered off her mother's plans for an uncertain future which Issy had decided there and then would not include her.

Now, looking at the honey-colored stone barn sheltered by the big chestnut tree, its windows gleaming, flowers blooming, instead of being angry at her mother's seeming inability to look reality in the face, Issy had finally to acknowledge Caroline had worked miracles. She wasn't sure about the restaurant but at least her mother had created this place.

She was still standing there, taking it all in, when she heard her mom crunching across the gravel toward her.

"It's lovely now, Mom," she called. "I think I'm seeing it for the first time, the way you did right at the beginning."

"At least now it's a home." Caroline linked her arm with Issy's and they walked back through the house to the terrace.

"I know about Asia," Issy said, "but something else is wrong." She dropped onto the yellow and blue striped cushion on the river wall. She almost didn't want to hear Caroline's answer. She turned away and threw a small stone into the water, saw the ducks come paddling, thinking it was food. Their own personal restaurant, she thought, wishing she could smile, but she knew this was something serious, she could feel it.

"It's about Dad, of course," she said. "Is it about Asia, too?"

"Not this time, sweetheart. This time I have to tell you that you were right. Your father did not kill himself."

Issy sat up straighter. *Thank God, oh thank God . . .* she thought. Then, "I'll bet I know who did. The ice-woman."

Caroline nodded. "Mark told me the police have a warrant for her arrest. I had to tell you before it's on the Internet, or the news or anything. I'm so sorry, baby, this is so hard for you."

"And you." Issy went and knelt in front of her mother. She put her head in Caroline's lap, felt her hand stroking her hair. There was just the sound of the river, the shrill whirr of a cricket in the grass, the rustle as the ducks paddled away . . . A feeling of peace came over her.

"It's all right, Mom," she said. "It's good that we finally know the truth."

chapter 68

Caroline woke late the next morning. The rattle of breakfast dishes and the smell of coffee and frying bacon came from the kitchen where Cassandra was obviously already at work.

She stretched luxuriously; the breeze from the open window brought a waft of hay and, pleasantly, of cow. *Her* cows, she now called them affectionately; her coppery-chestnut Herefords, creatures of beauty with their large soulful eyes. They even had long eyelashes. *And* enormous cowpats, but she knew that was a sign of good nutrition and therefore good milk. They were shooed out of the field every evening by the farmer and his black-and-white Border collie who was no relation to Frisky, old Laddie's dog, the one who just lounged in the pub and never so much as moved unless food came his way. The farmer's dog worked for its living and was a joy to watch. Of course Caroline had learned by now to avoid the lane at milking times; you could get stuck behind a slow-moving cow posse for ten frustrating minutes.

The smell of bacon finally got to her. She leapt out of bed and put on her old chenille bathrobe. She really had to buy a new one, not only was this falling apart at the seams but the chenille had worn in places, leaving bald patches. Cassandra would definitely not like it.

She leaped into the shower; two minutes flat, then out again, found her last pair of clean underwear—she really must do some laundry today; tugged the old yellow sweater over her head, then skinny black yoga pants for the yoga she had always meant to do but somehow never gotten around to; wafted the brush over her black hair, shoved up the bangs with her fingers, put on her glasses and ran down the steps in search of breakfast.

She paused, smiling in the kitchen doorway. "Good morning, Mom," she said. "Good morning, Dad." She went over and kissed them both.

Henry took the basket of croissants he'd bought an hour ago at Wright's in the village and put it on the table. He got the French butter and the Bonne Maman peach jam from the fridge while Cassandra doled out streaky bacon, fried crisp enough to fall apart when you touched it which was the way she knew her family liked it. She slid the over-easy eggs, fried in the sizzling bacon fat, onto their plates.

"Fried bread, anyone?" she asked making Caroline groan. "Mom, *no!* This is wonderful. Thank God for you."

"I think we have a great deal more to thank God for this morning than simply old me," Cassandra said, not looking the least bit "old" in narrow jeans and a blue shirt nipped round her middle with a thin gold belt.

"Asia, you mean?" Henry said. "Thank God for the successful resolution of that problem?"

"It's not resolved yet," Caroline said. "I have to take her home."

"No need to worry," Henry said, mopping up a bit of egg that had trickled down his chin. "Your mom and I will take her back."

"What? But you can't. James would expect me to look after his daughter."

"You already do," Cassandra said. "*Issy.* Remember?"

Caroline frowned. Was she ignoring her own daughter's feelings in all this? Issy had been so good, she had dried the child's tears, stopped her howling, even given her the precious cat to hold for comfort. Issy had told her it was easy being a big sister; she quite enjoyed the role, and in some odd way it seemed to Caroline that because of the new half sister, Issy had even come to terms with James. She couldn't simply allow her parents to escort Asia home. She would do it. It was her duty.

She squashed her egg onto a slice of toast, arranged a strip of bacon on top of it, cut the toast in two, folded it into a sandwich and took an enormous bite. "Great," she said with her mouth full. "God, Mom, your breakfasts are the best. We should serve them in the restaurant, they'll come from miles around for Cassandra's bacon and egg butties."

"Thank you." Cassandra anointed a croissant with the peach jam, and said, "Have you forgotten something important?"

Caroline stopped and stared at her. "What?"

"Finish chewing that sandwich first and think about it. Didn't I teach you any manners?"

Caroline grinned, feeling like a child again. "Sorry," she said. "It's just so good."

"Makes pigs of us all," Henry agreed, sopping up the last of his egg with his toast, then he remembered where bacon came from and said, "Oops, sorry, perhaps I shouldn't have said pigs, didn't make the connection . . ."

Caroline laughed, then suddenly realized what Cassandra was talking about. "Oh, God! How could I forget my own daughter's *birthday*?"

"I was wondering that myself." Cassandra poured more coffee then went and fetched a gaily-wrapped parcel tied with an orange ribbon bow. A birthday card was tucked into it. "It's a black dress, like the red one," she told Caroline. "I hope you at least remembered to get your child a gift," she added, because what with all that had gone down the last few days she was not at all sure Caroline had remembered.

"I did." Caroline thought of her gift, it was up in her room, waiting to be wrapped. Now, thinking about it, perhaps she would not wrap it. It was more appropriate, more significant just the way it was.

"What are we doing about a party?" Henry asked, because in his experience anybody with a birthday had a party.

"I was just thinking about that." Jim's voice came from the door, followed by a knock. "Sorry, am I interrupting?"

"Well, you've missed the eggs," Cassandra said, looking pleased to see him. He was a bit young for Caroline but she liked him, enjoyed his straightforward caring approach with her daughter. "Still, there's plenty of coffee and croissants."

"No éclairs, I'm afraid," Caroline said, remembering.

Jim took the chair next to hers and Cassandra handed him a plate with a still-warm croissant. Henry pushed over the butter and jam.

"Just the jam, thanks," Jim said. "Ahh, good, peach," he added, earning the reward of a smile from Cassandra whose favorite it also was.

She poured a mug of coffee for him and went to brew another pot. "You simply have to get one of those Italian machines," she said over her shoulder but Caroline wasn't listening.

She was watching Jim spreading jam on his croissant with the same precision he must use when he planed a piece of wood. He had the longest fingers. The few dark hairs on the back of his hands expanded into a soft crop up his lean but muscular arms, making her wonder about the rest of his body. She stopped that thought immediately. This was *breakfast* and she was having immoral thoughts. She laughed out loud, amused.

"What's funny?" Jim stopped what he was doing to look at her.

"I was wondering about the word 'immoral.' Thinking how I sometimes used it in the wrong context," she said, smugly because she didn't think he would know what she was talking about anyway.

"'Lustful' is the word you want," he said, quietly so only she could hear. Or that's what he thought.

"I always found 'lustful' to be a very opportune word." Cassandra had heard though. She was standing at the kitchen counter with her back to them and they looked astonished at each other.

"Hmm, well . . . 'birthday party' is the word on *my* mind," Jim said, polishing off the croissant and offering his mug for a refill. "I wanted to tell you my studio is available, rent-free for a special event like this. I even know a young guy round here who deejays, plus my sister has colored lights and I'm good at helium balloons. And you and Maggie are good at snacks."

"Me too." Cassandra came over to stand next to him. She put a hand on his shoulder. "Let's do it," she said, pleased.

"But what will they drink?" Henry asked. "Remember, they're only kids, Issy's turning sixteen not twenty-one."

"Fruit punch," Cassandra said.

Caroline wondered how they would get anyone to come at the last minute, but Jim said, "That's how youth operates, right here, right now, let's go . . . besides it's a Saturday night and they're always looking for somewhere to go."

"Somebody had better tell Issy," Caroline said. "And there's something else I have to tell her. I've decided *I'm* to take Asia back to Singapore and I want Issy to come with me."

There was a long silence while they all thought about Issy, then Cassandra finally said, "You're right, of course. *You* are responsible for James's child while she is here. And Issy is her half sister. Asia has no one else."

"It's only appropriate," Henry agreed.

"I'll miss you," was what Jim said, looking into Caroline's eyes. She was very glad she had not put on the old chenille bathrobe after all. But she did wonder what Issy would think about her plan. First, though, she had to give Issy her birthday present.

chapter 69

Caroline's phone rang. It was Issy.

"Mom? Did you *forget?*"

"Of course not." Caroline crossed her fingers behind her back and rolled her eyes at Cassandra. Little white lies made other people feel better. She said, "It just got a bit busy round here and anyhow now here I am singing 'Happy Birthday to You.'" She proceeded to do just that, with the added a capella of the others in the background. She heard Issy laugh and thanked God one more time that morning.

"Actually," she said, "we were talking about your party."

"*What!* What *party?*" Issy who was in the kitchen at the pub turned to frown at Sam who was standing behind her with Asia, holding Blind Brenda who did not want to be held and scratched as she wriggled out of her arms.

"Ow," Asia said.

"It's not Brenda's fault," Sam told her. "You picked her up and she didn't want to be picked up, that's all." Asia whined and rubbed the scratch and Sam said not to be a baby, so Asia didn't bother to cry and listened to what Issy was saying instead.

"*A party!*" Asia exclaimed when she heard, and so did Sam.

Issy grinned at Sam and gave her a thumbs-up. "Definitely," she said to her mother. "Seven o'clock tonight at the Thompson Manor stables . . . yeah, the studio I mean. I'll have to work the phones, call you back later, tell you how many."

"I need to see you before then," her mother said. "I'll come and get you in half an hour."

"I have to make phone calls . . ."

"It's important."

Her mother sounded serious so Issy agreed. "Wow!" she said, high-fiving Sam and then Asia so she wouldn't feel left out. *"We're having a birthday party."*

"Can I come?" Asia asked.

"Of course you're coming. Everybody is coming. Sam, you call your lot and I'll call mine. Except Lysander."

"Who is Lysander?" Asia never seemed to stop asking questions.

"Nobody you'd ever want to know," Sam told her, settling back to some heavy-duty iPhone work before Issy's mother arrived.

Issy flinched when Asia gave her a poke in the ribs. "I have a pretty dress," Asia said, gazing up at her, smiling.

"I'll bet you do," Issy said, smiling back.

Caroline was on the phone with Maggie. She asked her to get Sarah in to help and Lily if possible, and Maggie said she would send Jesus off to the market to pick up a dozen or so barbecued chickens and that she would make a hundred or so spicy tacos. Caroline would fix a couple of gallons of potato salad.

"Remember," Caroline reminded Maggie, "teenage boys will eat anything and everything you put in front of them. The girls will pretend they never eat but soon as the boys are out of the way they'll devour everything that's left. I'll also do hot dogs," she added. "And burgers. And I'll call Wright's and order buns, and also a cake."

"Don't forget the ice cream," Maggie reminded her.

"Chocolate? Or vanilla?"

Maggie asked the girls and they said both.

Caroline said Cassandra was in charge of the non-booze—punch she called it, though she thought they should check the boys for liquor on the way in. "You can't trust a teenage boy," she said. "At least, that's what I've heard. And by the way, Jim is in charge of decorations and the deejay."

There was a whoop of delight when Maggie passed that information on to the girls.

"All you have to do now," Maggie put down the phone and looked at her decidedly scruffy just-out-of-bed bunch, "is wash your hair and think of what to wear."

"What about presents?" Sam was bursting to give Issy hers.

"Later," Maggie said but Issy was already tearing into the blue foil-wrapped packet Sam had given her. Asia hung over her shoulder watching as she held up the little stretch-ribbed black cami. "*Perfect!*" Issy exclaimed. "Sam, it's perfect for tonight. With jeans, of course."

Maggie sighed, thinking back to the days when sixteen-year-olds wore dresses to parties.

"And heels," Sam added.

Issy beamed. "Right. Of course."

Maggie thought she might as well give Issy her present as well. "From Jesus and me," she said.

It was a pair of simple gold hoops, not too big, not too small; "Just big enough," Issy said, kissing her. "I love you, Maggie," she whispered.

"But *I* don't have a birthday present for you," Asia said, her narrow little face solemn, blackberry eyes gleaming sadly.

"*You* are my present. My new little sister," Issy said, then because she felt she was getting too soppy, she gave Asia a little shove and Asia shoved back and then they were racing up the stairs laughing.

chapter 70

Caroline came and picked up Issy, who hitched herself into the front seat of the Land Rover and leaned across to kiss her cheek.

"Sixteen! Imagine!" Caroline said, shoving the car into gear and driving back down the high street, automatically checking to see if Issy had fastened her seat belt.

"Did *you* ever imagine that? I mean when I was born, when I was just a little kid like Asia?"

"Of course not, nobody can ever picture their baby at sixteen. It seems light-years away, all those schools, the travels, the travails in between. *And* all those birthday parties."

She felt Issy's hand on her arm, and turned to smile at her.

"Thanks Mom, for the party," Issy said.

"It was Jim's idea. Well, Grandpa's really, but Jim was the one who sorted it out, said we could use his studio—which I know you haven't seen but it's a gorgeous space for a party, just big enough."

"Big enough for how many?" It was a Saturday night in summer and Issy knew everybody would be looking for some place to go.

"Oh, I thought maybe . . . forty?"

"*Mo . . . om!*"

"Forty's a lot. And let me tell you now, just in case you were thinking about it, a hundred is too many."

"Okay, around fifty." Issy compromised but anyhow she knew there'd be gate-crashers; they'd hear it from someone who'd heard it from someone else. "Anyway, where are we going?"

"Just for a walk," Caroline said. She drove out of the village and stopped beside a copse of beeches, where a trail led into the woods. They got out and strolled companionably for a while, not speaking. Finally, Issy said, "I know it's something about Dad again, I can just feel it when you're thinking about him."

Caroline stopped and faced her. "You're right. I'm going to take Asia back to her mother and I want you to come with me."

"*Mom!*" Issy glared, bug-eyed with anguish at her. "How can I go back there? And anyway, how can *you*?"

"Because Asia is your father's child, that's why, and we have a responsibility. This is your half sister we're talking about. Think about *her*. She has no one else and neither does her mother now that James, who really must have loved them, is gone."

"How do you know he loved her?" Issy had come to terms with she and Asia having the same dad, but going to Singapore—*her home*—and meeting some woman he had left her mother for . . . it didn't seem right.

"I know what you're thinking," Caroline said. "I've thought about it too. Issy, tell me what else we should do?"

Issy's shoulders drooped. "When will this ever go away?"

"It won't," Caroline said. "We leave the day after tomorrow. Grandpa's already booked flights.

"Anyway," she said, "I have something for you. Your sixteenth birthday present."

She took a folded paisley silk handkerchief out of her pocket and handed it to her.

Issy recognized it as one of her father's. She wondered where Caroline had gotten it, then remembered Mark had sent a box of James's personal things, which as far as she knew, her mother had never opened. Apparently she had been wrong. She unfolded the handkerchief and saw her father's gold signet ring.

He had always worn it. *As long as she remembered, he'd never taken it off*... until he was dead... memories flooded back, it was as though he were here with her now...

"I thought Daddy would have wanted you to have it," Caroline said, as Issy began to cry.

She took her in her arms. "He'd want you to keep it for him. I know he would."

"Oh I will, *I will*," Issy said. "I'm only crying because it makes me remember him." She tried the ring on her pinkie, but it was too large, so she tried the second finger of her right hand. It was still a bit big but it would do.

"We can have it sized," Caroline told her, still anxious about doing the right thing.

"Later," Issy agreed. "And then I'll never take it off. It's as though Dad's wishing me happy sixteenth birthday. Thank you, thank you," she said, hugging Caroline, grateful because she knew her mother must be reliving the same memories.

chapter 71

The party was to start at seven that evening and Maggie and Jesus pulled up in their truck at the Thompson Manor stableyard at exactly the same moment as Caroline and her parents. Jim was waiting for them at the door to his studio. He'd pushed back all the furniture, even removed some of it, so now there was a big bare room with rental tables and chairs round the edge of the wooden floor, which had been waxed to a dancer's dream.

Then Georgki arrived with Sarah and Lily and the two girls immediately got to work spreading red-and-white paper cloths over the tables. The deejay came and began fixing up his speakers while Jim took care of some fancy lighting which flickered and half-blinded Jesus.

"Strobes," Jim told him. "Heard they like 'em in clubs."

Maggie and Caroline were arranging the buffet on the trestle tables along the far wall with piles of paper plates (the sturdier kind that didn't bend when you put food on them) and plastic glasses. Cassandra stirring the cauldron of punch, floated slices of lime on it. She had also brought a bowl of olives which she told them would make the drinks look more grown-up, along with sprigs of mint. "They'll think they are drinking mint juleps," she told Caroline, who didn't believe for a minute they would, but smiled anyway.

Lily had decided to put nasturtiums picked from Jim's garden into tiny white bud vases on each table, a nice touch but unfortunately some of the nasturtiums still had their green caterpillars attached. She hadn't known they were notoriously fond of nasturtium leaves and now they were crawling across the tables.

Huge bags of ice cubes were at the ready, the lights were working, the deejay all set, and the food ready to go.

There was just enough time for them all to change.

Issy was wearing her grandmother's birthday present black dress that hugged her body as though it loved her, and the black "Lysander party" heels, with her dark hair swept up and skewered with a fake-tortoiseshell comb of Caroline's. She wore Maggie and Jesus's gold hoops and of course, her father's gold signet ring. Caroline thought she looked about twenty-two.

Sam was in a red cami, tight of course, like every other girl's would be that night, with skinny jeans and red platform heels that Maggie didn't even know she had and now wondered where they had come from, and which anyway made her about five inches taller. Her blond hair was brushed smooth around her shoulders. Both girls had on a lot of eye shadow and pink lip gloss.

Asia had on another "royal family" party frock, this time white with red polka dots. God knows where Melanie had expected to take the child, Caroline marveled, but anyhow it had turned out for the best because now here she was at a real party. Asia had drawn the line at the Mary Janes and ankle socks, though, and insisted on wearing her flip-flops.

The adults played it down in their usual casual attire, though Caroline did think Jim looked devastatingly attractive in jeans slung low on his narrow and very sexy hips, with a cowboy shirt and a leather belt with a silver horse buckle. He hadn't gone the whole cowboy hog though and wore brown suede loafers rather than boots.

Little Billy had been left with a friend and Sarah was wearing what she always wore, jeans and a white tee, because she had nothing else, and anyhow she was here to work; while Lily dazzled in a white mini (that reached, Cassandra told Caroline, just up to her bum but thank God still covered the important bits) with staggeringly high heels and a black top. Her hair was back-combed and sprayed into a cloud and she wore dark glasses.

"Jesus," Jesus looked at her, amazed. "It's a vision from *Transformers*."

They were ready to roll when the first loaded rented minivan arrived. Music was already blasting, the lights were strobing, and the food smelled great. The young guests looked wonderful and Asia was perched up on the platform with the deejay.

In an hour the place was happening. Maggie and Jesus left and so did Cassandra and Henry leaving Caroline and Jim in charge.

"Come dance." Jim offered her his hand but she smiled and shook her head.

"No, oh, no, I can't . . . not now . . ."

"Yes you can," he said. And before she knew it she was, and she forgot for a while that Jim was only twenty-seven and she was thirty-eight. For once, she was living for the moment.

Issy spotted her out of the corner of her eye and nudged Sammy. "Look at Mom," she said. "She looks quite young."

There was a roar outside as a motorcycle ground to a halt. "That's a Harley," Issy said. "I *know* that sound."

"How?" Sam asked, but Issy was already heading for the door, to check it out.

The young man on the chopper wore a black leather jacket, shades, and jeans. He swung his leg over and took off his helmet. His hair stuck straight up in gelled spikes.

Issy and Sam stared at him, thrilled; he was so grown-up, so different, so sexy!

"But who *is* he?" Sam asked.

Issy said, "I don't know, but whoever he is, he's wonderful. Where did he come from anyway?"

The Harley rider, who'd heard there was a party and decided to crash, took a quick look at them, put his helmet back on, got back on his bike and roared off. Despite the heels and the eyeliner, they were too young.

"He was *really* cute," Issy sighed, disappointed.

But Sammy grabbed her hand and headed back inside. "Better hurry," she said. "We might have missed something."

chapter 72

A few hours later, lights dimmed, club music blaring, Issy decided she was definitely a flirt and she definitely liked the guy she was dancing with. What's not to like? she asked herself: he was tall, and so skinny his jeans drooped over what looked to be a very nice rounded bum. And he was blond with it. His straight golden hair hung over brown eyes that were holding hers even while they danced. In fact he never took them off her.

She had never met him before but she knew his name was Alex because she'd asked somebody, and been told he was hot and that every girl was after him. Well, not her. She was not going there. He *was* awfully cute, though he'd never smiled, not even once and they had been dancing for ten minutes.

As if on cue, he stopped dancing and looked at her. *Really* looked at her. Issy thought his eyes were somehow full of meaning, and of course she knew what that meaning was. She was not a total innocent, she knew when a guy was coming on to her. And what's more, she knew when she wanted him to.

He took her hand and led the way through the dancers, past the bar with the now-empty punch bowl, past the table where Sarah was in charge of the buffet. There was a door next to it. He opened it, Issy went in.

Watching the door shut behind them, Sarah debated whether to go after them but thought oh well, it was a party and they were young and only having fun. After all, you didn't turn sixteen every day. Sometimes, though, she wished she could turn back the clock herself and be sixteen all over again. Have a fresh start. But that would mean no Little Billy and her life simply would not be complete without him.

She went over and replenished the punch bowl, rescuing the lime slices from the bottom and attempting to re-float them, but they refused and merged in a green heap on the bottom.

Good thing these kids were not drinking, she thought, checking round anyway. She was sure some of the boys had smuggled in some beers. She'd heard the rattle of cans and knew it wasn't Diet Coke.

Back at the buffet she checked the crowd for young Lily, saw her at the center of the dancers, light flashing off her short white skirt and long brown legs. At least she wasn't off in a corner with some hot guy, giving too much of what she shouldn't be giving, Sarah thought. Not yet, anyway.

That made her remember Issy. The door was still closed. They must have been in there all of ten minutes. She sighed, undecided, but then decided it *was* a party and went back to dishing out spicy chicken tacos with the hot tomato and onion and cilantro *pico de gallo* sauce. She ate one herself. It was good.

Issy trembled at the merest flicker of Alex's hand across her breast, she loved it when he did that . . . The top of her dress was elasticized and he pulled it down. She almost fainted as he cupped her breast . . . *oh God, oh God, she would do anything for him, anything . . .*

His lips were on her breast, her knees shook . . . she was a woman in the middle of an earthquake . . . and then his hand was under her skirt. It wasn't like with Lysander, this was some kind of heaven . . . she loved it when he did that . . . Or did she?

She pushed his hand away, tried to get her knees to stop shaking, told herself to take control, she was behaving like a slut and really what she wanted was for this guy to *like* her, not just have the hots for her . . . Still, she wanted more and yet she didn't because she didn't know how to deal with her feelings, and how to stop.

She had kissed boys before, been felt up a bit before, but the guys were always the ones begging her for it and she was always the one saying no. This was different. What did you do when you felt one way and then the other? What did you do when you were in a situation over which you had no real control?

In the back of her mind she remembered Cassandra telling her that one day she would find out about sex, and knew this was it. It was up to her to deal with it, not the guy groping her because he would go all the way if she let him.

He was trying to kiss her but she pushed him away. "Get off," she said, and saw his eyes widen with surprise.

"But you want it," he said. "Girls always do."

"Oh, bugger off," she said, suddenly angry with him and herself. "Sorry," she added as she hitched up her top and opened the door. "You got the wrong girl."

She heard his sigh as she slammed the door behind her. She couldn't resist the slam. It made her knees stop shaking.

She caught Sarah looking at her as she hurried past and gave her a wobbly smile.

"Everything okay?" Sarah asked.

"Yeah. Sure. Right."

Issy got herself together and went in search of Sammy who was dancing with a younger boy they both knew from school. She told herself she was okay now. I mean, whether she was *virgo intaco* (because of Lysander) was still a debate in her mind and Alex had been lovely really. It was *she* who wasn't ready for it, who didn't know how to deal with it, whether just to let it happen, let him touch her, get that great feeling when your whole body teetered on the brink . . . How was a girl supposed to know these things? Even if she was sixteen.

Cassandra and Henry had left early, and were in Issy's room, he in one bed she in another, still awake.

Henry looked up from his book. It was *Game of Thrones;* he'd seen the TV series and enjoyed it so now he was reading the original.

"I don't like sleeping without you," he said.

Cassandra checked the time. "The party'll go on for a bit yet," she said, climbing out of her bed and into his. They were a tight fit in a single but that's the way they'd started their married life: little money, a rented flat, and a narrow bed that made lovemaking even easier. Henry slid his arm round her and she snuggled in, the way she had for all these years.

"I still fancy you, y'know," she said, making him laugh.

"Thank God for that," he said. "Anyway, why are you wearing that nightie."

She glanced down at her white cotton nightshirt. "It's virginal," she said with a mischievous grin. "Anyhow, I always wear a nightie."

"No you do not. Not in France." Henry laughed out loud now. "It must be something in the air there," he said, kissing her.

chapter 73

It was one thirty and the party was still going strong. Sitting outside on one of Jim's sofas that had been removed to make way for the dancers, with Jim's arm around her, Caroline leaned her head into his shoulder. "Don't these kids have homes to go to?" she asked, through the ongoing throb of music and the haze of (forbidden) cigarette smoke.

"As long as they don't set fire to the place I'm not complaining." Jim pulled her closer, something Caroline decided she liked.

More than *liked*; she was enjoying having a man's arm around her; enjoying the girly feeling it gave her, like she was a teenager and not simply mother to one. Reminding herself quickly that a mother was *exactly* who she was and the reason she was here, she pulled away, sat up straighter and flicked back her hair. *Oh God, she'd done it again, the teenage hair flick!* When all she was, was a frustrated housewife making out with an attractive younger man on the sofa in the dark. *Making out?* Did she even *remember* how to do that anymore?

"Tell me about your husband," Jim said, out of the blue it seemed to Caroline.

"What *exactly* do you want to know?" She wasn't sure how to answer. Should she just say *"oh, you know young love, all that, then he cheated on me, and well, y'know how it is."* Or simply it wasn't any of his business.

"Why did you stay with him?"

Jim pulled her back and tucked her head into his shoulder again. She couldn't see his face, just feel the warmth of his body, his arm around her, his hand on her shoulder.

"I fell for James the moment I saw him," she said, deciding to come clean. "I never could resist him, even when I found out about his mistress. He told me that the affair was over, it was all about me and him, the two of us again."

"He must have been very charming."

"You would have liked him. Everybody did. You couldn't *not* like James, he was so . . . so *engaging.* When you were with him he made you feel you were the only person in the world that mattered, the only woman he wanted to be with. And I loved him for that."

"So, what happened, in the end?"

"He lied to me, kept on lying, I didn't know what was going on, couldn't understand why he was doing this. Of course I knew something was wrong, something more than a woman, though I didn't know anything about Melanie and Asia. I understand now he was under terrible financial pressure, bound to Gayle Lee Chen because she had brought underworld money into his business and then when that started to collapse, to save herself she threatened to lay the blame on James.

"Oddly," she added, after thinking for a while, "James was a loyal man. He didn't love Gayle Lee; never had I suppose, certainly not the way he'd loved me, and the way he loved Asia's mother. Mark told me Gayle Lee must have thought he would betray her and that's why she killed him. And then . . . when the underworld turned on her . . . she simply disappeared."

"You think she'll ever come back?"

"I don't see how she can, unless she reinvents herself." She shrugged. "Anything is possible."

"And you? Have you reinvented yourself?" Jim turned her face to his, took her chin in his hand.

"I hope so," Caroline said softly. *"Oh, I hope so,"* she said again as his mouth took hers.

"Mom? *Mom*?" It was Issy, looking for her.

They leapt apart.

"Here I am." Caroline got hastily up, smoothing down her skirt, rubbing her mouth on the back of her hand. "What's up?"

"Just that somebody's been sick all over Jim's bathroom floor."

"Great," she heard Jim say behind her. Then, philosophically. "Par for the course, I guess."

The first of the take-home mini-buses lumbered round the corner into the stable yard.

"Oh, shit," Caroline heard her daughter say. *"Already*?"

"It's two o'clock," Caroline said, surprised it was so late, heading inside to organize the departure.

The strobe lights were out and young people sprawled everywhere in the gloom, now lit only by trailing strings of red, white, and blue twinkle lights. Caroline saw Lily curled on some boy's lap, quickly hauled her off.

Sarah, who was throwing plastic glasses and plates into a big black garbage bag, told Lily she'd better stop it.

"Get over here, Lily," Sarah told her. "Or you'll end up in the same state I am."

"Not me," Lily said, pulling down her skirt and hitching up her top. "I just want to have a bit of fun."

Don't we all, thought Caroline, remembering.

The two girls at the door were doling out long lingering goodbye kisses to the boys when Georgki showed up in the Hummer.

"Who needs lift?" he asked, folding his arms and glaring at the crowd, scaring them half to death Caroline would bet. She'd also bet he'd been waiting round the corner for this very moment. Good-hearted Georgki, she gave him a smile of thanks.

"Mom."

Issy had come to stand next to her. "Yes?"

"It was the best party ever."

Caroline smiled and thanked God, one more time. "Of course it was," she said.

chapter 74

Two days later they were on a plane bound for Singapore. Asia had asked to sit by the window and after playing around with her food and playing games with Issy on her iPad, she had fallen asleep, stretched out and looking so tiny and skinny and vulnerable, Caroline knew she could never abandon her. In the space of just a few days Asia had become part of the family. It was up to Caroline to include her mother in that family too.

Issy's eyes were closed. "Mom?" she said.

Caroline looked at her. Issy didn't open her eyes.

"Yes?"

"Tell me about sex."

Caroline gasped . . . *of all things! Of all times! All places!* What was she supposed to do? Issy had brushed her off when she'd mentioned sex before, told her she knew all about that, they'd had the talk at school and the demonstration with the cucumber and the condom. Of course Caroline had taken her to the gynecologist, made sure she was safe, just in case . . . she knew "in case" loomed as a possibility. But what on earth had made Issy think about sex now?

Could she possibly suspect something about her and Jim? If so, how? Did she look different? Act different? She'd heard sex gave women a certain glow, an extra awareness of themselves, of their bodies. But she and Jim had not had sex.

"I know how it happens," Issy said, and Caroline breathed a sigh of relief that at least she did not have to give a whispered lecture on a plane of exactly how the birds and the bees and probably teenagers too, actually did it.

"Right," she said, and for the life of her couldn't think of another thing to say.

"I know how it *feels*," Issy added, shocking her. "I mean I haven't done it, if that's what you're thinking." She thought of Lysander and added, "Not that some people haven't tried, but you know, Mom, sometimes it's exciting. I *feel* it but I can't get my head around it. Is there something wrong with me?"

Wrong! Everything was *right*! How to explain? Caroline searched her memories, recent and past and out of the blue came up with a quote that once upon a time when she too was young, had seemed to her to explain sex.

"It's all about falling in love," she told Issy now. "A famous writer, his name is A. N. Wilson, once said that 'falling in love is the greatest imaginative experience of which most human beings are capable.'"

"So you have to love somebody to have sex?"

Caroline wracked her brain some more for the right thing to say. "Sex is a wonderful emotion," she said finally, hoping "emotion" was the correct word. "But you know Issy, sex can be really wonderful, when you're in love and in a relationship with a man you really care about. Then, it's a state of *being*, not just what you are *doing*. You can't even get close to the power of sex without your head—your *mind*, your other *emotions* being involved. Do you understand?"

"I think so. Is that what Daddy felt for Asia's mother then?"

"I hope so," Caroline said, and realized that now truly she did.

"And the Hong Kong ice-woman?"

"I believe that was different. It was an obsession."

"What about you and Dad?"

"For a long time it was wonderful," Caroline said simply. "We were very much in love."

Issy took her mother's hand and squeezed it. "I'm really glad you told me," she said.

chapter 75

Mark was waiting at Changi Airport when they emerged weary from immigration and customs, except for Asia who bounced out of there on stalklike little legs, all big eyes and big smiles that faded when Mark told her her mother was not there.

"She decided to wait at home for you," he said. "She told me to tell you she has a surprise for you."

He looked so good to Caroline, so familiar, big and burly and bearded, in a cream tropical-weight suit and even, for God's sake, a tie, though she'd bet it was ninety degrees outside and very probably raining.

"You never change," she said.

"But you do." Mark looked searchingly at her, saw a definite change; a softening, a lessening of tension, a womanly aura about her he hadn't seen in a long time.

"Where are we staying?" Caroline asked.

"My place, I thought it would be nicer for you than a hotel. We'll go there first, then we'll take Asia home."

. . .

Mark's loft was in the newly gentrified marina area with warehouses converted into boutiques, cafés and clubs and restaurants and apartments overlooking the river.

It was on the top floor, a tall, open space divided by opaque glass sliding screens. It was light, airy, and dramatic, sleek and modern with a steel kitchen that gleamed with the patina of the unused.

The guest room was stark like an illustration in an Italian décor magazine with a bathroom that was all white subway tiles and dark-tinted mirrors. Issy thought it was wonderful but Caroline found herself hoping that the beds, stretched tight with white sheets and hospital corners, were more comfortable than they looked. However, the shower's large raindrop head and the half a dozen other nozzles felt wonderful on her tired body, and fifteen minutes later, she and Issy emerged, airline grime removed, lotioned, scented, and refreshed.

Asia was waiting on the sofa, legs stuck out in front of her, watching TV. Caroline told Issy to give her a shower. She opened the child's suitcase and took out the new denim shorts she'd bought, and the pink T-shirt—Asia's favorite color. The flip-flops would have to do.

After the shower Issy brushed Asia's hair, braided it, and finished it off with an elastic band, though Asia told her disapprovingly her mother would have used a ribbon.

Caroline and Mark were drinking champagne over by the window, talking in low voices, so the two girls watched TV. It was in Mandarin, some of which Issy understood because, after all, she had been brought up in Singapore. Asia held Issy's hand.

"I don't know how to help Melanie," Caroline said. "There is no money."

"It's not as bad as it first seemed. Not that there's a lot, because of what happened, but James had in fact made trust funds for you and Issy, and also for Asia."

"Of course! Jackie must have known about that and thought she'd get her hands on it."

"It was the bank's fault," Mark told her. "'An error in accounting,' they called it. Anyhow, there's enough now for Melanie to buy their apartment and to live on, though she'll still have to work."

"So will I," Caroline said. "Nothing wrong with that. These days women have to fend for themselves."

"But not children. They must be looked after and however bad James was, he recognized that responsibility. Life goes on," he said. "And *your* life?" he added. "How's it going?"

"Good. Great." Caroline took a gulp of champagne. "Any time now, *partner,* our restaurant will be opening. I'm just waiting for the furniture to be delivered. Sarah's moving into the cottage while I'm away and she'll check out how well our kitchen functions. I know exactly what I'm going to serve, in the beginning anyway, and to start with I'm planning on forty customers, but only on Friday and Saturday nights."

"Hmm, we won't make our fortunes yet then." He smiled.

"Just you wait, before too long they'll be clamoring at the door," Caroline said, and with a sudden drop of fear in her stomach, she hoped she was right. Everything depended on it.

Melanie's apartment building was close to Orchard Road, near the boutique where she worked. Asia was quiet in the car and Caroline saw Issy squeeze her hand, heard her say it would be all right, her mom would be waiting.

But Melanie was not waiting for them in the foyer, and Asia pushed the elevator button for the sixth floor.

Caroline took a deep breath. *This is it,* she told herself. *Moment of truth time. I'm about to see the woman my husband really loved. No, that's wrong; he really loved me too, and then his love moved on, and because of that we have Asia as well as Issy.*

Melanie was waiting at the door. She was petite, with delicately boned Thai features, an exquisite skin the color of dark-gold honey, and long black hair in a neat bun speared with an ebony stick. She was wearing an amber-color lace top that left her shoulders bare, with skinny jeans and flats.

Issy held out her arms and Asia raced into them. Neither of them said a word, they simply held each other as tightly as possible. Then Melanie and Caroline looked at each other. "Welcome," Melanie said. "Won't you please come in."

The apartment was very small and simple with a dining area at one end and an open-plan kitchen. A pair of sofas in front of a large television set were piled with colorful Thai-silk cushions, and sliding glass doors opened onto a tiny terrace.

In a corner was a small red-lacquered kitchen-god shrine with a Buddha-like deity lit by a flickering votive. In the bowl in front of him was an offering of fruits.

"Please, sit down," Melanie said. "Can I offer you some tea?"

Her English was as flawless as her face and Caroline thought how could James *not* have fallen for her? She was gentle, beautiful, and anxious to please.

"It's difficult for me to meet you," she said now to Caroline. "I know you cannot like me, it is inevitable, but you took care of my daughter when I did something wrong and sent her there."

"You did nothing wrong," Caroline said, reminding herself she had already lost James by the time he met and fell in love with Melanie. "We were glad to meet Asia, find a new sister."

So far, though, Melanie had not so much as looked at Issy, who had shrunk into a corner of the sofa and was staring miserably down at her feet.

"Issy took care of me." Asia twitched at her mother's jeaned leg, gazing up at her.

"Then we must say thank you."

Melanie finally looked directly at Issy. "Your name is as pretty as you are," she said. "Isabel is beautiful. James told me that about you."

Issy lifted a non-caring shoulder and said nothing. She really didn't want to know her father's lover.

Melanie turned away from her and went into the kitchen and came out with a bottle of Portuguese Vinho Verde. She poured three glasses, put them on a tray with a can of Coke for Issy and a glass of orange juice for Asia.

Issy stared surprised. Her own mom didn't even know you served Coke in the can for chrisakes! And it was icy cold, exactly the way it should be. She looked at Melanie as she said thank you, observing how much younger she was than her own mother, and that she was lovely, like some girl from a Singapore Airlines ad, and also that she was so nervous she almost dropped the tray. Issy put out a hand to stop it tilting and received a grateful smile. The woman even had perfect white teeth, she'd bet she had never had a cavity in her life.

"Mommy," Asia said, sitting next to Issy on the sofa, "will you please love Issy."

Issy felt the mortified blush and gave Asia a nudge. Asia said "ow" and spilled her juice all over the sofa and the Thai-silk cushions.

Caroline laughed. "It's just like being at home," she said, and Melanie laughed too.

Then Mark had a serious talk with Melanie, telling her about the small trust fund that would enable her to buy her apartment, and pay for Asia's education. Melanie did not cry when she heard the news, but she put her hands together in that Thai way and bowed her head, saying thank you.

"Why don't we all drink to James?" Mark said, "taking the bull by the horns," as Caroline was to tell everyone later.

"James was a good man," Melanie said loyally.

"A good daddy," Asia said.

"Yes, to both those," Issy agreed.

Caroline raised her glass too, it was hard but she told herself she could get over it; she always had, hadn't she? Then she tucked the memory of James's and her life into the special place she would keep it forever. And Asia came and sat on her knee, and she heard Issy asking Melanie about the kitchen-god shrine saying she remembered one exactly like it in their old apartment, and Mark was sitting back with a Cheshire cat grin on his face.

She hoped he wasn't about to ask her to marry him.

chapter 76

Caroline realized, after an hour, there wasn't really that much to say. She and Melanie might have James's daughters in common but they were not women who would normally have sought each other out. They could never be real friends. She was just about to say it was time to leave when Asia remembered her surprise.

"Where is it, Mommy?" she demanded, jumping excitedly up and down. "Is it an iPhone?"

Mark laughed and said, "Didn't it used to be Etch-a-Sketch?"

"It's in the bedroom," Melanie said.

They heard her yell of surprise and *oh my oh my oh my,* then she came running back, clutching a sweet-looking black kitten. Issy was immediately on her knees and both of them stroking and coaxing. The kitten began to purr loudly.

"Oh, Mommy, it's the *best* surprise," Asia said.

"What will you call it?" Caroline asked.

"Why, Brenda, of course," Asia said, as though all kittens were automatically named Brenda. "She's not blind," she explained, "so I can't call her *Blind* Brenda."

Issy said, "But you'll have to promise to love her and look after her, and feed her properly."

"Oh, I will, I will," Asia promised.

It was a good time to say goodbye. There were hugs, there were kisses, Asia cried and so did Issy.

"Come back and see me, little sister," she whispered and Asia promised she would.

Caroline told Melanie it was wonderful to have met Asia, and she was sure they would see each other again.

"We will see her again, won't we?" Issy asked when they were in the car and Caroline reassured her, thinking, by hook or by crook, they would. She couldn't allow Asia to slip out of Issy's life now.

They were all hungry and they stopped off at one of the hawker areas with fifty or sixty busy stalls, where they ate spicy pork and noodles so thin they melted in their mouths.

On the way back to Mark's they drove past their old apartment building. "Why not stop and take a look?" Mark asked, casually. "I happen to have the key."

Caroline glanced at Issy who was looking longingly at her, and knew she had to let her go "home" again.

The elevator smelled the same, of polished wood and Windexed mirrors, and opened with the same perfectly smooth swoosh onto the big empty apartment that had been their home for so many years. It was the same but oh so different, empty and soulless without its family.

Caroline searched for the appropriate memories, but they refused to come. For her, it was in the past.

She waited while Issy went to look round, peering at the closet where she used to play with her father's ties, in the kitchen where they'd eaten dinner together, in her old "little girl" bedroom.

She walked slowly back and Caroline took her hand.

"It's over, Mom," Issy said quietly.

The past had finally become the past.

. . .

Later, when Issy had gone to bed, Caroline sat on Mark's hard modern sofa looking out at the lights of the marina. Music came faintly from a nearby club; there were snatches of laughter, a car horn . . .

"Is it all in the past, Caroline?"

She could feel him looking at her, knew what was coming. She removed her glasses, pushed back her fringe and took a deep breath.

"Yes," she said simply. "I don't belong here anymore. I'm not the person I was when I lived here. I don't belong, Mark."

"Then you won't marry me?"

She laughed. "Oh, Mark, you didn't even ask me."

"I was afraid to ask because I knew the answer."

"But we are still friends. I need you in my life." She took his hand. It was pleasantly warm, strong, like Mark himself.

"Is there someone else?" He needed to know the truth so he could give up hope.

Caroline thought seriously about his question. She thought about Jim and what was happening between them. It was exciting, nice, lovely. But was it the real thing?

She lifted her shoulder in a gesture that spoke words. "Maybe," she said.

Mark got up and poured a glass of the champagne left over from earlier that evening, when he'd still had hope.

"You'd better make a success of that restaurant," he warned and they both laughed.

chapter 77

To Caroline's surprise, when they arrived back at London's Heathrow Airport, Georgki was waiting for them. "Jim was going to pick you up, but last minute could not," he said, putting his arms carefully round Caroline so their bodies did not touch. As though he was afraid of her she thought, kissing his cheek. And maybe he was.

"Well, I'm glad it's you, Georgki," she said, as he hefted their bags from the luggage trolley into the back of the Hummer. "There's nobody else whose smiling face I would rather see."

She got into the front seat next to Georgki, turning automatically to check Issy. "Seat belt?" she asked.

Issy sighed loudly. Her mother always asked that.

"It's only because I care," Caroline told her serenely.

"Mom, of course I've fastened my seat belt. You don't have to ask me anymore, I always do and I always will."

"And I'll still ask," Caroline said, and then without waiting for the expected question answered, "Just because."

Issy rolled her eyes. "Because *what*?"

"Because I'm a mom and that's what moms have to do. Get a handle on it, Issy, after all these years I thought you would have realized that."

Georgki threw her a nervous look, worried they were having a fight.

Caroline threw him a nervous look back; shouldn't he be keeping his eyes on the road? She sighed and closed her eyes, deciding to allow her daughter and Georgki to take care of themselves for the moment. It had been an emotional few days, she was just off a long-haul flight and was exhausted. And of course, she thought repentantly, so was Issy, and now *she* was being bitchy with her. "Sorry," she called without opening her eyes but Issy was already asleep. And soon, so was Caroline.

They woke though, when Georgki turned off the motorway. Issy yawned and ruffled her hair.

"There you are," Caroline said, turning to look at her.

"You were sleeping too." Issy gave her mother's shoulder an affectionate pat. She looked at Georgki, at his stern face and his big hands clamped on the wheel, at the sheer height and size of him. He could play the bad guy in any movie.

"You know you're really *scary,* Georgki," she said.

Caroline frowned at her and she added quickly, "I mean you're just so big and you don't smile . . . much."

Georgki shrugged. "Is only I am Russian."

"From Estonia," Caroline informed Issy.

"From Serbia," he corrected.

"Right. Serbia." She would never get his story straight and nor, she suspected, would he.

He said, "I'm sorry, if I scare you. I care very much for you and your mother. I am good friend."

"You *are* my good friend." Caroline patted the hand nearest to her. "And you always will be." Mark and Georgki, she was thinking, two "friends" in love with me.

Issy was checking out the two of them, wondering. Her mother couldn't possibly have a thing going with Georgki, could she? Bloody hell, she hoped not! *No,* she told herself, *no, she can't.* If anybody it's Jim, who must be half her age anyway. She sat back in her seat, wondering morosely how to deal with her mother.

Georgki parked in front of the pub and took care of their bags while Issy barged inside. Caroline followed, remembering the two of them arriving at the pub that first night. She realized how much their lives had changed. They had new friends, family, affection, warmth, a security of the heart she had never known before.

Cassandra was behind the bar wearing a black low-cut V-necked dress that could only be called a "barmaid outfit." She was leaning on one elbow as she pushed a pint across to a very interested older man, a widower whom Caroline recognized, and who she knew lived in the Old Rectory with a married daughter and her husband and small child.

They were so caught up in their conversation her mother didn't even notice them, until Issy yelled, "Here I am," and almost galloped across the room and into her grandmother's welcoming arms.

Cassandra kissed her and said, "Get out of this bar, you're not allowed in here," gave her a pat on the rear and walked over to greet her own daughter, while Issy ran off to see Sam.

"You look tired," she said, holding her at arm's length for an inspection, the way she had ever since Caroline was a little girl. "But wonderful," she added. "As though everything is right in your world. Is it now?"

Caroline nodded. "Yes, I think so. Our world seems pretty good to me right now."

Maggie came out from the kitchen. "I missed you," she said. "And I wasn't the only one."

She gave Caroline a meaningful smile but Caroline pretended not to know what she meant and they both laughed. The regulars in the pub waved hello and even Frisky ambled over for a pat and a sniff. Then Georgki came in with the bags, and then they went into the kitchen where Jesus got the wine open and Sarah wanted to show her the pies she'd made. She would be moving into the cottage tomorrow, if that was all right with Caroline. Blind Brenda went and sat on the table in the middle of everything, then Little Billy gave a wail, seeking attention which he got immediately from both Issy and Sam, and Caroline thanked God Lily was not there tonight to drop plates.

It was, though, she thought, almost perfect.

chapter 78

Everybody's heads turned later, when Jim walked in, all except the dog Frisky, whose head stayed on its paws, though it did lift an eyelid to check him out. Jim stopped to give it a pat, said good evening to the other customers, and ordered half a bitter from Cassandra at the bar. He bought a chicken taco and threw it for the dog, who caught it in one lightning move, chomped, swallowed, and settled back down, head on paws again. There was a round of applause and laughter and Jim took a bow.

"Hi," he said to Cassandra. "I saw Georgki's Hummer outside, thought the travelers must be back by now."

"They are, and I'll bet *you're* glad." Cassandra pulled his beer gently so the foam could subside.

"What makes you think that?"

She shoved the beer across the counter and gave him a steady look that meant she knew what she was talking about. "Just you be careful with her," she warned, but she was smiling as she said it and Jim breathed again.

He was in love with Caroline; he had not stopped thinking about her; he was enraptured with her, for want of a better word . . .

actually *enraptured* was a very good word, it described exactly the way he felt. He was under some kind of spell.

Cassandra said, "Caroline's in the kitchen. It's a bit crowded in there so I'll go get her."

She disappeared through the swing door and minutes later Jesus emerged and took over the bar. He and Jim said hello and passed the usual time about the weather and business, then the door swung open and there Caroline was.

"Hi," she said. Jim thought it was the most wonderful word he'd ever heard.

"Hi, yourself," he replied, as she came closer. So close he could smell her perfume. "What is that?" he asked, nuzzling her neck.

"It's called So Pretty," she told him and he said he agreed *she* was. "Can I give you a lift home?" he asked, still not taking his eyes off hers.

"What about your beer?" She saw he had hardly touched it.

He shook his head, it didn't matter.

He held out his hand and she took it.

They didn't even notice the curious glances that followed them all the way to the door and missed the buzz of interested speculation about them afterwards. Anyway, they wouldn't have cared.

Caroline sat demurely next to Jim while he drove. They barely spoke, only a quick question from him about her trip and her answer that she was exhausted.

He drove past the manor and down the lane and she was home. Cassandra had seen to it that lights were left on and the old barn looked squat, solid and welcoming, settled in by the river.

"It looks like home," Caroline said, making no move to get out.

"I don't suppose you'd feel like a walk?" he said. "There's a full moon. My grandfather used to call this a 'bombers' moon' in World War Two, not that they had many bombers this far from London."

Caroline turned to look at him thinking she knew so little about him; about his family; who he *really* was. What she did know was, he was only twenty-seven and single, and she was thirty-eight going on -nine, married, divorced, and with a child. She told herself this could go nowhere, and that it should *not* go anywhere. But she still said, "I'd love to go for a walk, get some fresh air."

Jim hurried round to open the truck's door. He put his hands on her waist to help her jump down, sliding them up over her rib cage, holding her steady. Electricity, that sparkle Caroline had always looked for, flashed between them. They stood for a second, eyes linked; he let go and took her hand.

"The river's beautiful in the moonlight," he told her. "We used to come and swim here when we were kids, there's a little tributary that forms a pool, deep enough to dive in off the rocks."

"Scary," Caroline said with a shiver that made him want to put his arm round her again. "I hate all those weeds that float and reach out to entangle you."

"I promise not to allow them to entangle you."

They took the path that led from her terrace along the riverbank, disturbing a duck, that set off a racket of quacking, then there was only the rustle of their feet on the grass, the run of the river, somewhere a cow coughed.

They stopped and took off their shoes and walked barefoot until they came to the pool. Dark and smooth, it glimmered in the moonlight.

Jim led her onto the grassy bank above the pool. He said, "Come, let's sit here."

Caroline eyed the grass dubiously. "Do you think the cows were here?"

Jim laughed, delighted. "I didn't know you were that practical," he said, pulling her down with him. "No cows have ever been here, this is virgin territory."

Caroline thought if anyone felt "like a virgin" it was her. Madonna certainly knew what she was talking about, and she'd bet Madonna would not have been able to resist Jim's arms pulling her to him, nor his mouth covering hers in a long kiss, the kind of kiss she had kept in her memory because she'd told herself she would never feel it again. *Liar,* she told herself now. *Oh wonderful, wonderful liar.*

"I'm too old for this," she told him when he lifted his face from hers.

"Too old for what?" He was unbuttoning her shirt and she was letting him . . . so much for all the sex talks she had just given Issy, the condoms and the cucumbers, and about her head being involved as well as her body. Had she even mentioned anything about the heart? Hers was thundering as Jim slid her arms out of the sleeves, then took off his own shirt and wrapped her in a close embrace.

Caroline ran a hand down his back, she could feel the ridges of his muscles, the smoothness of his skin. His hands were on her breasts, his mouth so tender as he took her nipples, she flung back her head and allowed the moment to take her. Then she was lying on her back in the cool grass and his body was covering hers and he was kissing her again.

He held himself up on his arms to look at her. "You're beautiful, you know that," he said. "Lovely. And I'm in love with you."

She wondered, Did *in love with her* mean the same as *I love you*?

"I'm *enraptured* by you," he added, making her laugh.

"And I'm enraptured by you," she said, "I must be, just look at me lying on my back, half naked in the grass, out in the open air . . ."

"Let's try for full naked," he said.

Caroline hadn't remembered she could get out of her clothes

so quickly, and anyhow thanked heaven for the forgiving moonlight. She was nervous about him looking at her body.

"You have a wonderful bottom," he said, cupping it in both hands. "*Wonderful.*" He opened her legs, put his hand there, and heard her moan. "Like a flower," he said, touching her, bending his head over her. "It's like unfolding rose petals."

Caroline lay on her back, staring up at the stars and then the stars were exploding; she was in another world, one she half-remembered, but now thought heaven must be something like this. "Heaven," she murmured later, in between kisses. "Tell me this is what heaven is like."

Had she made love for hours? she asked herself a long time later. She had fallen asleep in his arms at some point, and then woken up "enraptured" again? It didn't seem to matter; he was a wonderful lover—an indefatigable *young* lover, she reminded herself. And she was the older woman whose body still tingled with the remembered pleasure of the feel of him hard inside her.

They were lying side by side on the grass, holding hands. The moon was a lot lower in the sky than it had been.

Jim sat up and looked at her. Uncomfortable, she crossed her arms over her breasts which left the rest of her exposed and she giggled, not quite knowing what to do.

"You don't have to cover up," he said. "I've seen everything." He laughed as he stood up, naked and so goddamn sleekly beautiful with his tight muscular body she wanted him all over again. "Let's go for that swim," he said, pulling her up.

"But the weeds," Caroline protested.

"There are no weeds, and if there were I would save you from them."

He stood posed at the edge, then dived in. Without a second's more thought, she followed him. She cried out, the pool was icy . . . delicious. They swam side by side across and back again.

"Happy?" Jim asked, taking her in his arms under the water.

"Happy," she agreed. After all, life was meant to be lived in the moment. Wasn't it?

chapter 79

That same night, back at the Star & Plough, Issy and Sam lay in bed talking with the lights out and Blind Brenda making her purr sound, curled between their pillows. The curtains were open and so was the window and moonlight poured in, along with a warm breeze.

"Missed you," Sam said.

"Missed you too," Issy said.

"I missed you more."

"You did not!"

They laughed and the cat, disturbed, swatted at them.

"Ow." Issy rubbed her head. "I'd forgotten how touchy she is."

Sam said, "I heard that guy Alex is going out with a girl from St. Mary's."

Issy knew the school she was talking about. "She must be older then," she said. "At least eighteen." She thought about the night of her party and her talk with her mother, and felt thankful for her reprieve. "He's just some guy," she said, forgiving Alex for coming on to her, because after all she had met him halfway. "He needs an older woman."

Sam giggled and told her some more gossip about their school friends. It was so comfortable, so homey, so back-where-she-belonged, Issy almost forgot about Singapore and Asia.

"She's such a nice little kid," she said suddenly to Sam.

She had no need to explain what she really meant; they always knew what the other was talking about, sort of like texting.

"Little *sister,* you mean," Sam corrected her, leaning on an elbow to look at her friend. "I was worried when you were gone, I thought you'd be jealous, I mean about your father going off with somebody else and having Asia."

"She's nice and so's her mother Melanie." Issy didn't say "my father's lover" but she thought about it and was glad Caroline had told her how much she and her father had loved each other when *she* was born.

"It's over about my dad and her, at least for me it is. I won't think about it so much anymore. And at least I have a sister."

"And a friend," Sam said. Issy thought she sounded a little bit jealous. She took her hand to make sure she was all right. Blind Brenda was jealous too, and pushed her way from the pillows and stretched lengthways in between them.

"If Blind Brenda were fatter she'd look like one of those plush pajama cases you zip up the belly," Sam said, making them giggle.

But then Issy fell silent, thinking about her mother, and the barn and the restaurant plans. Caroline was getting old, she'd be thirty-nine next birthday, and still struggling to get her life in order. Alone. Dreaming her dreams with no one to help her. Well, only Cassandra and Grandpa but they lived in France and would soon go back there. It was as though things suddenly went into reverse in Issy's mind and she knew that instead of her mother always looking after *her,* it was now her responsibility to look after Caroline, to help her, make sure she was all right, and that she was never "alone."

"I really have to go home," she said to Sam, meaning the barn.

"I wondered when you'd come around to it." Sam leaned on her elbow again, looking at her. "I'll miss you," she said.

"I'll miss you more."

"No you won't."

They collapsed into giggles and Blind Brenda swatted at them again, making them laugh even more.

chapter 80

The next morning Caroline woke in her own bed. They had walked back along that riverside path, barefoot, holding hands, dazed with sexual longing, touching, affectionate, stopping to kiss. Light kisses though; nothing too passionate, they were too worn out. At least Caroline was. Fatigue had hit her hard; Singapore; the meeting with Asia's mother; the long-haul flight back . . . the empty barn . . . and her overwhelming desire for Jim Thompson, he of the lovely body and sensual mouth that knew exactly what to do with her. He'd begged to be allowed to stay, to sleep with her, wake with her in his arms but she couldn't let him. She had to think of her daughter, as well as her reputation.

They had kissed goodnight—or good morning, at her door, then she'd climbed the stairs to her room, she'd pulled off her clothes once again and fallen into bed. What woke her later was the spurt of gravel as a vehicle meandered up her drive. She climbed out of bed, got her head together and went to the window to look.

It was a delivery truck and two men were already manhandling an enormous wooden crate down the ramp. She quickly climbed into her jeans and a T-shirt and ran to open the door.

"Ms. Evans?" The truck driver checked his invoice, then her.

"Right, that's me. What is it though?"

"Furniture, ma'am. From Singapore it says here."

Of course! It must be the console tables and the other things Mark had kept from her old apartment. She tipped the driver and his mate to lever open the two crates for her. They dumped the two narrow nineteenth-century elmwood consoles and the Chinese chairs in the restaurant, and left her to deal with them.

Excited, she put both tables against the wall opposite the windows that led to the terrace, then stood back to take in the effect. Their simple elegance was beautiful against the rough stone. She thought Jim would appreciate them.

Rummaging through the crates, she found the lamps that had always stood on them; tall, clear glass columns with plain cream shades, lined with gold so they gave off a warm glow.

Tired, she eyed the other bubble-wrapped packages still in the crates, debating the merits of a cup of breakfast coffee. Coffee won and she went to the kitchen to fix it, praying it wouldn't rain until she had time to get everything out of the crates and into the house.

She had just poured the first cup when Maggie drove up.

"Thought I'd get here before your ma and pa," she said, hugging Caroline then holding her away to get a better look.

"Smug," she said. "That's how I'd say you look."

"What *smug*?" Caroline grinned, lifting a shoulder in a who-cares little shrug. "Okay, so I'm smug. Very happily smug, if you want to know."

"Oh, I do, *I do*." Maggie got a mug from the shelf and poured herself some coffee. "Sit. Tell me all." She patted the chair next to her and Caroline sat.

"Mags," she said. "I was absolutely shameless, and I loved every minute of it and I want to do it all over again. He's beautiful, perfect, and I haven't felt like this since . . ."

"Don't even mention his name, you'll spoil it."

"You know how it is, Mags, when a man looks at you, when he kind of holds you with his eyes . . ."

"And you couldn't let go."

"Should I have?"

Maggie considered while she sipped her coffee. "Truthfully," she said, "I don't see any reason you should. And nor, probably, did most of the customers at the pub last night. You two made quite an exit," she reminded her.

Caroline grinned. "I told you, *shameless*," she said and they both laughed. "Just between you and me, Mags," Caroline lowered her voice and leaned in closer, as though someone might overhear, "I asked myself before . . . you know, well *before* I ripped off my clothes."

"You *ripped* them *off*?"

"Well, Jim started and then I went on . . . or *off* I suppose you might say. But I did ask myself how I felt about him, you know, with my head, my heart, and not just my body. And I do care about him, Mags. I might even love him. I'm just not sure yet. But I am *involved*. Totally. Completely. Absolutely. Right now, anyway."

"Then you were right to take what he offered and give him what you offered. Not many people get to feel that way in life, in fact some go through their *whole* lives without ever feeling that kind of passion."

"Jim said he was in love with me." Caroline looked searchingly at Maggie. "I know that doesn't mean the same thing as 'I love you.' Does it?"

Maggie set down her cup, exasperated.

"Caroline Evans, you are a thirty-eight-year-old woman who just had great sex with a man she cares about and who cares about her. You are not a teenager, you don't need instructions in life. Haven't you learned by now that the course of life and true love cannot be planned? Take it for what it is right now, and let the future take care of itself. Somehow, it always does you know," she added.

They heard the sound of a car on the drive and recognized the trundling weight of the Hummer.

"Here's Georgki." Caroline got up and was going to the door just as he drew up behind the open crates. "Oh, he's brought Sarah and Little Billy," she cried, spotting them wedged in the back amid a load of plastic bags and cardboard boxes. "Of course, she's moving in today."

Georgki got out first, then Sarah handed him Little Billy in his car seat, then she climbed out too.

"I hope we're not too early," she called. "I wanted to get away before that bastard landlord came and forcibly ejected me. I mean, I've paid my rent and all that, he just wants to move the new people in because they'll pay more. *And* the roof leaks," she added, picking up Little Billy and depositing him on the doorstep. He gazed up at them, and kicked his socked feet, chewing on a rusk, dribbling happily. "Teething," Sarah explained, just as another car turned into the drive.

Caroline recognized her parents' rental and told Maggie they'd better put on some more coffee. She waved, then took another look. Could that be *Issy* with them?

"Hi, Mom." Issy wriggled out of the backseat then leaned in to get her bag. "Thought you might need some help. So, here I am."

For a moment Caroline was speechless: her daughter was *here,* at the barn she despised, the place she was never going to live, that would never be her home . . . *and* she was offering to help . . .

She told herself not to make too much of it, play it cool, like it was normal, an everyday occasion . . . She said, "Well, wonderful. All hands on deck."

"Grist to the mill," Issy retorted, and they both laughed. "You are silly, Mom," Issy said. "Nobody else talks like you do, you know, with all those silly sayings."

"I got it from your grandfather." Caroline grabbed her daughter in a hug, savoring the perfume of her just-shampooed hair and her clean fresh skin. It reminded her of when Issy was a baby.

"I'll take my bag up," Issy said. "By the way, Cassandra and Grandpa can have my room, I'll sleep on the couch."

"Oh, but . . ." Caroline started to say, but her mother held up a warning hand.

"Take what you can get, when you can get it," Cassandra said. "It won't always be like this. Things will get back to normal before you know it."

"*Normal?*"

"Like Issy rebelling and you two butting heads. *That normal.*"

Another truck chugged along the lane. It went past her turnoff and had to back up, making Caroline wonder if the Place in the Country sign Jim had made was big enough after all. Then it swung into the driveway and parked in back of her parents' car, which was parked in back of the Hummer, behind Maggie's truck, and the two massive wooden crates.

It was her other furniture! Her "ghost" chairs. Her tables. The makings of her restaurant!

"Better come on in and have some coffee," she told the delivery men as they swung open the back and began to haul stuff out. "Everybody else is."

She walked into her suddenly busy house, people hanging around, chatting, enjoying the morning, enjoying themselves. Everybody was there, she thought, smiling. *Except Jim.*

chapter 81

Jim could not get Caroline out of his mind; sleep had not found him the way he knew it must have her; he was too keyed up, too excited by her. It wasn't only her lovely body and the way she had responded to him, not in the knowing way some women he had known had, asking *would you like me to do this, does this excite you,* telling him what and how they wanted it.

He had been in love a couple of times before. Two to be exact. The first was when he was eighteen and she was seventeen. His sister called them the "Romeo and Juliet" of their year, because they were both still in school and looked too young to know what love was. But then of course, the young always knew what love was when it smote them over the head. It had gone the way of most young love when they had moved on to different colleges, and distance parted them.

Experience followed experience; girlfriends were just that until a few years later he'd met the girl of his dreams. They had been so wrapped up in their passion for each other, nothing else mattered. He'd thought this was it, he could never live without her, and he asked her to marry him. She said no. Turned him down flat. "I love you," she said, "but I'm not the type to be buried in the country, I don't ride, I don't garden, and most of all, I don't cook." She had gone on to become a quite famous movie actress, almost a star, and was married to a famous actor. At least right now, she was. You never knew with her, the press said: Jim guessed they were right.

And now there was Caroline.

He'd decided he'd walk over to the barn, see if she was up yet, see how she was feeling—about him especially.

He came to Caroline's turnoff where the sign he'd carved for her as a surprise swung from a wrought-iron hook hitched onto the old dry stone wall. The cows were back in the meadow, tearing great tongues-full of grass and he smiled, remembering telling Caroline the grassy bank was "virgin cow territory" because she was worried about cowpats.

He'd remembered he'd had to take off her glasses and put them in his pocket . . . she was so blind without them, she probably couldn't even see him, but it hadn't mattered. There was just the sweet dampness of the grass, the shimmer of the pool in the moonlight, the rustle of the trees. It wasn't only great sex, he told himself, it was the emotion, the tenderness, as well as the passion.

He parked behind all the other cars and he spotted Issy and Sam sitting on the doorstep with Little Billy in his chair between them. He also saw two enormous wooden crates and Georgki's Hummer, and remembered Sarah was moving in today. And wasn't that Maggie's truck? And the parents' car?

He stood for a moment undecided, this might be the wrong time. But looking at the packing cases, he thought she might need some help. He and Georgki could take care of everything. Anyhow, he couldn't just leave, because now the girls had seen him and were waving.

"Morning, girls," he said, stepping past them and over Little Billy whose head rotated to watch him.

"Morning everybody," he said again, walking into the wanna-be restaurant, where "everybody" was standing around with mugs of coffee in their hands, admiring a couple of exceptional elmwood tables that he'd bet were nineteenth-century Chinese and crafted by someone who knew what he was doing.

"Perfect," he said, looking at Caroline.

"Just in time to help," she said, smiling into his eyes in a way that locked out everyone else in the room. He definitely liked it.

chapter 82

It was Maggie who, a week later, suggested Caroline should have a practice run and invite friends and the locals who had helped her, to a special dinner at A Place in the Country.

Caroline looked doubtfully round her restaurant. An upholstered taupe banquette was now installed against the far wall, long enough to accommodate four tables; two tables would seat four and two were for couples. There was a long low mirror behind, French brasserie style, so guests sitting facing the wall could still catch all the action in the rest of the room.

The other tables were mostly for four but could easily be adapted for two, or added to to seat six, or even eight at a pinch, because flexibility, Caroline had been told, was essential. You had to think of groups as well as couples having a night out, Cassandra had explained. Of course Caroline should have remembered that, she had been to enough good restaurants in her life, but she needed that extra help in thinking right now because she had so much on her mind.

Her see-through lucite Ghost armchairs had had their backs upholstered in the same taupe that played so well off the honey-color stone walls, with matching seat cushions. As yet there were no table-cloths, no lamps, no votives, no flowers. Even the tables under the new coffee-colored awning on the terrace were bare naked. Caroline's heart sank. The place felt suddenly "empty" and not just because there were no customers. Somewhere, it had lost its "soul."

"I can't ask anybody here," she said to Maggie, "it's not ready. And I don't know how to make it 'ready,' and I never will. I've lost it, Mags, and so has my Place in the Country. Oh, I know how to cook and I know what I want to cook but I have no experience and, Mags, I'm scared."

"That's exactly why you have to do it." Maggie scowled at her. "Get yourself together, Caroline," she said firmly. "Your future depends on this."

Of course it did. Once again she was the one in charge. "So what'll I do?" she asked.

"First you decide who you're inviting, then decide on your menu, and when you do remember *who* you are cooking for and what they would like to eat, and get cracking. Friday will be a good night, people are always eager to get out at the beginning of the weekend."

"Friday! But that's three days away! *Oh my God,*" Caroline said feeling faint at the thought.

"You getting religious or something?" Maggie went to the door and flagged down Sarah who was walking across the drive with Little Billy strapped to her chest, carrying a bunch of flowers picked from the hedgerow. "Opening night, Friday," Maggie called to her. "You ready?"

"Wow!" Sarah's eyes opened wider and she pushed a hand worriedly through her pale blond hair. "Sure," she said, uncertainly. "Of course," she added, eyeing Caroline who looked as worried as Sarah felt. "We can do it." She gave Caroline an encouraging smile.

"We'll do the cheese soufflés for a starter." Caroline made a sudden decision and immediately felt better.

"Isn't that a bit ambitious?" Now it was Maggie who was getting worried.

"Not the way I do them, it's not," Caroline said. "Come on, let's get my mother and Issy and get to work."

Of course her partner Mark was the first person she phoned to tell him of the opening night, and of course he agreed to come.

By Wednesday all the necessary ingredients were purchased, save for the salad and vegs, which would be delivered fresh-picked from the local smallholder Friday morning. By Thursday, the tables were covered in taupe-colored cloths (the hell with the laundry cost, Caroline told herself she would just have to build it into the price) and laid with large bronze-color chargers and the mismatched but lovely old cutlery, rescued from a restaurant auction. Pale robin's-egg-blue plates went on top of the bronze chargers; old-fashioned cobalt blue glass salt and peppers; a flat pale blue bowl in which to float a single flower; and small clear crystal holders for sepia votives.

After a quick visit from the electrician, the amber wall sconces suddenly worked and Caroline's lamps lent a warm glow. The cream canvas sail billowed in the breeze coming from the open French doors, while out on the terrace, amber globe lanterns had been slung from beams and brackets and in the trees. Caroline had flung cushions on the riverside wall and set the tables with the added luxury of an inexpensive pashmina draped over the chair arm in case the breeze got a bit much later.

By Friday evening all was ready; the *mise-en-place* with its stainless steel bowls of diced onion, celery, carrot; the breads that came from Wright's bakery, the good sweet butter stamped with the image of a cow in small brown bowls. Cloves of garlic, pots of fresh herbs and containers of dried ones; the salt, the pepper, the flour. There was a basket of tiny pansies, as well as sprigs of thyme and rosemary to decorate the finished plates.

Remembering she was cooking for locals and friends, Caroline tailored her menu accordingly: nothing too experimental, she needed to "get her hand in," and so did her guests. Besides, simple food was always *good,* and often more enjoyable than the more daring techno-gastronomy of the new young chefs.

She had made a sorrel soup, a delicate darkish green, to be served with a tiny pale-orange scallop floating in the center, so sweet it still smelled of the bay where it had been that morning.

The "special" cheese soufflé mixture waited in the refrigerator, and small dishes already buttered and dusted with grated Parmesan rested on baking trays, ready to be filled and put in the oven for half an hour. Salad greens crisped; asparagus waited to be rolled lightly in olive oil, dusted with salt and pepper and more of that good Parmesan and then also put in the oven for ten minutes or so. Grated courgettes had been sliced, sautéed in butter, salted, peppered, a hint of dill, and whipped lightly with a dollop of cream. Peas, fresh from the garden, awaited a brief dousing in the minimum of sugared water; a couscous "salad" with fresh spinach and Meyer lemons smelled so fragrant several people had already tested a spoonful in passing. Wild rice had been cooked and then mixed with tiny stewed tomatoes and now brewed slowly in the oven. And in a pan with lid firmly on, were the smallest new potatoes cooking gently in only a knob of butter.

Chocolate brownies, made by Cassandra, had been frosted with even more chocolate, and Caroline had made the French pear tart she had learned in French cooking school, and had been famous for at dinner parties in Singapore.

For the main course, Dublin Bay shrimp, the colossal kind, were to be floured, and sautéed with garlic, shallots, and white wine; and chateaubriand steak was being kept at room temperature, to be anointed with oil and salt and pepper, quickly browned, then roasted for barely twenty minutes, then sliced and served with a sauce prepared by Caroline, spiked with champagne because that's what she was drinking at the time. And, most exotic and a true test of something "new" for her guests, were her own handmade fine rice noodles, served with tiny marinated shrimp and spicy chicken, and the special Singapore hawker-style seasonings Mark had sent her.

Two waitresses had been hired away from the local tea shop for the night and were specially outfitted in taupe cotton aprons. Issy and Sam were still hustling anxiously round the room, checking that every knife and fork was set at exactly the correct angle. They were to act as "busboys," in copper-colored T-shirts and black jeans, and wore sneakers so they wouldn't slip.

Cassandra was hostess and greeter in her black "barmaid" low-cut dress that Caroline told her would wow the men, at which Cassandra simply smiled and said "Great." Of course she wore her kitten heels too.

Henry in black cords and a white shirt was in charge of wine. Georgki, in a blue pinstripe suit, was already out in the lane ready to direct traffic, and Jim waited outside the door, in jeans and a blue shirt, ready to valet park. "Think they'll tip?" he asked Cassandra with a grin.

"If they do it goes in the tip pot, and everybody gets a share." Cassandra knew her stuff. And she also knew Jim was dying to be with Caroline, who with only ten minutes to go, was up in her room with Sarah, getting into their new "chef's" suits.

"I hate these pants," Caroline said, scowling at herself in the mirror. They were polyester with an ugly black and white pattern and drooped over her bum.

"They make me look fat," Sarah agreed.

Of course nothing could make Sarah look "fat," but anyhow they decided against them and opted instead for black yoga pants. Caroline lent Sarah a pair, and then they put on their new white cotton double-breasted chef's jackets.

"Top two buttons left open, like Gordon Ramsay," Caroline instructed. She enjoyed seeing her name and rank, EXECUTIVE CHEF CAROLINE EVANS, embroidered in blue. This was the real thing. No getting away from it now.

Sarah ran a finger over her own name, and her title, CHEF. "How did this happen to me?" she asked, awed.

"All I know is we had better live up to it," Caroline said, as they put on their white chef's clogs and headed down to the kitchen.

Caroline paused at the door. She looked at her restaurant. At the beginning of her dream. Votives flickered on the tables, lamps cast a glow against the stone walls, and globes of golden light illuminated the terrace. The lovely old stone, the taupe cloths, the robin's-egg-blue plates, the shining cutlery, the river drifting past, the breeze just stirring . . . the scent of food coming from her kitchen, the sound of a champagne cork popping, and then the gravel spurting as the first car arrived. And the old sign over the barn door. *Bar, Grill and Dancing.*

This was the real thing. No getting away from it now. This was her new beginning. And she was ready.

A PLACE IN THE COUNTRY
Grand Opening Dinner Menu

❧

Red's individual cheese soufflés

OR

Rosette's sorrel soup with scallop

OR

Caroline's butter lettuce salad with frisée

❧

Piazza Navona colossal shrimp with shallots in white wine, served with wild rice and roasted asparagus.

OR

Richard's roasted chateaubriand finished with a champagne sauce and served with the newest of new potatoes, fresh spinach, and lemon couscous and new peas.

OR

Mark's favorite fresh-made noodles in the true style of Singapore with Dublin Bay shrimp, spicy chicken, and sautéed vegetables, served with a creamy side dish of special courgettes.

❧

Cassandra's chocolate fudge brownies with butter icing

OR

Caroline's French pear tart with almond crust and Devon cream.

❧

Coffee and brandy snap tuiles

❧

Wines

Rosé Champagne
Chardonnay from Bordeaux (just to be different!)
Napa Valley, USA, Cabernet
Monbazillac dessert wine

❧

With respects to Julia, bon appétit from Executive Chef, Caroline Evans, and Chef Sarah

Turn the page for a sneak peek at
Elizabeth Adler's new novel

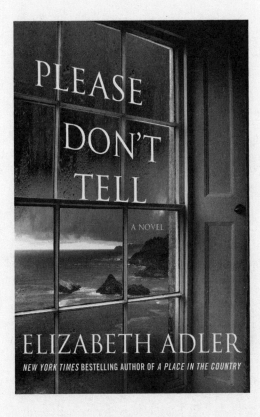

Available Summer 2013

Prologue

It was a winter afternoon, and a stormy sky was looming. The man was waiting in the black Range Rover, parked in the darkest part of the coffee shop lot away from the lights, when he felt the pain again. A pressure in his chest, a floating sensation in his head, only a few seconds, though. The first time he'd felt that was when he'd lifted a table to move it to a more prominent position. Fool; he should have known better. He must have pulled a shoulder muscle and now it was acting up, just when he needed to be at his best. His brain cleared, the pain left. He forgot about it and concentrated on the work at hand.

The lot was almost empty, just a couple of vehicles belonging, he knew, to the kitchen staff. Customers always parked round the front. It was one of a popular chain in California, right off Highway 1, south of San Francisco. He knew exactly what time the girl's shift finished, knew how she would burst out of the staff door, bubbling with laughter and relief at getting out of there, sometimes with others, but more often on her own. He knew her car was the ten-year-old Chevy Blazer that often broke down and for which she had no insurance, and which she always left in the same spot in back of the café so no nosy cop, dropping in for a cup of coffee and pancakes with phony maple syrup, would take notice of and maybe ask questions about a vehicle that looked as crappy as that.

He knew exactly where she lived. In fact he knew exactly what her small studio apartment looked like. He had been there, easily forcing the cheap lock when she was at work, looking round, touching her things, inspecting the tiny bathroom and the plastic shower stall with the plastic curtain that must have stuck to her naked body when she took her shower. He had run his tongue over her toothbrush, sniffed the underpants she'd left on the floor with the rest of her clothing, exactly where she'd stepped out of them the previous night. He had lain down on her unmade bed, rested his head on her pillow, surprised to find the sheets were clean. She was not a dirty girl, just sloppy and untidy and careless.

He'd marked her as his victim when he had gone into the coffee shop and she had made eye contact, ready to flirt with a customer in the hope of a good tip, though any tip she'd get was probably negligible. He'd liked her fresh clean skin, the pinkness of her cheeks, flushed from rushing between the customer and the kitchen. She worked hard, she was willing. Her name was Elaine. It said so on the badge pinned to her shirt and she was pretty enough to qualify. He had even chatted to her, learned she had quit community college where she had been studying, of all things, biology. She'd said cheerfully she would go back there when she could afford it, which both he and she knew meant never. Still, he liked her plumpness, her long brown hair, her brown eyes and pink cheeks and her jolly girl demeanor. He always liked the nice girls best.

Now he saw her come bursting out the staff door. Alone. She was wearing a black skirt, a too-thin black jacket. He put on his fine, supple latex gloves, got quickly out of his car, called her name. "Elaine." She turned, surprised. He knew she couldn't make out who he was, in the shade.

"My door seems to have stuck, could you help me?" he called, just loud enough, that, thinking she must know him, she came.

He liked the hurried way she walked, half-running.

Her long brown hair swung over her face as she neared. In one smooth move he grabbed it in his fist and slammed the side of his hand hard on the carotid. She went limp and he pushed her into the car, flung her handbag in after her. In seconds he was out of the lot and onto the highway.

He looked at her in the mirror, facedown on the plastic cover he had carefully arranged so that his leather seat would not get stained. She was not moving. At the next exit, he pulled off the road into a quiet place, got out and checked her. She was still breathing. Low hurting breaths. He'd hit her exactly hard enough. He knew what he was doing. He'd done it all before. He stuck a needle in her arm; a quick shot to make sure she would not wake suddenly and surprise him. Her erratic breathing slowed.

He got back into the car and drove on. He'd already picked out the place he was taking her, on the edge of some woods. When he got there he sat for a moment or two, anticipating what was to come. No rain yet, only the harsh sound of the wind gusting in the trees, presaging a storm and sending a shower of leaves over him and the car, and over the girl as he opened the back door. It was still light out but dark in the woods.

He took out the lightweight black messenger bag containing the small video camera, its tripod and his night-vision binoculars—his "equipment" he called it—and slung it round his neck. He pulled the girl out of the car and carried her into the woods . . . not too far, no need . . . nobody ever came here. His heart gave a little bump again: she was heavier than he'd thought.

There was a method to these things, a ritual he had to respect. Everything must be in sequence. He spread-eagled her on a pile of rotting leaves. Nice and soft. He thought she would like that. Next, he took the tripod and the video camera from the messenger bag and set them up next to her, making sure to get her properly in focus. He pulled on the black woolen ski mask, covering his face. Now, he was ready. It was the work of moments to undress her, tugging off her skirt, her white shirt, her underwear. She was not wearing a bra and her small breasts looked very white in the dense blackness.

He pulled the knife from its custom-made leather sheath that he wore strapped to his leg. It was a slim fileting knife, around eight inches long, the kind used by chefs. Pure, hard gleaming steel. Power in the hands of a man who knew exactly how to use it.

Kneeling over her, with surgical precision he slit each of her wrists, then sat back watching the blood ooze, her life begin to drift slowly away. She had not opened her eyes. The supreme moment was almost here. All it would take was one more cut, soft as butter, across her throat. She was limp, unresisting as he raped her, the knife at her throat, just the first small incision . . . waiting . . . waiting . . . he groaned in triumph, slid the knife across her throat, saw the blood spill though she wasn't dead yet . . .

He sat back exhausted. There was nothing to equal that moment, that feeling. The sheer sexual power of it. There was one last thing though; something else he was compelled to do. He took the green Post-it pad from his pocket and using his left hand, printed out a message.

He checked her again. Her mouth hung open. He snapped her jaw shut, then he stuck the green Post-it over her closed lips, added a strip of duct tape, just to make sure it didn't fall off. He had the knife on her neck again; he knew where the carotid was.

He thought he heard something, sat back startled. He had not finished yet . . . A car stopped, then started up again. Unnerved, he grabbed the camera and the bag, crouched low, made a run for it . . . The pain hit his chest and his heart thundered so loud he could hear it, a million beats a minute . . . he was falling into blackness with the pain . . . and the fear that he was caught . . . fear won . . .

He concentrated all his being on driving. It was raining now . . . the pain hit again, lesser this time, not really his heart, more his shoulder . . . exactly where he'd pulled the muscle yesterday, shifting that table.

Should he go to the emergency room? Why? He was fine now, breathing, okay, heart steady as a rock. It was a minor mishap and a spoiled "event." He checked the bag on the seat next to him, felt for the camera. It was there. His knife was there. Everything was okay, but it had been a close call. He would be more careful, find somewhere more remote next time.

He already had his next girl picked out. It made him feel secure, knowing the future, his plans. He'd been watching Dr. Vivian for weeks. Now though, he'd get out of here, fast, get a drink and something to eat. He was always hungry after his little "experiences." He would avoid the freeway, stick to the side roads. He hadn't reckoned on a storm, though, on the bad visibility, the sudden slickness. And then he hit something.

Big Sur, California

It had started out as an ordinary morning for Fen Dexter. She had gotten up late—nineish, something like that. It was Hector who woke her, putting his big paw on the bed, giving her a nudge and drooling on her arm. Labradors always drooled, and they always had to be let out first thing before they burst. Nine was late for Hector too. She opened the door for him, then, when he'd finished, let him in again and went back to bed, feeling lazy, just lying there listening to the boom of the waves hitting the rocks at the base of the cliffs.

Cliff Cottage, Fen's small California house, stood in what Fen had always termed "isolated splendor," on a bluff between Big Sur and the village of Carmel. The "isolated splendor" was meant as a joke since the road was a mere hundred yards away and the "cottage" was far from "splendid." It wasn't even "grand" *and* it was pale blue stucco.

It had been her home for twelve years, bought on an impulse after her husband died suddenly and to her, inexplicably because he was such a fit man, always exercising, running, he even played a three-hour game of tennis the day before. Then, after a morning cup of tea, he looked at her, surprised, she thought, and quite simply crumpled to the ground. And life as Fen knew it ended.

Greg, the "all-American boy" as she always called him teasingly, was in fact her third husband. The first had been the Frenchman, when she was twenty and making a somewhat precarious living in Paris as a dancer, on stage in stilettos and a minimal amount of sequins and wearing the short Sassoon bob wigs all the girls wore. It wasn't what she'd hoped for after all those years of ballet and training but not everyone could be a star, and she met so many people. Including the husband she only ever referred to now as "the Frenchman," the hand-holder, the gentle kisser, the leaver of romantic messages, the donator of generous bouquets of white roses. They were not her favorite flower but soon became so. He was older, thirty-five to her twenty, divorced and with baggage but he wanted to marry her and who was she to say no to a life of romance and kisses. It lasted a year. And then he was on to someone new. That's just the way he was.

The second husband was Italian-Jewish. Who knew there was such a combo? Certainly not Fen, but without any family of her own, she had fallen in love with *his* big gregarious in-your-face family that took over their lives and before she knew it she was trying to decide between a Catholic Italian ceremony or a Jewish wedding with all the trimmings. In the end they sneaked off and got married in a civil ceremony and that was that. And finally when, to their great disappointment, the expected children did not appear, the family decided it was all her fault. Fen knew from their silent looks across the table, the sudden diminishing of jolly family meals, that was what they thought, and when she finally was worried enough to get checked out, to her horror, she found they were right.

Since it was a civil marriage divorce was easy but it left Fen brokenhearted and lonely. She was alone in the world. Again.

On an impulse she flew to California, went to stay with an old friend at her small vineyard in Sonoma County. Her name was Millie, and Millie produced a Chardonnay that was just coming into fashion in the way certain wines did. Fen invested her small savings plus the money she had been awarded in her two divorces (in both of which she was the innocent party) and ultimately financially it was the saving of her. It was also where later, she met her third husband. The American.

Greg was thirty-eight, Fen was twenty-seven. She was living in San Francisco in a small pastel-color Victorian in the Mission District that was only just starting to come into its own and still had rough edges. Too rough, Fen worried sometimes, for a woman living alone. But then she didn't live alone for long. She had a part-time job at the university teaching her specialty, the evolution of dance to its modern form, while also donating her services free to an animal rescue charity, when she got the call from a Mr. Herman Wright, attorney-at-law, asking her to please come to see him. It was very important, he told her and no he could not discuss it on the phone.

Oh shit, she remembered thinking as she dressed in her most respectable outfit, black slim pants (she had good long legs) a soft white linen shirt and an Hermès orange cable cashmere sweater, a long-ago expensive gift from husband number one, when he was still courting her, that is. She powdered her nose, a daring slash of fire-engine red over her full lips, a quick flick of the brush through her golden blond hair. She took a final look in the mirror, wondering if she looked respectable enough for Mr. Herman Wright attorney-at-law and his secret message. She grinned as she waved herself good-bye. Fuck Mr. Attorney at Law. Nobody was suing her. Maybe she had come into a fabulous inheritance from some long-lost relative. Yeah. Right. A kiss for the ginger cat named Maurice who hated to be left, and she was on her way.

She took a taxi to the lawyer's, not wanting to get all mussed up on public transportation, even though she could really not afford it. Mr. Wright's offices were imposing, three floors in a good building downtown. Mr. Wright himself was not so imposing, small, square and ginger as the cat. But what he had to tell her was. It shocked her to her very core, more than anything else in her entire life.

That's what she said to him, then. "But I'm too young!"

Mr. Wright shrugged a shoulder, smoothed his floral silk tie, looked kindly at her over the breadth of his oak desk. "Many women have several children by your age, Miss Dexter." Fen had reverted to her own name after the last divorce. "Surely it can be no hardship for a healthy young woman like you to bring up two girls."

"But they are not *my* girls," she cried, shocked. "I don't have a husband! How could they do this to me!"

The "this" she was talking about and that had come at her like a bolt from the blue—not just any old bolt but a *thunderbolt*—was that a remote cousin Fen did not at first remember having, though they had met once when she was dancing in Paris (the cousin and the husband had come backstage and introduced themselves, had a glass of Champagne then smiled their goodbyes . . .), had perished in a plane crash, flying a small Cessna over a mountainous area where they'd been caught in a lethal downdraft. Their two children were still at their home in Manhattan.

"Of course with the children comes the wherewithal to keep

them, there's certainly enough to see them through childhood and college."

"*College?*" What was he talking about? *She* had not been to college!

He said, "The two girls are ages six and four. Their names are Vivian and Jane Cecilia. Miss Dexter, I cannot emphasize enough that they have no one else to turn to. Without you it will be foster homes. I'm afraid they are rather too old to be popular for adoption."

He sat back looking at her stunned face. "I know, I know," he said gently. "It is a great shock and a terrible responsibility, but your cousin mentioned you specifically in the will, said you were her only relative and therefore she would leave you her most treasured possessions in the hope that, should you be needed, you would know what to do."

Fen said nothing.

Then, "Here are their pictures." He slid a few photos across the desk.

Fen did not pick them up. She simply stared down at them, at the two young faces of her distant relatives, one dark haired, stony-eyed, kicking the grass with a sandaled toe, unwilling to smile for the camera; the other a blond blue-eyed angel beaming for all she was worth.

"That kid's a natural," she heard herself saying. And then quite suddenly she was crying, sitting there in the lawyer's smart office looking at pictures of two little kids who had no one. They were so innocent. She had been alone herself from the age of eighteen. She thought what she was being asked to do was not a lot different from the work she did with abandoned and abused animals, it all came from the same love source.

"I could love these girls," she said finally, collecting the photos and putting them in her bag. "When can I have them?"

And that was how she, Fen—short for Fenalla, a name she'd always hated because she thought it sounded like a stripper—became "aunt," never "mom," to "her girls." Who now, after all the growing up—Fen as well as them—through all the schools and ballet classes, the childhood illnesses, the terrible teens, high school, college, boyfriends, lovers, had become a family.

Vivi the oldest was thirty, an emergency room doctor in San Francisco. JC at twenty-eight was out there somewhere, still trying to become a "star," singing in small clubs and in Fen's opinion, going exactly nowhere. Both girls had their own lives and Fen had decided to let them get on with it. She had probably interfered enough over the years.

· · ·

Another hour passed before Fen finally got out of bed and walked downstairs. The kitchen's dark planked floor felt cold under her bare feet. It was going to be a chilly one today. She put on the coffee— how she loved that morning coffee smell—then showered, and got herself generally together in jeans and a gray V-necked sweater, first brushing off the dog hairs. She checked the weather again—also gray and with a cold buffeting wind she didn't like. Nor did the dog. Fen had considered naming him Hercules because he was strong, a survivor, but Hector had seemed to fit the bill better. And now here they were, twelve years on. Alone, together.

Then the phone rang. "Fen," she heard Vivi say urgently, "I need to see you. Tonight. I have something I must tell you."

Fen recognized the sound of trouble when she heard it but refrained from asking what was up on the phone; she would save the questions for later. Vivi was a third-year resident at a San Francisco hospital's emergency department. She worked long hours and she and Fen didn't get to see much of each other anymore. Now, though, Vivi said she would stay the night. Which meant Fen had better drive to Carmel and get in some supplies.

She put on her old dark blue peacoat, bundled Hector in the back of the Mini Cooper—no mean feat since the dog weighed in at a hundred pounds. The dog usually preferred to stick his head out the window and sniff the passing scenery but today was too cold.

Twelve years ago Fen had found Hector abandoned at the top of her driveway. When she first saw the brown paper bag she thought, irritated, somebody had littered her property. She got out of the car intending to pick the bag up and dispose of it properly. Instead, there was tiny Hector, gazing mournfully up at her with his big brown eyes. I mean, what could she do?

In Carmel she got lucky, a Range Rover slid out of a parking spot just as she arrived, giving her plenty of room. It was spitting rain and Fen wished she was not wearing her new suede boots. Suede and rain did not go together. She'd worn them because they were flats and she never could manage Carmel's cobbled streets in heels. In fact there used to be a Carmel ordinance that only flat shoes could be worn in the village, since there were so many accidents.

She eased Hector out of the car and dashed to buy a newspaper, then thinking of Vivi's supper, picked up a crusty loaf, some good aged Manchego and a silky goat cheese, as well as a chunk of Parmesan to be grated onto the salad. Two bottles of the Napa Pinot Noir she liked, plus of course she had a couple of cases of her friend Millie's Sonoma Chardonnay. She was pleased when she also managed to find the nice rosemary-raisin crackers which went so well with the cheese.

She had already made a *daube*, her French-style beef stew (she used filet steak and about a gallon of good red wine and let it brew down for long slow hours, adding tiny pearl onions and fresh carrots when the original ones turned to mush) a few weeks ago with Beethoven's Fifth blasting from the stereo, completely drowning out the boom of the waves on the rocks below. She made so much she had to freeze it in separate batches, which meant that tonight she could unfreeze some and serve up a spontaneous meal without any effort.

By the time she finished her shopping the rain was coming down hard. The wind pushed at her back as she shoved Hector into the car, along with the groceries, and when she turned off the road and into the gravel drive to the cottage, it was bending the Monterey pines sideways. Below the house the gray Pacific roared over the rocks even louder than the wind. Still, she was home now. Safe and sound.

• • •

By seven o'clock, the fire was lit, the beef daube was simmering on a low light, the kitchen table was set with the knives and forks with the aquamarine plastic handles that Fen had bought in Leclerc, an inexpensive French maxi-market, and which were still a favorite. She'd put out the plates with the pictures of parrots on them and the decent wineglasses. The crusty loaf sat on a wooden board, cheeses warming to room temperature next to it while the rain hurled itself with gale-force ferocity at her big windows, which opened onto the small ocean-view terrace.

In fact the weather had turned so bad Fen began to worry. She tried calling Vivi on her mobile to advise her to turn back but could not get through. She went and looked out of the window; all she could see was her own reflection against the black of the night. She put another log on the fire, shifting Hector with her toe and making him grumble. Hector liked his warm spot. Actually, so did she; she was glad not to be out there herself on a night like this.

Restless, she paced back into her bedroom and checked her appearance in the long mirror on the closet door: jeans; the new suede boots that pinched her toes; the gray V-neck that almost matched her silvery hair, cut in a shortish bob to her chin.

For fifty-eight she wasn't half bad, though not nearly as good as she would have liked. Were those new lines, there, above her nose? Wasn't that what Botox was for? She must ask Dr. Vivi about that when she got here. *If* Vivi ever got here was more like it, which Fen doubted, the way the wind was howling now. Gale force was increasing to hurricane, here on her little spit of a cliff, with the waves boiling on the rocks below and rain that had turned into a deluge.

She went to the pantry cupboard and found the hurricane lamp, just in case, trimmed the wick, checked the oil, carried it into the sitting room and put it on the glass coffee table. She turned up the stereo to combat the growl of the wind and sat there, sipping her wine and listening to Beethoven turned up loud, belting out over the rattle of the rain against her windows. She never closed her curtains because the view of the Pacific in all its moods, with its passing gray whales and sporting dolphins, was what had brought her to this place anyway. Seeking solitude, she had found it. And then she had found Hector. And together, they had found "aloneness."

Tonight though, there was something unnerving in the power of the storm. The sheer ferocity of it rocked around her little house. Windows rattled, beams creaked, doors shuddered on their hinges. Even Hector seemed worried, lifting his head and looking inquiringly at her, as though she should stop it or something.

"I wish I could, Hector," she said, interpreting his look. She and Hector always knew what the other was thinking.

She picked up the phone to call Vivi but her line was dead. Of course it was; the phone was always the first thing to go in bad weather. She tried her mobile but there was no reception. Now there was no way to contact anyone.

Frowning, she sat back against the sofa cushions, hoping against hope that Vivi had had the sense to turn back. Surely, whatever it was she needed so urgently to talk about could wait till tomorrow.

She'd finished her wine and had just gotten up to pour a little more when the lights went out. Everything went out: the stereo, the refrigerator, the TV.

Fen froze, glass still in hand. There was a thickness to the darkness, a *texture* to the sudden silence. Even the usual almost imperceptible hum of household gadgets was gone.

She felt Hector standing next to her. She said quickly, reassuring herself as well as him, "It's okay, Hector," pulled herself together, clicked on the lighter and lit the hurricane lamp, relieved she had thought of it earlier because she surely would not have been able to find it now in that cupboard in the dark. She lit the stubby green candles on the kitchen table where dinner was set, then went round lighting up the votives she kept around, mostly as decoration, but now happy to have their small light also.

There was nothing else to be done. She went and sat with the dog in front of the fire, welcoming its flickering glow and thanking heaven it wasn't electric. The wind seemed even louder. Or was it because she was so aware of the house's overwhelming silence? She walked over to the window again. Rain sluiced down the glass in sheets.

She went back and sat near the fire. The dog put his head on her knee, drooled on her jeans. A log slipped in the grate. Fen could even hear herself sipping the wine from the glass.

The sudden knock at the door sent her leaping up, heart jumping in her throat. Her wine slopped all over Hector. Hackles raised, ears pricked, the dog stared toward the kitchen door. There it was again. Someone knocking. *Of course, it must be Vivi. She had made it after all.*

"I'm coming," Fen yelled, shoving Hector out of the way, battling the wind to get the door open. A gust snatched it out of her hand, slammed it back against the wall. Beside her, Hector's lip rose in a snarl.

A man stood on her porch. His wet dark hair was plastered to his skull. Blood trickled down his forehead. And in his hand he held a knife.